Accidental Pasts

Lisa Keifer

To those who struggle with mental health issues, including anxiety and PTSD. I know the world can sometimes seem like a harsh place, but you are not alone.

LISA KEIFER

Chapter 1

Rhett

I'D GIVE ALMOST ANYTHING for my body to be numb again. These aches aren't helping the situation any. Every muscle movement makes me wish I could lie down and rest.

Being in this microscopic shed isn't helping either. It's bare bones. Nothing like what's back home in Georgia. No organization of any respectable means. No organization whatsoever. No heater. No fireplace. Maybe ten feet by twelve feet. Most likely broken windows under the haphazard, rotted wood covers. It's difficult to understand if the pile of stuff taking up half the floor space means anything to anyone or ever did. Yet the longer I stare at the junk in here, the clearer an idea becomes in my mind. Thank God my mind is actually clear right now.

"What are you doing?" These words are spoken slowly.

"Thought you were unconscious," I say to Gwenn, who lies over on the floor to my left. I slowly turn my body in order to face her.

I realize how creepy my words sound to her when a gasp escapes her mouth, followed by a sharp intake of air. She unsuccessfully attempts to pull herself up and scoot away.

"Thought you were sleeping," I correct myself. "You were exhausted." So am I, but there isn't anything I can do about it.

There also isn't anything I can do about the burning ache spreading through my sore back.

"Rhett? What are you doing with all that stuff?" Overhead branches from a nearby tree scrape against the roof in the whistling wind, making so much noise I barely hear her. Still, her uneven voice scratches against my eardrums. Gwenn sits up from the spot on the dingy wood where I carefully left her and points to the tattered tarps and rope in my hands. Her hand trembles as she does so.

Now I know I've freaked her out.

I toss the long ropes and ripped plastic sheets aside to show her I mean her no harm and start pulling broken pallets away from the wall. "Making a tent or some kind of cover we will use to trap as much heat as possible."

"You mean body heat," she corrects me. Though I can't see her features well in this dim light, I hear the unsteadiness in her voice. She breathes quickly, almost uncontrollably.

"That—I didn't say that. That isn't what I meant." I stumble over my words in horror.

"Isn't it?" Her tone is not accusatory, but is also not trusting.

I wish she could see more of my face to understand I won't hurt her. It's hard to convince someone to put their faith in you when you've only just met.

I release the pallets in my hands, allowing them to fall back against the wall. Then I turn toward her and put my hands up in submissiveness. "Gwenn, I swear I won't touch you. But we need a shelter to keep warm together. This place is hardly better than a pile of sticks." The wind gusts in through a hole, proving my point. "I refused to let us freeze out in the forest. I still refuse to let that happen now."

I think she nods, but there's no way to be sure.

"Are we clear on this?" I make my tone as gentle as possible.

"Okay." Gwenn's voice is small and barely audible. I can't say how much she trusts me since she remains on the "far" side. She doesn't move, which makes perfect sense.

However, I cannot stay still. I have work to do.

Chapter 2

Gwenn

I'M SO HUNGRY. No clue when I ate last or when Rhett did, for that matter. I can't tell if Rhett is hungry just by looking at him. Maybe I should ask him, but I don't think I can do anything about it if he is. I can't even help myself. I am still freezing. Literally. Icicles hang in my hair. The snow hasn't melted off of my boots or outerwear.

I remember only bits and pieces of Rhett dragging me through the eerily quiet, snowy woods when I could no longer walk, after hours of wandering after the crash. He was too strained to carry me, and yet here he is taking control of this harrowing, bitterly frigid situation.

Rhett seems to have the tent formation figured out. A pallet scuffs against the floor as he readjusts its position. I've already offered to help three times and got told no. Whether he wants me to rest or is afraid I'll be in the way, I have no idea.

Then there's the worry about what comes next for two strangers who are desperate not to die once the tent is finished.

The best idea I come up with is to start digging through the mismatched, ramshackle cabinets over on the opposite side of where I sit. To get there, I have to crawl on my sore hands and knees, as my rubbery legs refuse to hold my weight. One of my legs seems like it should be in pain, but I don't actually feel anything. With increasing heart palpitations, I ignore this and instead, try to come up with a plan. I need to squeeze my way past Rhett. It's impossible to not touch his body with mine. This ridiculously small, cluttered building won't allow us to avoid any contact.

"I'm sorry. Pardon me," I tell him as my lower back and bottom brush against his, my upper body turned away from him.

I thought back-to-back was the safer, less invasive choice. However, this forces me to protect my chest from all the rusty, broken garbage hanging on the walls. Sliding a little at a time is the only way, and yet it isn't helping much. This hard yet hardly solid, cracked wood floor is killing my knees. It's also depositing dirt, dust, mouse droppings, pine needles, and I don't dare wonder what else all over me.

"Yes, ma'am," Rhett says in return while he works.

It's a little jarring for my rescuer, my hero of sorts, to call me "ma'am." Makes me feel like even more of a stranger to him.

There are a lot of gardening tools in this first rusted-out metal shelving unit. Spades, two intact terra-cotta pots and one broken one, and some tiny rakes I don't know the name of. I also spot two small paint cans whose contents spilled out long ago, soaking a couple paint brushes. Nothing useful for surviving a blizzard. There is a long, empty shelf where Rhett might have found the rope, which means he's probably checked this one already. No sense in me going through it. Rhett curses under his breath as I carefully crawl/climb over an abandoned pile of something soft yet stiff. Not quite sticky. I dig out my phone from my coat pocket and shine its flashlight on the pile to find it's actually dirty, greasy gloves and coveralls.

Ew. Hope I don't have to touch those again.

I quickly move on. Past the nasty pile of used work clothes stands the wall of cabinets, five tall, thin ones and one that's short and wide. I see no locks. In fact, a few of them don't have doors. Most are made of metal, but the short one is wood.

I open the decrepit wooden cupboard first. It's in the corner. The hinges give a worn-out, rusty squeak. I planned on working my way down the row to the end, but I find something we might actually be able to use.

"Jars!" I exclaim.

"Pardon?" Rhett asks behind me, still at work.

"Ugh. Jars full of screws. And bolts. Washers." I check each one in my phone's light. "Wait. And food," I tell him with excited relief. "Tomatoes, what looks like apple butter, pickles, green beans, beets, sundried tomatoes, and some dehydrated fruit rings." I rummage around a little and find some dried meat jerky. "There aren't any labels or dates written down."

My phone light hits the first food jar again, and I let out a groan. There's a visible greenish mold mixed in with the once-red tomatoes in juice. "They've gone bad. All of it." I push on each seal to check for sure. The putrid odors reach my nose, making me gag. "Everything but the dehydrated items is ruined."

Rhett doesn't acknowledge this.

There is a loud crack nearby, and a violent boom sends vibrations into the shed with the strength of an earthquake. I jump in fright, then freeze.

"Explosion?" I ask Rhett, hoping he understands enough that I won't need to say the rest of the words that debilitate me just thinking about them.

He shakes his head. "Would've happened already. Probably a tree got knocked down."

But now I'm trembling.

I have to go back to the food. At least it's something to focus on.

I guesstimate the amounts of the dried meat and produce. "We should be okay food-wise for a few days."

"Let's hope we won't be here too long. But it's good to know."

"The apples are all yours, so long as you aren't allergic to them, too." As carefully as I can in order to not jostle the stinky items, I slide the jars with spoiled food into the far back of the shelves. I remove the good stuff-filled jars, placing them all on the floor. Then I shut the cabinet doors.

I turn around to face Rhett.

He has stopped what he was doing and is now turned toward me, tarp and ropes in hand again. His face is scrunched up. "You're allergic to apples?"

"It's strange, I know. For most people, it's just a lot of swelling and itching, but last time, I had an anaphylactic reaction. My epinephrine was in my suitcase, on the tiny plane. Lost to the abyss now, I guess." I take a moment to turn back to the jars. "I'll avoid the pears as well, just to be safe. I'm stuck with dried tomatoes and meat. Good thing I'm not a vegan. I hope they didn't cross-contaminate anything."

Rhett still isn't moving. I shine the light on him again. His pinked-from-the-cold complexion has paled a bit.

"Are you okay?" I halt my movements, hoping there isn't some giant creepy-crawly nearby. Slowly, I flick my light all around me on the floor. I don't find anything. Then I aim it up, just in case. All the old cobwebs tell me that was probably a bad idea. "Was there a spider? Please, just tell me it wasn't too big, even if it was. I can't handle a giant arachnid right now."

He pulls himself out of his trance. "Yeah. No. No spider. I just—I've only known one other person who was allergic to apples. We were as close as two people could be."

"You understand." I smile in relief, though it's possible he can't see it because of the darkness. My light is not shining at my face or anywhere near it. "Good. It isn't a common allergy, or at least it isn't one that's talked about. Most people think I'm making it up or tell me I'm crazy because of it."

"No. You're not," he whispers. He turns slightly, takes one more look at me, then goes back to work with the wooden pallets.

I, on the other hand, have no urge to continue sorting through the cabinets after the moldy jar experience. "We have food and shelter, such as it is. What do we do about water?"

"What do you mean? Snow's right outside."

His words make me stop. "And full of pollutants. Benzene. Toluene. You know, paint thinner. I am not drinking paint thinner. There has to be something else we can do."

Rhett keeps sorting and stacking pallets. "How did you think this was going to work? I doubt there's a filter in here anywhere. Where else do you suggest we get water from? Back at the plane? We looked there and didn't find any. Remember?"

"Of course I remember." Despite his derisive tone, I try not to snap as I speak. My frustration is vocalized, anyway. "I never imagined I'd have to consume something so dirty. Its color doesn't matter. It's filthy. And poisonous. We could die from it." Just the idea of it is making my head swirl. I look over at him to make sure he isn't swirling, too.

Rhett shakes his head. I assume it's in exasperation, but I can't see his facial features well enough to be sure. "You're telling me you'd rather risk dehydration? Which death do you think will come sooner?"

My heart beats faster. I stand, then kneel again. "Do we at least have anything to boil it with?" I finally manage to make these words leave my mouth.

"Why are you asking me? Aren't you the one in the cupboard?"

Oh. Right. That means I have to check more shelves. But what if I find more mold? Or worse, a dead animal? Oh gosh, I can't risk finding a dead, decaying mouse, can I? Or risk one crumbling to pieces on top of my head, or even all of me, trapping me under the weight of rusted-out metal or rotted wood.

But I have to.

Yes.

I have to.

Ew, ew, ew, ew, ew.

"So. Okay." I can do this, I remind myself as I blow out a hard breath.

With only my thumb and index finger, I tentatively open the door next to the one with the nasty jars, holding my breath, except this cabinet is empty. I exhale and take another breath in. The next shelving unit only has tools, no containers.

"Well, we could empty out one of the jars. One with jerky inside would be easiest. Do you have a lighter?" I ask.

"Don't smoke, and we were just flying on an airplane." Although Rhett sounds calm, I sense he's getting annoyed with me. There has been an almost deepening growl to his words. He's mad at me for asking all these questions. He thinks I should be able to figure this out as easily as he can.

"Right. You're right."

How did I forget about being on the plane?

Oh gosh. The plane. In a million, billion pieces up here in the middle of I don't even know where with those—

My face is hot. The warmth burns from having been so cold not long before.

No. Nope. Don't do that.

Focus.

"So. Water. We can let it melt. But boiling would be better. We can't boil without a heat source. So." My lungs start working harder. I put my right hand to my forehead. My fingers just graze the bottom of my damp, gray knit hat.

"You feeling all right?" he asks.

"Mm-hmm. Fine."

I'm not even close to fine.

Chapter 3

Rhett

"Tent's done." I gesture at my handiwork.

"Will we be able to breathe in there?" Gwenn asks. Her phone flashlight is still on, giving me a view of her face. She has wide eyes, raised eyebrows, straight lips, and an extra paleness in her skin.

I bend my knees and motion to the bottom of the tarp. "See? It doesn't go all the way to the floor. Plenty of oxygen for us both."

Though she nods, she isn't satisfied with this answer. The fact remains there isn't anything else I can do. "I can't rip a hole in the top, since doing so would let all the warm air escape. The bottom does allow a sufficient amount of air both in and out."

Another wordless nod.

"What other choice do we have?" I try to be gentle with this question, but it's difficult. Surely the answer has to be obvious to her, right?

"I kind of hate how right you are."

"I can tell." I hold in a chuckle. She might not find this as funny as I do.

"We should clean that." She motions toward the cut I feel on my cheekbone. There's another, I think smaller one, on my forehead.

"It doesn't hurt," I lie. "And we have nothing to clean it with. You ready?"

Gwenn and I gather the jars of still edible food and put them down around the base of the makeshift tent. She empties one container of jerky and shoves its contents into the other jar of jerky. We agree slowly melting snow is better than no water at all.

There's just the matter of getting the snow. I can't make Gwenn do it. Mama and Granny raised me better than that.

After sucking in as much air as possible, I quickly open the door, kneel down, and scoop some clean, untouched snow into the jar. In a rush, I secure the door once more. Although I hurried, snow managed to force its way inside. It blew in the immediate vicinity of the door, including near the base of our tent. I sweep up the snow with my hands, shoving it off to the side near the front wall. I don't care if it melts into a puddle in here.

Then I turn to Gwenn. "Hat, coat, and gloves off."

She scoffs as if I just told her to get naked.

I stand another pallet on its end. "So they can hang to dry. You'll become hypothermic if you stay in those wet things any longer." I should probably remember what the symptoms of hypothermia are, just in case because we might need to know before too long. I hope it doesn't get to that point. My mind is a blank in that department, unfortunately.

Gwenn reluctantly complies as I remove my own winter gear. However, we keep our coats, as I'm too scared of what might happen if we take them off. Then I think maybe the coats are too wet. It would be nice to stay in them, but I'm afraid they might be too damp from the snow. It's better to try to allow them to dry out as much as possible but keep them nearby in case we need to cover up.

"Now, let's get in there before we freeze," I say.

She takes in a breath, as if to steady herself.

We crawl under the tarp. Then Gwenn crawls back out.

"You all right?"

She doesn't answer.

"Gwenn?"

I hear her doing something out in the open part of the shed. Should I crawl back out after her?

"Hey," I call again. "You don't have your coat on. You'll get too cold outside of the tarp."

It's dark where I am, since she took the light with her. I try to kneel down far enough to look out the gap, but her back is to me, blocking what she's doing.

"I got it," she replies.

I'm leaning over to duck below the bottom of the tarp when Gwenn returns with an armful of dirty coveralls. "Closest thing we have to blankets."

She and I both put on a pair. I make her add a second pair on top of the first. Coveralls are under us for cushion and on top of us for warmth. Good thing they have sleeves, which makes it less necessary for us to chance wearing our wet coats. I just hope these things warm up fast and we don't lose too much body heat in the process.

We huddle near each other without touching. We have no candles, no fire. Our only source of light is her cell phone, but she has only eight percent battery life left, I notice as I look at the screen. With it constantly searching for the signal I'm certain it won't find, it'll die soon. My battery crapped out before the plane lost control.

Gwenn's trembling is more pronounced than when I half-dragged her to this shed. I'm worried this tarp "tent" may not be enough to keep her warm. I just don't know what else to do to prevent her from developing hypothermia.

"This is wrong," she says suddenly, though I'm sure it doesn't seem sudden at all to her. "This is wrong. We shouldn't have left them. We shouldn't have left them. We shouldn't have left them." Her voice rises with every sentence uttered.

"We stayed with them for as long as we could." Only there wasn't much reason to.

"There was no fire and no explosion. Maybe they stood a chance. There were seven of them. Maybe some of them are still alive, and we left them. We left them."

While no longer there, I see flashes of the shredded metal that used to be an aircraft. The scattering of suitcases and personal belongings, none of it ours. The lone boot I know had been worn by a fellow passenger. I hold back the urge to cry. "None of them made it. The pilot was gone before we ever found his body. The other passengers just happened to be in the wrong seats. They were already dead or bleeding to death when you and I were trying to rescue them. There was nothing we could do. We would have died with them if we'd stayed."

"No." She shakes her head. "No. We have to do something. They were so bloodied and— and broken. They need our help."

I keep my voice steady. "We can't. Not now. It's too late for them and too risky for us. We'd never find our way there or back here. This is where we are safest."

"We have to do something!"

"Gwenn, relax. We'll be fine. In here is better than out there." The wind whipping against the walls and creaky roof of the shed prove my point.

I'm not sure Gwenn hears me as she pulls a small, round plastic container from her pocket. After opening it, she gulps down a little white tablet. She doesn't even bother taking some water with it. Not that we have any yet, but damn.

Am I stranded with a junkie?

She avoids my gaze. "We have to go back to them. We can't be the only survivors. It's too awful." He breathing is the fastest it's been since the crash.

I don't respond to what she just said. I can only think about what she just did. "Look, I don't know what you're into. I'll help you if possible. But right now, I can't have you freaking out on me. I need you to stay clear-headed enough so we can get out of this alive. Will you do that for me?"

In the phone's light, I see her eyes go wide. "I'm not an addict."

"But you just—I mean, I've never seen a normal person take a pill like that before."

"This isn't about what's normal or abnormal."

I beg to differ, but this isn't the time to say so.

"I almost died once. It wa—" She stops herself with a shudder.

There's a hard knot growing in my stomach. "You almost died before the plane crash?" I barely manage to get the words out.

"Anyway, I have PTSD."

She breezily yet pointedly ignored my question. I doubt she'll answer if I try again. I let it be for now.

"The pill I took is an SSRI, for my anxiety and panic attacks. Like the one I'm trying to stave off right now. I already feel like I'm losing my mind."

I let this slide. Probably best not to focus on the fact that the person I'm trapped with might be losing it right in front of me. "Aren't you supposed to take medication with water?"

"Nope. Not if I don't have any. And I can't stop the anxiety by doing nothing. I can't keep myself from completely breaking down if I don't do something now. We'll see how well it works if I sleep for the next twenty-four hours straight. Or possibly not wake up at all."

Does she mean this as a joke? I don't laugh. I can't bring myself to laugh, assuming it was supposed to be funny. She might have that kind of sense of humor right now, but I sure don't.

I look at her phone to check the time. It's been about six hours since the plane smashed to pieces somewhere in the Adirondacks, maybe four since Gwenn and I began hobbling through the darkening skies and whipping snow to shelter, and most likely an hour since we got here. We aren't in the more mountainous area, which means we may have a chance of surviving. If only we could go out and find the house that has to be around here somewhere. A town is nearby as well. There is more than trees in this area. There has to be.

"Why did you get on the plane?" she asks.

"I don't know. The pilot offered us a way out." This is only part of the truth.

"But he was a stranger. We were all strangers accepting a ride in a private plane from some guy telling us he could do what the professional pilots couldn't. They didn't have cancellations for no reason."

I stay quiet. Nothing I say right now is going to calm her mind.

"We never should have been on that plane. We never asked if he was certified or, if he was, for how long. Did he secure approval from the tower? I don't remember hearing any conversations between the pilot and the tower."

"Now that you mention it, I don't remember hearing any, either. Or radio calls with other pilots."

"He put all our lives in danger to make a few bucks."

"Maybe he did it for free. I didn't pay him. Neither did you, that I know of, anyway. You and I were together when we met the pilot."

"Because we had just met, too. He took advantage of the situation."

"He might have felt like he had no choice but to help us."

She huffs. "I think you're giving him far more credit than he deserves. He had a stupid, selfish idea, and we stupidly, selfishly bought into it. There was no co-pilot, only a passenger in the seat where a co-pilot should have been. That rogue jackass basically killed himself and six other people."

"In an accident," I gently remind her as she begins to roll forward and backward on her bottom.

"A reckless, preventable crash. Why did we think we'd be safe in a low-flying plane? We were never going to get out of the snowstorm. The pilot must have known. We all should have." She quickens the forward and backward rocking as she speaks, the pitch of her voice higher than it was not long ago. Her shivering has become almost violent by this point, but I'm not sure she'll let me help her.

"Wallet. Do you have your wallet? Of course you have your wallet. You didn't put that in your suitcase. Why couldn't we find our suitcases? I didn't have a purse. I have my small coin purse with my ID. It's good to have ID. If we die here, at least they'll know who we are. Not that I have anyone for them to notify. You have people for them to notify. If we die, at least we have that." This is said at a faster and faster pace until I wonder how she can even breathe. She never paused for me to answer her questions or reply in any way.

Then she slows down the rocking and blows out a breath. "Sorry. I'm sorry. This is bringing up a lot of bad memories for me." This is still said faster than normal.

I nod. Her accident must have been more traumatic than I can imagine.

"Can we talk about something else?"

"What topic would you like?"

She takes a few moments to think. "Your choice."

I decide to tell her the story of how I named our cat when I was five—the same story Mama liked to relate to any guests we had come over for months afterward. One look at the almost brown ring of fur around Thimble's otherwise orange neck made it easy to see why I was aiming for Simba but didn't quite make it all the way. Mama always made it seem like my misunderstanding was magical.

Gwenn tells me how cute that story is, and her rocking has slowed even more, so I give her another story, this time about the food I used to sneak out of the house and leave in the yard for the rabbits when I was no older than five. My dad caught me one day, but instead of scolding me, he helped me research the right kinds of foods they could eat and safe places to put them.

Now that Gwenn has calmed down a bit, I scoot closer to her, softly pulling her toward me, my hands at her shoulders.

She jerks away, kicking a leg out in the process, which knocks into a jar. "What are you doing?"

"I'm sorry, but you're too cold."

"No, I'm not. I'm fine."

"Do you always lie just to avoid uncomfortable things?"

When she huffs, I know I probably shouldn't have said that. I have to figure out a better way to keep her from developing hypothermia. "You need to warm up. Your skin is too cold, which means it'll be harder for everything else to retain heat. Can I please help you?"

After a few seconds of biting down on her bottom lip, she replies, "Fine." Mama would call her tone "snippy," but I'm trying not to judge her.

Gwenn and I move so our hips are touching. She pulls her knees back up and embraces them. I then wrap my arms in a circle around her limbs, creating almost a human bubble with her in the middle. Carefully, I begin stroking parts of her legs and up onto her arms with my hands, being mindful to avoid any area I have no right to be near.

"How do you know any of this?" she asks as she starts rubbing her hands on her knees. "Were you some kind of survival scout?"

"After my dad died of heart failure when I was eight, my mama and granny wanted me to know every possible way of keeping myself alive. We never bought or ate any food that was pre-packaged or non-organic, and we also kept our minds and bodies healthy with games and puzzles. Spent lots of time outdoors. Mama took up yoga. I was in different scouting groups growing up. When I got older, I took survival classes to learn as much as I could."

"So, you'd survive on a desert island, too?"

"I'd like to think so."

"What about zombies or the apocalypse?"

"Both. The only thing I think might take me out is a formal dinner party."

Gwenn laughs.

I'm not sure what to say. At least the laughter relaxes her. She'd been tense since I first held her. But the relaxation doesn't last long. She's worked up to almost the point of panting again.

"Tarp. Phone. Light. Shadows." These words come out short and staccato.

"What are you doing?" I ask.

She lightly puts her hand up on my arm. Though it had just been on her leg, it's still cold. "Grounding exercise. Rhett. Floor. Cold. Getting rid of panic." For a moment, she's silent. "Wind. Walls creaking." Then she sniffs. "Cologne." Her exhale is long and mostly quiet, aside from a small *hmm* sound at the end.

"Better?"

"Not yet." After another breath in, she starts again, with the same pattern of taking in air between each grouping. "Wooden boards. Tarp. Snow in a jar. Light. Warm Rhett. Hard floor. Cold. Blowing wind. Respiration. Cologne."

"It's actually deodorant."

She lets out a sharp exhale after my interruption.

"Sorry." I don't know what else to say. I'm feeling pretty damn stupid right now.

But then she laughs. "Either way, I like it."

"Why is it important? What are you doing with all those things?"

"Four things I see, three things I feel, two things I hear, and one thing I smell."

She doesn't say anything for a while. She's also removed her hand from my arm. Based on her previous behavior, I believe her silence to be a good thing. More like the Gwenn I met in the airport. There is no longer any frenetic energy. Still, I'd like to know for sure.

"You okay?"
"I'm better now. Thank you."

Chapter 4

Gwenn

I HAVE NO IDEA what to do. I'm sitting here in a shed under a makeshift tent with a mostly unfamiliar man's arms around me. Even fully clothed, it's odd. Then again, there is something not quite cozy but comforting about it. But still. It's been months since a man's body was up against mine.

When I add in the fact that he still thinks I'm a druggie no matter how much I've sworn I'm not, I wonder if maybe I've said too much. How much is too much when it comes to something like that? How does someone convince someone else they genuinely are rational, albeit anxious to the extreme?

But he offered to help me warm up. Well, perhaps this is because I asked him what we were supposed to do about being in an unheated shack. Maybe this is my fault, this situation of our bodies draped around each other.

It's all so awkward.

"So," I begin, "where do we go from here?" My head rests against his shoulder.

Though the questions continue their assault on my mind, I'm managing to keep my internal conflict internal and not flying out of my mouth in a word vomit of worry. That jumble of panic from what feels like both seconds and eons ago but was most likely a few minutes cannot happen again.

The last time I needed my meds, it only took thirty minutes for the calming effect to kick in. Shouldn't be too much longer before I'm not so jumpy.

"Warmth first. We aren't as warm as we should be. And food. We'll have to eat. Our water will melt soon enough." Rhett lets go of me to look at the jar of snow. Then he moves it from the floor to the top of one of the crates inside our tent before holding me again. "Then we ride out the storm."

"But it's a blizzard in the Adirondacks. We already know there's at least two feet of snow out on the ground. There will be more by morning. Snowstorms like this don't let up without dumping several feet. It could take ages for someone to find us. We could die in here and no one would know."

"Going outside is not an option. The cold alone could kill us."

"Isn't that what bravery is for? I don't want to die in here, and I'm sure you don't either. It's going to be too late soon. If we don't go out now and try to find help, how else are we supposed to be rescued?"

"We wait."

He can't be serious. "With all your skills, that's the best you can come up with?"

"Yes. It's the right thing to do."

"But—" I stop myself.

"But what?"

My mouth opens with a yawn. I think about his words again. "Do we have options?"

"Nope."

Annoyed, I stifle yet another yawn. I could sleep for days. Did I bump my head in the crash? My body stiffens. Another brain injury could be a disaster for me. Potentially fatal, depending on severity.

"You all right?" Rhett asks.

Since I can't stomach the thought of telling him the truth, I simply don't. "Yep. I'm fine. You were saying?"

"We wait until the wind dies down. When we find help, we'll tell them where to find the wreckage and the victims, if they haven't already."

He's offered up a reasonable plan. This levelheadedness of mine in acknowledging such logic lets me know the medication is starting to work. So does the fact that I no longer feel like my skin is crawling. And if I'm honest with myself, Rhett's idea is the only choice we have.

I don't why I thought there might be a different answer.

No, wait.

That isn't entirely true.

It's this tranquility here with Rhett, like I could snuggle with him for days on end without growing tired of it. He has surprisingly figured out how to hold me without hurting what feel like major bruises. Not good. It's the perfect reason to want out of here as soon as possible.

"I need to go home. My clients need me."

"Are you a therapist?" he asks.

"Real estate broker."

"Then they'll live. We are literally in a life-or-death scenario. You need to focus on you, not them."

"What do you do?" I ask, tilting my head to one side. As I do so, a thought crops up that perhaps I shouldn't put my hair in his face. He doesn't seem to mind, however, since he moved his head closer to mine after I repositioned myself.

"Mechanic."

"Don't you hate being away from your work?"

He laughs. "I'm not the only mechanic in the shop. If the customers have made it three days without their cars, they certainly can make it another two."

"Wow. How generous of you."

"It sucks for them, but it's true," he adds in a softer but still matter-of-fact tone.

"What did you have planned in Boston before he who shall remain nameless because he never told us his stupid name offered us a ride to a different airport?" I ask.

"I had tickets to the basketball game between the Celtics and the Hawks."

"Hawks?"

"Atlanta. NBA. I've been a fan for years. What about you? Where are you supposed to be right now?"

"There's a new exhibit at the Museum of Fine Arts, but first I had a meeting set up with a client. They're from Syracuse, staying in Boston for the month. They wanted to talk about the land they're trying to buy for a new-construction house."

"They couldn't come back to meet you?"

"If only. I'm always supposed to be available to them, not the other way around."

"So your vacation was only because of a business meeting?"

I nod. Now not only do I seem like an anxious druggie to him, but it turns out I'm also a workaholic. Just great.

We grow quiet again, except the silence is an excruciating kind. Other than the wind, the only breaks in the silence are the growls of two ravenous stomachs.

I lean forward and grab the jar of jerky. After removing a few slices, I put the lid back on and reach for the sundried tomatoes. Along with the jerky, I make two sort-of sandwiches, then offer one to Rhett. He accepts with a nod of gratitude.

"Do you play basketball, too, or just watch it?"

He shifts his weight again, pulling me with him in smooth motions. I'm leaning against him more now than I was.

"I liked playing basketball as a kid. As I grew up, I preferred football, but I do shoot hoops every once in a while. 'Course, Mama has never been a fan of me playing any contact sports."

"I believe it. I know what anxiety does to the mind. She probably hated you taking any risk you couldn't control."

More quiet. Our makeshift sandwiches are quickly gone. There is a nervous chatter about to bubble up out of me.

"Let's talk more," I say, knowing this is all far too intimate. "Tell me something personal about you, and I'll tell you something about me."

But not everything. There's no way I'll ever be able to admit the horrific truth of my first brush with death. I barely let myself think about it.

Rhett shifts once more, tenderly, seamlessly moving my body with his, but he doesn't say anything. My left hip isn't comfortable this way, so I move away a bit. He stays where he is. I am, after all, only two or so inches from where I was.

"Okay, look. You don't have to worry. This isn't a 'get to know each other romantically' type of situation. Obviously. We aren't going to fall in love just because we were involved in a traumatic event together. That only happens in Sandra Bullock movies," I say.

"You've seen *Speed*?"

"Of course. Who hasn't?"

He makes no reply.

"I can't keep sitting here cuddling with a stranger. I need to know something other than your name and how you like basketball and football and survival skill classes and cute animals." And I know how his dad died and the fears of his mom. So, okay, we aren't really feeling like strangers anymore. However, that's what makes this more unsettling. I decide to correct my previous sentences. "We just survived a terrifying accident and are now forced by circumstances to talk to each other. So talk, please."

"I had a fiancée," he tells me slowly. "Her name is Edin."

The "had" and "is" together are jarring to my ears. I'm not sure I can come up with an acceptable question or comment that doesn't feed into my desire to know what happened and why he speaks of her with both past and present tense. So. Many. Questions. "Edin is a pretty name. What does she do?"

"She owns a bakery. She's a couple years older. We were engaged for five months."

"Did you set a date?"

"No. I never wanted to, even if it took me a little too long to realize this. With Edin, it was easy just because I didn't bother thinking or feeling anything. I let her decide everything. 'Want to go out to dinner?' 'Sure.' 'Want to have sex?' 'Sure.' "Can I move in?' 'Sure.' I never asked myself why. In the last few weeks, it's really hit me how miserable I am. I just broke up with her before our flight."

He doesn't sound the tiniest bit upset. I'm not sure how to verbally react to this or what to say. My brain is in a bit of shock. I can't image how shitty that must have felt for her, especially since she was the only one in love. But then, maybe I can. Maybe I'll be able to not hold this against him.

And yet.

Well, it's "be honest with myself" time again. I am a little giddy from being told he is actually single, and for that, I'm deeply ashamed. I cannot let myself get carried away. No attraction allowed, no matter how good his deodorant smells and no matter how much his Southern drawl sounds like heaven to my ears with every word he speaks. I can't explain or even understand why it does, but I have to let it go. This situation we are in is the complete opposite of romantic. I'd like it to stay that way.

I rub my hands together and blow on them to warm them. I need more feeling in them in order to eat some more of the jerky my stomach is gurgling in pain for.

"I was in love with a woman once." He whispers this. "The woman who was allergic to apples. She died."

Every part of me sinks a little. "I'm sorry."

He sniffles and tightens his arms around me. "I have only what she gave me through the years of growing up with each other and a few gifts from when we were finally adults, ready to take on the world. Her parents lost their damn minds and threw away everything else she owned. It's gone, all of it. Nothing else left for me to cherish."

"That's awful," I whisper. I can't manage to say more. Words don't come to mind.

"After Jill died, my world fell apart. There's no other way to describe it. I mourned her every day. Still do."

"How long has it been?"

"Almost seven years now. Feels like seven hundred. When Edin came along five years later, she was the first woman to catch my eye since Jill. I jumped in with Edin before realizing what was happening. It was just so fast. She fell in love. I didn't."

"And then you were engaged to be married. Suddenly?"

"What do you mean?" His tone isn't as soft as it was a few moments ago.

I suppose it doesn't really matter which one proposed if the end result is the same. "Does or did Edin know any of this? About what you never felt for her?"

"You think I'm not being fair to her."

"I also think you're not being fair to yourself." And to Jill's memory, but I don't add this. I wait for Rhett to speak or not speak.

He chooses the latter.

Even with all my effort of rubbing them back and forth, I can't put any heat into my hands. Rhett removes his arms from around me and takes my hands in his. He rubs and blows just as I did. It works. We sit side-by-side, knees bent, one leg of each touching the other's, Rhett's hands around mine.

There's a thought I have that won't go away. "You still love Jill."

"Every damn day. I listen to our song twice a day, when I wake up and before falling asleep."

"Oh? What's your song?"

"'I Won't Give Up.' Jason Mraz. She said it was perfect for two fools who fell for each other as kids and were madly in love at nineteen."

"She was nineteen when she died?"

"Yeah. I didn't get to say goodbye to her. Her parents didn't even have the decency to hold a funeral. Just cremated her and stuck her up on the fireplace mantel like a trophy."

I watch him for a few seconds. If Jill died when they were nineteen, seven years ago, that makes him twenty-six. My age. How sad that we've already experienced such heartbreak.

Chapter 5

Rhett

"HAVE YOU ALWAYS LIVED in New York?" I ask. "Wait. I'm sorry. That was presumptuous. Do you live around here?"

Gwenn laughs. "I live here now. In Syracuse. Haven't always. After my injury—well, injuries—I wanted to move as far away from my old life as possible. Didn't have any family or friends, anyway. This seemed like a great place to try a new life on my own."

I realize it would be wrong of me to now ask where she originally came from. Far too many people must have already done the same thing. I feel an ache thinking about how much that must have hurt her. I don't like the thought of anything causing her agony.

"How long have you been up here?" she asks me.

"Accent's a clear giveaway, huh?"

"Little bit."

"I moved up here from Georgia after Jill passed. This was a place she always wanted to visit. She never got the chance for one reason or another, mostly because of her mom and dad. They refused to let her come up even when she was an adult, despite the fact that she should have been able to make her own decisions. Her parents had total control of her life."

"Oh my. That sounds awful." Gwenn's tone indicates she's as disgusted by this as I am.

"It's hard to break away from something so toxic."

"I believe it." Her voice is soft.

Based on both her words and her tone, I sense she's hiding more pain than her previous accident caused. I give her hands a gentle squeeze. A few seconds later, she moves her leg so more of it is touching mine.

"Once I was up here, I decided to stay, though I still consider Georgia home. Then I met Edin. I guess I'm here for us all now."

"Except you aren't."

Chapter 6

Gwenn

I know I shouldn't have said anything when Rhett's hand muscles tighten, though not enough to hurt me.

"What do you mean?" he asks.

"Well, first, it wasn't your dream to move to upstate New York. Second, you don't love Edin and won't marry her. You're only here for Jill. New York was her dream. You're just too afraid to admit that because it would mean she's controlling your life, and not you. That's different than admitting you miss her."

Rhett looks at me like he'd love to let go of my hands right now, but he doesn't. "I don't expect you to understand."

I save him the trouble of trying to be a gentleman and pull my hands away for him. "It isn't my business to understand, but it is yours."

"You are determined to lose your fingers." He grabs my hands and rubs them with his again.

I decide to stay quiet for now. Rhett chose to open up to me. The rest of the story is none of my business.

Against my last decision, I break my silence to tell him so.

"Thank you," he replies. "I appreciate you acknowledging that it isn't any of your business." Yet none of this is said in a harsh or snarky tone.

Our eyes meet.

This man certainly has a way about him. I don't blame Edin for falling for him. If circumstances were different—well, if my entire life was different—I might be open to doing the same.

He flicks his eyes to my cell phone. A tightness overtakes his face.

"Wha—" I look at my phone's screen. It still hasn't gone black in order to preserve its charge, most likely because of the flashlight app. Only four percent battery left and no signal. Then I look back up at him. "What do we do when my battery goes out?"

"I don't know." He shakes his head and releases a deep sigh before he starts blowing on my hands again.

"Are you afraid of the dark?" I ask. I mean it in an ironic, teasing kind of way, referencing a TV show I used to watch, but the words sound troubled as they leave my mouth.

"Nope," Rhett replies confidently. "Are you?"

More than I'm willing to admit.

No sun, no moon, no stars. The whipping wind, blowing snow, and thick clouds have taken away any hope of even a trace of lingering light. Rhett and I will be trapped in the pitch black night, warm only because of an aging tarp and each other.

I gasp and gulp in rapid succession, over and over. I don't do it on purpose, and I can't slow it down.

Rhett leans over to me. "Just relax, Gwenn. We're going to be okay. We won't freeze or suffocate or starve. We won't die of thirst. We won't die of anything. We are going to live through this and for many days after. You are my partner in this. Don't give up on me."

Chapter 7

I WASN'T SURE HOW Gwenn would react when I whispered in her ear. I just didn't want her to be scared anymore. Now I'm holding her in my arms again, and for the first time, I don't one hundred percent want this person who's so close to me to be Jill.

How is that possible?

"You okay? Your heart is racing," Gwenn asks.

I could make up a simple excuse, but I don't want to lie to her. "I'm not sure how I feel."

"Me either." Her voice is quieter, as mine was.

"Can I tell you something?" I ask.

"I think we've reached the point where you can tell me anything."

"In the airport, when we made eye contact, I about fell over."

She quietly asks why with a bit of a laugh to her tone.

I work up the nerve to finally say it. "Because I noticed that your eyes are the same color as Jill's."

"Oh." This is barely more than a whisper.

"It was alluring and unsettling," I add.

She doesn't reply.

"Can I tell you something else?"

Gwenn makes a soft "mmm" kind of noise that I take to mean yes.

"Before the pilot offered us a flight, before our original flight was canceled, my only concern was whether I'd be able to sit next to you. So there's that."

"There is that." She speaks in a hush. "Is that why you chose a seat by me on the small plane?"

"I wanted to be with you," I tell her in the same soft tone she's been using.

Our bodies have relaxed, one into the other. We begin breathing in sync.

It's like the yoga breathing Mama taught Jill and me when we were still in elementary school. Jill loved it and used it as a way to deal with her unbearable folks. It kept her calm and prevented her from acting out as much as she might have. Jill was such a sweet girl that Mama even took both of us to her classes sometimes. If it had been Jill with me now, that's the first thing she would have thought to do once we were safe inside the shed.

"You know what this reminds me of?" Gwenn breaks through my reflection.

I clear my throat. "What's that?"

"A meditation technique I learned in therapy."

"Oh yeah?"

"Yes. Calm, controlled respirations. It allows one to be mindful of themselves and their surroundings in order to drown out any bad thoughts. I like that we're doing it together."

I nearly choke while swallowing. Now Gwenn has me on edge for a whole 'nother reason.

"The breathing," she quickly clarifies. "Breathing together." Her chest rises and falls faster.

I need some physical distance from her, at least for a few moments. There has to be a way to silence the dramatic, increasing change in energy between us. "You know, I've heard it's better to face someone and breathe rather than look away from them."

"That so?" Her voice sounds odd. Different than it has been. It's almost raspy.

"No idea, but it couldn't hurt to try."

"Yep. You're right." Gwenn nods, never turning to look up at me. "Couldn't hurt."

We peel ourselves away from each other and shift to sit cross-legged, face-to-face. Gwenn guides us, slowly vocalizing.

"Inhale. Exhale. Inhale. Exhale."

Eventually, her voice goes quiet. Can't have been more than a minute or two. Our eyes were closed, but I open mine to watch her.

She's just as beautiful in the dark as in the light. When we met, I never imagined I'd be alone with her, and certainly not like this. It has been a hell of a day for us in each other's company. Her expressions are soft as she continues the meditative breathing. With all the shadows, the tiny scratches on her face look gargantuan.

I reach over toward the only one she let me clean at the crash site with what I could salvage from the plane's damaged but still usable first aid kit. Could've used those supplies on me, but it hadn't occurred to me then. The adrenaline kept me from feeling anything. It also hadn't occurred to me to bring it with us. My fingertips make contact with her skin, startling us both. Her eyes rush open. Our respirations increase yet again.

"I'm sorry. That was stupid. I—" I stop talking.

While watching me, her eyes slightly wide, Gwenn continues the exercise. In. Out. In. Out.

Then she slowly leans forward. She moves her gaze from my eyes to my mouth and back. I close the distance between us. Our lips touch for just an instant. She is so near, I feel her take another breath in and let it out, the air lightly brushing against my skin.

Gwenn gives me a nod of permission. Then I gently put my hands on her face, plant my mouth on hers, and kiss her with the kind of passion I've never kissed anyone with but Jill.

Chapter 8

Gwenn

I PULL BACK, MY hands up. "We can't do this. It's—we shouldn't. We have to stop."

I know this makes no sense. We've been making out for at least thirty minutes, and I've enjoyed every second of it. I even had my body pressed up against Rhett and my fingers wrapped up in his hair, for goodness sake. It isn't like I wasn't an active participant. But it's wrong for so many reasons.

"Okay." Rhett immediately moves away from me. "I'm sorry."

"Don't be," I tell him. I put my hands down and wrap my arms around my knees again. "We just have to keep reminding ourselves this isn't *Speed*. This attraction isn't real. Our close proximity should not factor into how we react to one another."

"Maybe—" He stops and pauses. "Agreed."

I'm not sure how much we are being truthful with each other, but under the circumstances, I think we're awfully close. Only there is the way he introduced himself to me in the terminal.

No.

Not again. I have to stop any and all of those thoughts.

Rhett's greenish-brown eyes lock onto mine. He scratches through his dark beard to his chin. "Would you rather eat right now or sleep?"

Before answering, I reach out to grab the water jar. It's a bit slushy. I take a sip of the small amount of liquid and offer the jar to Rhett. He takes a tiny sip as well.

"Sleep," I tell him.

"Then you should shut your phone off." He motions to it. "Better to sleep in the dark than waste the rest of your charge."

"It has only one percent left, anyway." Despite knowing it won't last another minute or so, I turn off the battery-killing flashlight app, then the phone altogether. Rhett and I are suddenly ensconced in an inky black.

"We should have discussed how we're going to sleep first," I whisper.

Chapter 9

Rhett

"There isn't enough room in this tarp tent to lie down," Gwenn continues. I think I hear her breathe a sigh of relief.

"Sitting upright is probably our best choice even if we could lie down," I tell her. I say this from a scientific standpoint, but I also know it most likely eases her fears.

"Holding each other?"

I can't decipher by her voice if she's only a little scared or completely terrified by this prospect. Being so close was what led to all the kissing, but lying to her about make-believe choices won't do any good, despite her trepidation.

"We'd stay warmer that way." I want to reach out to comfort her, but that isn't a good idea.

She audibly blows out, takes another inhalation, and then speaks. "You're right. I hate it, but you're right."

"Are you ready?"

Gwenn scoots over close enough to touch my shoulder with a reaching hand. Before I know it, she slides one hand across my chest and the other across my back. Her head rests on the same shoulder she first touched.

After repositioning my body closer to hers, I wrap my arms around her as well. The coveralls are stiff and a little crunchy under my hands, but I don't mind.

This is nice, I decide.

Really nice.

I fall into the same rhythm as Gwenn's inhales and exhales. We don't speak, but the quiet is more comfortable than I could have imagined. I pull her nearer to me, not wanting her arms and hands to grow too cold. Soon, she's asleep.

I haven't really been a praying man for years. Not since. . . But I'm deep in prayers tonight. Praying to survive with Gwenn. To see my family again. For the agony and ache to go away.

Gently, I kiss the top of Gwenn's head, then lean my own back against a pallet and close my eyes.

Chapter 10

Gwenn

WHAT'S WRONG WITH MY neck? I can't feel anything. Why can't I move? Then the pain hits like I've been smashed by a fifty gallon bag of bricks. I try to transfer my weight from one side of my body to the other in order to roll over, but nothing happens. I'm stuck.

"Help! Someone help me!"

"Hey." A deep, soothing voice answers me. "Gwenn? It's okay. Open your eyes."

"What? I did." Then my eyes flutter open. "Oh! Oh."

Rhett assists me in carefully sitting up a little further. Nausea grabs hold of me. It feels the way it did each morning I woke up in the hospital.

My senses are being assaulted the way they were back then: the cleaning-solution smells, the fresh yet somehow bitterly stale flowers that perfumed my room thanks to my well-meaning nurses, and the clumpy, bland pasta Alfredo I ate every day, which tasted overwhelmingly of disinfectant from the odors having infused themselves into everything. All of this and more floods my brain.

I'm safe, I remind myself. I. Am. Safe.

My companion puts a hand on my face and turns my head so I face him. His scrunched brows and wrinkled forehead catch my attention.

I smile shakily, sheepishly, quite ashamed at first of losing control of my anxiety. "Just a dream."

"Or a flashback."

He is probably right, much as I don't want to admit this. I take his hand off my cheek so I can stretch my arms. Every part of me hurts.

"Sunlight." I suddenly notice it through the cracks in the wood as I stretch out my legs as much as possible and try not to cry out in pain. I promptly discover stretching was a bad idea, but it's too late. "That's, uh . . . That's a good sign." I struggle to speak. My body is telling me I shouldn't have moved so soon.

"It is." Rhett nods, then grows serious.

Uh-oh.

"Hold that thought," I quickly tell him. Then I rush out of the tent to the door, open it, and breathe in as much cold air as possible. I'm on my hands and knees in the shed, facing the outside. The moment I opened the door, I was almost immediately covered in snow. More snowflakes land on me with every second I sit here.

Once I can function again, I shove a handful of frigid white stuff in my mouth to cool off the alarming heat I feel in my head. Pollutants be damned.

I brush as much snow off me as possible, excruciating as this action is, then Rhett helps me push the door closed once again.

"You all right?" he asks with a raised eyebrow.

"Fine," I lie. "Please continue with what you were saying."

He pauses, then walks to the window on the right. There is a large gap in the wood covering it. "We got too cold during the night."

"How do you know?" I ask. I suspect I shouldn't have bothered. The tips of my fingers and toes are mostly numb. It's difficult to wiggle my toes as well. Has been since I woke up, even after I remembered I'm not actually paralyzed.

Rhett kneels, reaches into the tent, and pulls out the jar. The snow is more like a slushie than a glass of water. Wasn't it like that before we went to sleep?

I look up at him. "What does this mean?"

Because of his furrowed eyebrows, I assume he is trying to find the right way to tell me.

"There isn't an easy way to say it, is there?"

He shakes his head. "No. There isn't. Between the wind and the snow, with the visibility the way it is, we're trapped."

I open my mouth, but my voice catches. After clearing my throat, I try again. "How are we supposed to stay warm in this broken shack?"

Again, I assume by the look on his face that Rhett is deep in thought.

"Tell me what you're thinking," I tell him. "I have a say and also a stake in this. Not just you."

"Maybe. . . a fire would work, but. . ." He again turns to look at the accessible window on the right. This window is awfully close to the tarp tent. "We have to vent the smoke and carbon monoxide the fire will create. Not doing so will kill us, but opening a window too close to our tent might freeze us before the fire has a chance to warm us."

"But the fire is still a good idea," I say.

"Yes."

Then he glances over at the cabinets. I'm guessing he hopes there is a window behind all that mess.

Numb as I am, I still walk over and do my best to clear a space in front of the side wall. The coveralls and gloves are already gone, except the two pairs he and I put on in order to work. Rhett and I toss aside a few more warped and cracked pallets, and then we work on the cabinets themselves. I place all the jars into the far corner to keep them from breaking. The only thing worse than not being able to eat the food would be having to smell the decay.

We rip apart the wooden shelves first. This takes us—well, mostly Rhett—nearly no time at all due to all the rot. The giant metal one, however, is trickier than we suspected.

"How is this rust holding it together?" I shout. I want to kick at the cabinet with what little strength I have, but refrain. Don't want to risk further injury or possible tetanus.

Rhett is calm. He adjusts his filthy work gloves, grabs hold of one side of pitted, dented steel, and tugs as hard as he can. He groans from the effort as the cabinet creaks and finally starts pulling away from the wall. It's enough to reveal another awkwardly covered window.

"Does that help?" I ask. I would think so, but then, I'm not the survival specialist.

His face remains scrunched.

"What exactly are you going to make a fire in? And will the open window be enough of a vent source? How will you start a fire? We don't have any lighters or matches, remember? You made that perfectly clear to me last night."

"I don't know what to do. I'm not a fire expert, but I'll figure it out. Or we can figure it out. We can't do nothing."

I'll give him that.

"Okay," he says, running a hand through his hair. "Random pieces of scrap metal welded what looks like ages ago."

I am about to ask him how he knows this when he begins shaking the cabinet with one hand. It creaks and groans from the strain. To my ears, it sounds like it's about to crumble at any moment, especially with the crunches of rust I hear.

"Is that wise?" I ask.

"If it's going to hold a fire, I need to know it won't collapse. And it needs to have legs or something to keep it off the floor." He becomes quiet again.

I try thinking the way Rhett is.

We don't want the entire shed to catch on fire. We don't want to breathe in the smoke and carbon monoxide. If we make a fireplace, we need a chimney, which we don't have parts and tools for.

While contemplating all of this, I hear Rhett mumble something.

"What?"

He turns to face me. "Shit. I said 'shit.' We can't stay here." He puts a hand up before I have a chance to speak. "I realize I said we needed to be here. We did. But I'm afraid we won't last much longer in here without losing some fingers and toes."

Oof. That is not what I want to hear. I don't want to risk escaping death for a third time. I'm not sure I have it in me to try. What if I fail? But then, I suppose I am taking a risk either way.

"What will you do if we make it out of this?" I wanted to add the word alive at the end of my question, but there was a choking feeling that crept up on me with that thought.

"Call Mama and Granny. You?"

I don't have any family to call. Except that isn't strictly true. I have blood relatives who left me in my time of need, though I've only admitted this to one person. If I can face this catastrophe and survive, I can face them. "My bestie Lourdes is probably worried since she hasn't gotten any texts from me yet. I'll have to call her. And our friend Lucy. Lucy doesn't worry as much as Lourdes, but I'm sure if Lourdes can't reach me, Lucy has already been told something is wrong."

"Here." He hands me the jar of jerky. "Eat up. We're leaving soon."

"What?" I stop moving in the middle of opening the jar lid.

Rhett doesn't answer with his voice, but his expression says everything. We have no choice. I open the container the rest of the way and eat a piece of what I think is venison. Rhett munches on the tomatoes. He hasn't touched the fruit rings.

"So, we eat, drink what little water we have, and then what?"

He closes his eyes for a second before turning to me. "Then we head out."

"We keep the coveralls, of course," I say in between bites. "Put our hats and gloves back on. Then. . . look for a house? A barn? We know something must be nearby."

Rhett nods.

Once we finish eating, when the sun looks at its highest as far as we can tell, we pull down the tent and move everything aside, away from the door. Our gloves and mittens are only partially dry and a little frozen.

"Greasy gloves it is," I say. We have been wearing them so long, it doesn't matter, anyway. Then I look at my frozen hat, which is in no way wearable. It's as slushy as the water we'd hoped to drink.

Rhett hands me his dry stocking hat—gray, like mine—and places a ball cap from his inside coat pocket on his own head.

I resist. "You don't have to do that."

He shrugs. "I had two. You need one. And I have a hood."

We both shove our hands into a "fresh"—i.e. different—pair of work gloves and make sure we are as bundled as we can be. I put my still turned-off phone into the middle coverall pocket up by my chest. No point in wasting battery life since we know there won't be a signal.

"All right. Let's go."

I brace for the bitter cold waiting for us on the opposite side of that rickety door. "Wait. What about bears?"

"What about them?"

"Aren't they out there? Is it dangerous?"

"It's winter, for one," he says in an annoyed tone.

"But they don't actually sleep the whole winter. That's just a myth."

"Most likely, they will run off before we ever see them."

"Most likely?"

"You really want to look deeper at our chances of being attacked by bears? Especially when we know we will probably die if we stay here?"

"When you put it that way, no, I don't." I move to the exit.

"Wait." Rhett puts one hand out to me and one on the door to stop me from opening it.

"What's wrong?"

He drops his hands and steps closer to me. With the little light that filters in, I detect the tenderness and also fear in his eyes. "We're partners in this."

I nod, breathless and also understanding what he means. If I fall behind or give up, he won't go on without me. I move nearer to Rhett, wanting him to understand I know I already promised not to quit. Despite my serious reservations, I accept that this excursion is our only hope.

We gaze into each other's eyes for a few more seconds. In all honesty, this might be our last time alive like this. We might not find help of any kind. But no matter what happens, we'll be together. This thought gives me a terrifying yet exhilarating rush.

I'm just working up the nerve to lean forward and kiss him when he places his left hand on the door-knob.

"Ready or not, here we go."

Chapter 11

Rhett

I SHOULD HAVE KISSED her. I know I should have kissed her. As we trudge through snow up to the tops of my thighs, I can't stop thinking about her soft lips. I haven't yet turned back to look at her for fear those lips will be blue or purple-tinged. But I know she's still with me. We are holding hands. The work gloves we wear are large and bulky. Nevertheless, I feel when she reciprocates my hand squeezes.

She and I got lucky last night. Upon leaving the shed, we saw just how close that fallen tree was to ending our stay early. It looked large and heavy enough that it might have crashed all the way through.

While it's true the sun is shining and the sky is clear, there doesn't appear to be any visible buildings. Gwenn didn't need to worry, because I don't see any animal tracks. Due to last night's storm, everything is white and mostly nondescript. I can make out the pine trees, but their boughs are so heavy, they sag almost to the ground. I know Gwenn and I would love nothing more than to rest on the ground, too. We drag forward, anyway. I'm a human bulldozer, pushing through massive snowdrifts with my body.

At least my steps make a path for her. The snow in some spots is about as high as her waist. Even with me in the lead, this isn't easy for her. She falters every so often, her footsteps unsteady. Gwenn's leg is beyond sore. Possibly a torn muscle or ligament. It's been at least an hour since it began to hurt so bad, she started to cry. She's still crying and whimpers now and then.

But we can't stop. Not for anything short of a rescue, despite our exhaustion. I asked Gwenn not to give up on me. I cannot give up on her.

The sun shifts its position in the sky, and still we plow on in the snow, through the small clearing. It's no bigger than half an acre and a beast to advance across. Somehow, we make it far enough to move into more woods, with what could be a wooden fence. It's what it looks like, as far as I can tell, but I'm opening to the real possibility I could be wrong.

As in all the other woods we've walked through, all the tree trunks and branches are white with snow. Some of what's under us may be overgrowth or exposed roots, since several snow-covered spots have us up higher or off balance. It's difficult to know where property lines begin or end. Hell, we could have passed near a handful of houses and never seen them.

Parts of me are numb or almost numb. The snowflakes burn when they hit exposed areas of my skin. Moisture from my breath is freezing into ice crystals in my beard.

Then, Gwenn yanks my arm. Instead of advancing another step ahead, I stop with alarm and check behind me to make sure she's okay.

"Look," she whispers. She points her right index finger off to what I know to be the northeast, based on the sun.

"The blowing snow?" I move my eyes to her.

"It's smoke. Look."

I turn again, and I'll be damned if I don't see smoke billowing in the distance. The wind lightened just enough to make the grayer smoke visible.

Gwenn moves her legs so she stands right next to me. We turn to face each other. Her skin is pinkish-red from the cold, but I also think it's a little from excitement now. For the first time since we met, I can look into her gray, hauntingly familiar eyes without feeling like I've had the wind knocked out of me.

With my hand still gripping onto Gwenn's, I use my other hand to press on the small of her back, moving her to me. She gives me a nod and moves closer. I touch my lips to hers, and I can't say I'm all that gentle or reserved about it. Gwenn gives me as much as I give her. Her free hand has hold of my coat sleeve. She tugs it, urgently moving my arm around her more as she moans.

She pulls back after about a minute and says my name breathlessly.

"What's wrong?" I barely manage to reply.

"Let's keep going. Walking," she adds.

It's a good idea to not stop too long in this frigid weather, especially when we're so close to our goal. So close to being warmer and safer than we've been in the last twenty-four hours. But then she doesn't let me remove the arm surrounding her body.

"We're okay," I whisper in reassurance. "We made it. Together."

Chapter 12

Gwenn

THE SNOW-COVERED WOODEN DECK is sturdy beneath our boots. Neither Rhett nor I have much energy left after plowing through feet upon feet of the fluffy white stuff to make it to this point, and the throbbing in my leg is almost unbearable, but we've finally arrived. A house. Another person. Thank God.

Rhett manages one knock on the shabby screen door, his hand unable to complete a full fist. I still hold the other. No way am I letting go now.

"Who's there?" A thin, older woman with deep brown skin, short, curly, salt-and-pepper hair and thick-rimmed glasses opens the inside door.

I point to myself with my free hand. "Gwenn." Then I motion to my companion. "Rhett. Some people might be looking for us."

At this, the woman backs away, but Rhett quickly adds, "There was an accident. A plane crash. Not sure how far away. Gwenn and I survived and stayed the night in a shed. We need help."

The woman takes in our wind-burned, snowy faces and coveralls, and then she looks behind us at our tracks in the deep snow. Her hardened expression softens. She nods and opens the screen to let us in. "Don't bother about taking anything off or of making a mess. Just come in and warm up."

Rhett helps me hobble inside the faded yellow house into a comfortable, well-used but clean foyer.

"I know of the blizzard, of course, but I had no clue of the plane going down or of anyone being out there in this mess. I'm Adelaide, by the way," the woman tells us once we are in and the door is shut.

"Thank you, ma'am," Rhett says. "We sure appreciate it."

Adelaide waves him off, but she also gives us a smile that says it's no bother helping us.

She pulls a cell phone out of her sweater's large, rectangular pocket. "Yes, this is Adelaide Trellix," she says to the person on the other end of the call. She provides them with her address and the information Rhett told her. "I see. Yes. Thank you."

Adelaide turns to us after ending the call. "There were reports of the plane going down, distress calls, whatnot. No one has been able to search for the wreckage due to the blizzard. An officer is coming by to take you both to the hospital. You'll be examined for injuries and give your statements regarding the crash."

"Thank you so much, Adelaide." My eyes well up with tears.

"Where are we?" Rhett asks. I'm so glad he has the presence of mind to, because this question completely slipped mine.

"Near Lake George," she tells us.

Not necessarily off course, but not where we should be. The tears begin to spill.

"Are you all right?" Adelaide asks me.

"You have no idea how scary this has all been. Truly, thank you for helping us."

Rhett squeezes my hand again.

I turn toward him and pull him in for a hug. "Thank you, too." Though I manage to stifle any sobs, my voice can't seem to register above a whisper.

His arms are wrapped around me as far as they can go. His breath is on part of my neck, but it isn't the only body part feeling warm because of this. It takes us a moment to remember where we are and with whom. We let each other go—reluctantly, on my side.

"Might as well wait in the kitchen," Adelaide tells Rhett and me. She heads in the opposite direction from where we stand.

Rhett and I follow her. I have to lean most of my body weight on him, as the warmth is making the injured, numbed parts of me thaw, and therefore ache with excruciating pain. All the walls of Adelaide's kitchen are decorated with what appear to be antique utensils, tools, and so on. The shed we stayed in is possibly Adelaide's. I'm too afraid to ask her in order to be sure, but then she answers my question, anyway.

"Any of the food in that rickety shed still good?"

"Not much, ma'am," Rhett replies as he helps me sit in one of the upholstered dining chairs. "Just the dried stuff."

"I figured. My sister's husband canned everything in there years ago, just before both of them got sick. Lost him not too long after. She died just over a year ago. Haven't managed to force myself out there in order to clean it up. Too sad. The shed was theirs. All of this was theirs," she adds. "Just before she passed, my sister wanted to fill every nook and cranny of this house with her dearly departed husband's things, but she was too weak to make the trek out. I couldn't bear to bring it all in. Only a few items he especially loved or used the most. The ones she would notice were missing if I hadn't gone down to retrieve them."

Rhett and I glance at the gloves and coveralls we are wearing.

Adelaide ignores this. Rhett chooses the seat next to me as she continues.

"Pack rats, the both of them. I don't like the idea of throwing it all away now." She motions to the kitchen décor, but I suspect she's including the contents of the shed in this as well. There's a reason it's all still out there. She might view it as her only way of keeping their memories alive.

"The stuff in the shed kept us alive." I smile at Adelaide.

"True. True." She turns away and starts a pot of coffee.

I can't shake the guilt of still wearing her brother-in-law's work clothes. Even if these items did save our lives, it feels like such an intrusion into his life and his memory. I wouldn't blame her for hating to see us in these clothes, despite all the good they've done.

Then Adelaide offers us glasses of water.

We greedily drink, barely letting the last gulp of water slide down to our stomachs before taking new gulps. After removing the crunchy, ancient, grease-soaked gloves for the first time since putting them on, Rhett and I also nearly inhale the food she offers us at the same rate of speed. Fresh bananas, roast beef sandwiches, and cheddar cheese sticks. I can't speak for Rhett, but I know I hardly taste any of it before chewing and swallowing.

Thoroughly stuffed, I finally realize none of us have spoken in several minutes. Adelaide must think we are so rude. "How often do you have visitors in the winter?" I ask her.

"Oh. More than you might imagine. Just depends on who is willing to face the outdoors. I'm happy either way. Mostly, though, I spend my days reading a good book in bed or in my overstuffed chair by the fireplace."

"Sounds lonely."

Adelaide grins. "On the contrary. I never married, never wanted to. My sister and her husband moved me in when they developed those health issues and some financial difficulties due to so many medical bills. I ran a quilt shop in Vermont for twenty years. When I moved in here, I did my best to keep them as healthy as possible. But I hadn't lived with anyone since I was in college, and certainly not with those who needed round-the-clock care. It was a trial adapting to the noise and the habits of others."

She pauses with a chuckle, temporarily lost in her memories. Rhett and I don't speak. I don't dare to.

"After they were both gone, I realized it was the first time I'd lived in a quiet house in three years. I'd also grown accustomed to the bustle and felt I had nothing more to do. I lost my purpose for quite a while."

I'm just about to ask how long it took her to acclimate to solitary life again when there is a knock on the front door.

"That must be your ride." Adelaide looks at us with a kind smile.

We all step to the front foyer once again. Rhett is basically a human crutch for me, as I am unable to walk on my own. I'm getting used to the touch of his hand on my body.

Not good.

Our ride, meanwhile, is not an ambulance, but a police car.

The drive to the hospital, after many thanks to and hugs with Adelaide, is a fast one. It isn't, however, an easy one. On top of my leg problems, my digestive system is in shambles. I glance over at Rhett. He looks the way I feel. Scrunched up features, pale, almost green coloring.

"I hope Adelaide isn't as bad about checking her food as she is about her sister's." Rhett tries to grin at his joke.

I can only blink in reply.

The police officer supplied us with plastic bags just in case. I sincerely hope neither of us needs them.

Once we are at the ER, Rhett and I are taken directly to separate rooms. It's the first time we've been apart since the airport. After explaining to the doctor and nurse on duty exactly what happened with the accident and snowstorm, some of my blood is drawn and I'm hooked up to an IV. Each pinch of a needle feels like it's ten times bigger than I know it is.

A nurse or tech or someone I don't remember or know the title of tends to my injuries. I'm at the point where I don't care about job descriptions. I just want help.

Thankfully, I'm told I need stitches on only one of the several cuts I sustained in the crash. Then I tell the nurse who stops by about the pain in my leg. After checking it and noting her findings in my chart, promising it will need tests of some kind, she gives me something for the nausea and looks closer for any signs of frostbite.

With us having come in at the same time for mostly the same reasons, I assume Rhett is receiving the same treatment, though I hope he's feeling much better than I am and in far less pain. Any wounds he suffered from the wreck were well hidden behind his wall of confidence and composure.

I still have to disclose my previous traumatic injuries, which is never easy. This conversation leads to extra X-rays, CT scans, and an MRI, just to be on the safe side. At least my leg doesn't need surgery, although it will be sore for a while. Mobility aids were mentioned, but I'd rather not have to deal with those again. Too many bad memories of hobbling around with no clue what to do with them or any hope of things improving.

After hours of waiting and testing, I am wheeled back to my "room" in the ER. Though the nurse let me take my anxiety medication, it isn't working yet, and I really, really need it to. Actually, what I really need is to get the heck out of here. Every sound of a door opening or closing makes me jump. Doctors being paged over the intercom system has me covering my ears every time. There is a strong odor of antiseptic everywhere, including my room. It's a different hospital, but the smell is exactly the same and just as alarming.

A squeaky wheel passes by now. I go to scratch at my plastic ID bracelet, then remember I'm not wearing one this time. Haven't even been admitted.

It seems like eons before I can let my body relax and loosen up the tension I've been holding on to. When my eyes will no longer stay open, indicating the medicine has kicked in, I decide to let them have their way and rest.

Chapter 13

Rhett

I'VE NO IDEA WHERE Gwenn's room is. If I could be with her, maybe there wouldn't be any unexpected complications. I could hold her hand or wrap my arms around her. I could offer her some comfort instead of her having to go through all this by herself.

I need to see her.

Some would call this an obsessive need. I don't care what it's called so long as it happens. The nurses can't or won't tell me anything because Gwenn and I aren't related or married. I have to be sensible, though. Gwenn needs to feel better. I need to let that happen, and harassing the ER staff doesn't seem like it'll help.

As the evening wears on, I'm interviewed by several different officers and detectives regarding the plane crash. They grimly nod at my words. Eventually, I'm told the wreckage has been located. When one policeman mentions recovering the bodies of the other victims, my eyes burn. I wish as much as Gwenn does that we could have saved them, some way, somehow. I also remember Gwenn is doing these awful interviews as well.

"Excuse me," I say to the next nurse who comes in. "When might we—I mean I be released?"

"You'll be kept a few more hours for observation," he says. "It's a cautious move. Then you'll be free to go. You're lucky you weren't out there longer."

"I know it." I wait a second or two. "I'm sorry, I have to ask. Will Gwenn Rhys be released the same time I am?"

"Who?"

"She and I were brought in together. She was in the crash with me."

He gives me a look, with one eyebrow arched and the other pushed down.

I understand this expression. "You can't tell me. Rightfully so. But if she leaves before I have a chance to speak to her again, well, I'm not sure I'll be okay with that. We survived because of each other. I need to know that she's going to be okay. It was a difficult night for both of us. And I—"

"I understand," the nurse replies before I finish. He pauses for a few seconds. "I can't break any laws, of course, and we have to respect her privacy. But I will see what I can do."

"Thank you."

· ♥ · ♥ · ♥ · ♥ · ♥ ·

Hours pass.

I've been waiting for word about Gwenn. Her cuts might mean stitches, but her leg might mean surgery. I hope she tells them if she's allergic to the anesthesia. What if she can't tell them? Or what if she has more complications than we suspected? What if her previous injuries were silently bleeding all night? Would they be able to fix her? Would they be able to save her?

I need to see her.

I can't stay in here.

When I try to look for her, one of the staff happens to be in the hall at the same time and asks me to go back to the exam room.

All my test results have been what both the ER staff and I have hoped for. There is no reason for me to stay, but I don't want to leave. I'm not sure what—if anything—the nurse is doing for me. Maybe he's too afraid of getting in trouble.

When he returns to my room, I can tell by his expression it's time for me to go. He doesn't mention Gwenn, so neither do I. No sense in asking if he isn't comfortable enough to bring it up first. I reluctantly sign all the papers, put on the clean scrubs one of the staff gave me from their locker, grab my bag of personal items and dirty clothes, and head for the door out of here. I know they don't want me hanging around in the waiting room, hoping for word of her.

Then I see her.

Chapter 14

Gwenn

I instinctively put my hand on his arm once I reach him. The meds I was given have taken away most of the pain in my leg, but I still hobble with my new crutch as I move.

He takes a few steps closer and hugs me, being cautious to not knock into the crutch. I hug him as tight as I can in return, knowing this is most likely our last embrace.

My developing feelings for him surprised me as much as anything else from the past thirty-six hours. After having time to sleep and think on my own, I've realized I got carried away with the attraction. I didn't want to rush into, well, all those very hands-on activities we engaged in, both in the shed and out in the snow, but I also let myself do that, anyway.

"I'm perfect now," he replies into my neck. His breath is hot on my skin, yet it gives me electrifying goosebumps and sends a quick shiver through my body. Rhett makes a soft, content kind of sound. It's almost like he's figured out how much I like this.

"I am so happy we were released together."

In order to say goodbye, I want to add. No, need to add. I just cannot force myself to say those last words.

"Let's go," I tell him.

Taking Rhett's hand in my free one, I cautiously lead us to the exit. Though our progress is slow, there's no use in prolonging the inevitable. We can't stay here any longer, even if we wanted to.

As we shuffle through the doors to the outside, a blast of cold air makes me flinch with a start. I hadn't expected it to affect me after being out in it so long before, yet I'm already shivering.

"You want my coat?" Rhett asks.

I decline. The sidewalk is clear, so I have no trouble maneuvering this damn crutch on the concrete. What I do have trouble with is the desire to keep Rhett's hand in mine for much longer than I should. He offers me help, but I'm an old pro at this now. As unwelcome as those memories are, at least I still know how to use the underarm crutch in the most comfortable way possible, if one could call it comfortable to have a hard object jammed into your armpit.

We make it into the nearest parking lot without having any idea what we will do next, except maybe call a cab or a rideshare, when there is a loud squeal nearby.

<h1 style="text-align:center">Chapter 15</h1>

Rhett

"RHETT LIAM MASON, WHAT happened to you?" Edin runs up and grabs hold of me.

Behind me, I hear Gwenn stifle a laugh and move away. Her boots crunch on the snowy pavement, as does the bottom of her crutch. I wish I could turn to watch her, wanting to be able to run to her side if she slips and needs me.

"Look at you," Edin says, not that she can actually see me. "You have giant gashes on your face. How much blood did you lose? Why didn't they stitch you up?"

"What are you doing here?" I manage as Edin tightens her grip around my middle.

"I thought you might have . . . Oh, Rhett, the awful things that went through my mind when you disappeared. You didn't answer your phone. The people at both airports were no help. Then I got a call from some nurse." She finally sucks in a breath. "Rhett Mason, I'm so glad you're okay."

Damn. I forgot she's my emergency contact.

I pull her away from me so we can be face-to-face. She still has her arms around me, so I gently remove them. "Edin, I—" Then I choke. Just completely choke, unable to mention having dumped her before my flight. "I have to talk to Gwenn before we leave."

Edin flicks her eyes to Gwenn but remains silent.

Chapter 16

Gwenn

I SHOULDN'T LAUGH. I know I shouldn't. That woman has a lot of heartbreak coming her way. But seriously? For one thing, his injuries don't look anywhere near as bad as mine. It isn't just that or her way of saying his full name that's annoying me, though. As beautiful as she is and as much as she clearly cares for him, I don't understand why he doesn't love her—apart from missing Jill—and this bothers me.

Once Rhett makes it over to me, I ask, "Does she always call you by your full name?"

"Pretty much."

Anything else we could add right now would be awkward and perhaps forced. There's only one more thing I need to say. I decide to face it with honesty. "It was nice to know you. I'm glad we met, despite the circumstances. Thank you for everything."

"That's it? Are you serious right now?" he asks with a tilted head and raised eyebrows.

"What do you mean?" I ask innocently.

Rhett makes no reply. He only stares at me.

We both know that I understand despite my reluctance to admit this. He stopped feeling like a stranger to me long before we left the shed. He felt, and feels, more like—well, it doesn't matter. I can't let it matter.

I heave a sigh. "This is the way it has to be."

"Gwenn, I can't let you go now and have this end."

He watches me shake my head. "I told you, Rhett. We are not going to start up a relationship or whatever it is you think you want solely because we now share a similar traumatic experience."

"I don't want a relationship. It doesn't have to be romantic between us. Can we please keep in touch, even as friends?"

Despite his words, the look in his eyes tells me he is thinking of our kisses.

Thing is, as knee-weakening as those kisses were and as much as I'd love to repeat them, I doubt they were about me. I doubt they were about Edin, either. The only way I can allow myself to view them is to assume those kisses were about Jill.

I want to tell Rhett no, we can't be friends, though we practically are now. I really do. It's what's right.

Then I look in his beautiful eyes again. They watch me with more optimism than I've ever allowed myself. They also hold a desire I have yet to see from any man, including those few I welcomed into my bed. Maybe it's because, unlike those men, Rhett is also hoping to be accepted into my heart.

I've endured two harrowing, brutal near-death experiences. Rhett is one of the few people in my life who might actually understand the dynamics of this situation and what it is doing to me both mentally and emotionally.

"You have situations you need to move on from." Which is rich coming from me, but I can't say that out loud.

"Maybe you can keep me accountable," he suggests, hope in his eyes.

I don't think he understands what I meant since he is clearly talking about Edin and not Jill.

I glance over at Edin waiting by a car. How would I feel if I were her? "You owe her an explanation before you are allowed to call me."

"I don't owe her anything. I've told her I don't love her. There isn't anything else to say."

"Apparently, there is. Otherwise, why would she show up here?"

"Can I at least have your number when you're satisfied that I've sufficiently told Edin off?"

A lightheadedness starts to overwhelm me. "I can't," I whisper. My head throbs.

Edin isn't your only problem, I want to add. Those words won't leave my brain. My mouth won't even start forming them.

"At least take mine."

"I can't," I repeat, as quiet as I did the first time I said it.

Rhett doesn't reply. He simply nods his head and walks across the hospital parking lot to his possibly ex-fiancée.

Chapter 17

EDIN CAUTIOUSLY DRIVES ALONG the icy, barely plowed roads, heading to my apartment in Auburn. "Are we going to talk about that voicemail now?" she asks.

I never told Gwenn about the message I left Edin. Too ashamed.

"So, you haven't forgotten it?" I ask Edin slowly. Although I'm looking at her, it's too dark to see her gorgeous, creamy, freckled skin. I envision her face up against mine, along with her soft skin, but I'm not sure I want those memories at the forefront of my mind. Knowing she's damn sexy just isn't a good enough reason to stay with her anymore.

"Of course not. My fiancé broke up with me in one of the most cowardly ways possible. Not easily forgotten." Edin's voice is tight, but her tone is not harsh.

I know better than to trust this. She's holding in a lot of anger. "I'm sorry. I truly am."

She lets out a sharp exhale. "I'm sure you are, and given recent events—"

While I felt the urge to interrupt her, this pause is not because of me. Edin stopped herself. If only she would tell me why, maybe we could get the fight out of our systems and be done with the whole thing. Unfortunately, it's never as easy as that with her.

After another deep breath in, Edin continues. "Well, maybe we can just move past the message. Move past the ugliness."

Despite, or maybe because of, our history, I can't believe I'm hearing her right. "You mean stay together? Are you for real?"

"Why not? Rhett Mason, you almost died. Everything that happened before this weekend has been flooding my mind ever since the hospital called me. I would have lost you forever and only had those memories to keep you alive. I, for one, am not willing to let a brief moment of misunderstanding ruin what we have. How about you?"

"You think it was just a misunderstanding?"

"How else do you explain dumping me without a reason?" She remains in control of herself while battling for control of this conversation.

"I gave you a reason."

"No, you did not. 'I can't do this anymore' isn't a reason. It's an excuse. One I absolutely forgive you for, so long as you apologize."

I watch her weave around a large pile of snow that juts out a few inches into the road. "What do you mean it's an excuse? What kind of reason do you want? How does it get any clearer than I don't want to be with you anymore?"

"But that isn't what you said."

"You want me to take back the words I meant, and still mean, by the way?"

"Yes. Will you?"

She gives me no more than half a second to form a reply before speaking again. "Well, who am I kidding? I forgive you no matter what. I love you, Rhett. More than anyone I've ever known and more than anyone else could. I know you love me, too." Then she makes this sighing noise she knows usually has me offering her any damn thing she wants.

There's a whole heap of trouble coming my way if I give in to it this time.

Chapter 18

Gwenn

"Lourdes?" I call out as soon as I open my door in Syracuse. I know she is here. Her car is parked across the street from my apartment building's entrance.

Her quick footsteps on the ceramic tile reach my ears. She appears in the doorway of the kitchen, runs the short distance to me, and we embrace. It's a total best friend movie moment. Then she pulls back, careful not to knock into my crutch.

"Why the hell didn't you tell me when you were released from the hospital? You didn't have to order a car. That must have cost a fortune to come all the way here."

"I don't care. They didn't tell me in advance when I could leave. I was so happy to not stay there any longer."

Lourdes nods in comprehension.

Because I had plenty of time in the hospital by myself, I texted her the whole ordeal while my battery charged thanks to the custodian's charger. Lourdes and I both know I don't want to discuss it any further right now. She's the only one I've ever told about all the gory details of my last brush with death. Other friends know simple highlights. This weekend's events are not anything I'm in the mood or the right mental place to rehash. Not yet. The time will come, along with the rest of my past.

"I realize it's pretty much the middle of the night, and your appetite level could very easily be at a zero, but I saved dinner for you. Your favorite." She watches me and waits for a reply.

I temporarily close my eyes and take in a deep breath through my nose. "Do I smell tamales from that little blue place on the corner?" Opening my eyes again, I look to my friend.

She smiles. "Yep. Keeping warm in the oven."

I'm a little wary of eating after my previous brushes with nausea earlier today. However, the nurse practitioner promised the meds she gave me should allow me to eat if I feel up to it. I decide to take her word for it. I am genuinely hungry. Perhaps one or two tamales will be okay.

My bestie and I head to the kitchen. She selects a square, gray-and-white swirled plate out of the cabinet as I pull out a fork from the drawer. I totter my way to my tiny two-seat kitchen table, where Lourdes and I both take a seat.

"Nice, warm meal on a cold night." I sigh before I even dig in, and it remains untouched on my plate.

I needed this last night. Actually, what I needed last night was the lobster dish I'd been looking forward to in Boston after an evening of fantastic art. I needed to not be in a plane crash. I needed for all those people to not die.

Tears start burning my eyes, then my cheeks.

Lourdes leans forward and puts her hand on mine. I use my other hand to wipe away the warm moisture on my face. My dearest friend sits with me and lets me cry as long as I need to. I no longer care about my food or my hunger. The only thing I care about is letting the almost toxic energy out of me. Every last drop of it.

Eventually, I sniffle and give her a smile before sighing again. My face is hot and still a little damp. I dry off what I can with napkins.

"Better?" Lourdes asks.

"Better."

"So, about that guy."

"Rhett?"

"He saved your life. Is he some kind of emergency worker or military guy or just an average, real-life hero?"

"He's a mechanic with super survival skills. We actually met just before the charter flight."

"How did that happen?"

I explain the circumstances of how Rhett and I conversed with each other in the terminal after he approached me by the large wall of windows. I hadn't noticed him before, but then, I didn't pay much attention to anything except the snow outside.

"We made small talk. He gave me a cute half-smile. And then that son-of-a-bitch promised us something we should have known he couldn't deliver."

"It isn't your fault for trusting the pilot," Lourdes reminds me for what feels like the sixth time.

"I let my guard down. I was so excited and probably a little anxious about my trip—the first trip I've taken in years—that I didn't allow myself to be cautious. I didn't use common sense. Look what that got me."

Lourdes stands instead of answering. "Thirsty? Would you like tea, coffee, some Pinot, or a hot buttered rum?" she asks.

"I'll have water for now," I tell her. "I'm not in the mood for anything stronger."

She takes my plate still full of now-cold food and walks to the sink. The fork she deposits into the sink basin, and the plate she sets on the counter next to it. Then she steps over to the cabinet.

"You know, it wasn't long. Only one night. Damn if it didn't feel like forever. I thought—" I can't hold in another sob that's desperate to escape my mouth. More sobs follow before I have a chance to regain my composure. "I thought I was waking up from the accident all over again."

"Not the plane." Lourdes says this rather than asks it. She knows.

I nod as she turns and fills the glass with cold, filtered tap water. "I escaped death twice. Twice. How many more times am I going to experience something so terrifying? And before you ask, no, I didn't tell my hero any details. We had enough shit to deal with. The last thing I needed was him being sad for me because I didn't have anyone in my life before I met you." Many more hot tears stream down my face. "What is the point of my survival?"

Lourdes hands me the glass of water and returns to her seat. "You haven't had any train or car accidents yet. Maybe fate wants to you experience them all first."

I can't help but chuckle. It's twisted, but I kind of love it. "If that's the case, we might as well throw in bus and motorcycle, too, right?"

"Don't forget ATVs." She laughs a bit more, then takes a breath. "I won't give you any 'grand scheme of things' BS. I don't have the answers. I'm just glad you're alive."

Lourdes moves up out of her chair in order to hug me again.

I ask her to stay the rest of the night with me. I don't want to be alone. Too many thoughts of death swirl around in my brain.

Some people would call all of my experiences fate. Despite joking around with Lourdes, I can't say for sure fate exists. If it does, what on earth does it want with me?

Chapter 19

Rhett

I'm finally home. Edin reluctantly left for her own apartment. The one she hasn't slept at in three months. Apparently, she slept here last night, too. Never really answered her on whether I want to stay together. She was always one to overlook my flaws, but forgetting how I dumped her? That's a kind of grace I'm not sure I deserve. Not sure I want it, either.

My phone dings with a new text. Late as it is, I know who the message is from. The same text she sends me each time we are apart, which isn't much, thanks to her.

Edin

> Call me tomorrow. Luv you

She added a heart and a kissing emoji at the end. Like nothing happened.

Except something did. Something, or rather someone, I can't get out of my head.

I glance at my new text from Edin again before turning the phone off. I know the staff was kind enough to let me charge it, but I still don't care to check all the messages I missed. None of them are from the one person I want them from. She doesn't even have my number. Wouldn't let me give it to her.

I'm sure most of my missed messages are from Edin. She doesn't know my family, so she wouldn't have bothered contacting them. There's probably a couple from my online chess-game partner. Though I've been working with him on how to be a better player, he struggles sometimes. When we left off, almost all his pawns were still blocking his bishop. I know he must be uneasy, but also maybe a little eager to start playing again. As it is, I'll win in less moves than it took the last game.

Probably should read Edin's texts, just in case.

Tomorrow.

I lie in bed after showering but can't sleep.

Gwenn won't talk to me unless Edin is clear I'm not interested in her anymore. But doesn't Edin deserve more of me after sticking around so long? Does that make either or both of us complete fools? Maybe I'm too tired to know the answer.

I do know what Jill would say. She would have the perfect answer to both of those questions. She'd also tell me to quit being so wishy-washy and make up my damn mind right now. Honestly, Jill would probably tell me I already have.

·♥·♥·♥·♥·♥·

"Mason, where the hell have you been?" My manager nearly growls this as I hang up my coat in my locker at work Monday morning. He follows me to the break room, huffing the whole way.

"Been a little tied up," I say. I know he knows about the crash, but I don't expect any sympathy from him. It would be stupid to. Sure as hell can't tell him how much I'd rather be back at the crash site than this place, much as I want to. Can't afford to look for a new job.

I originally wanted to drink some coffee while looking over the work orders, but now I realize Giovanni is going to make that impossible. He's standing with his arms crossed not far from where I planned on sitting. I head straight for the 2009 Malibu I was working on before I got on that stupid airplane. Giovanni follows me yet again.

The Malibu is still here and still broken. Surprise, surprise.

"Why haven't the axles been replaced yet?" I ask Ricardo, a fellow mechanic at the shop, although I actually mean the question for my new shadow.

Ricardo shakes his head and moves his eyes toward Giovanni.

Of course. It's been untouched, waiting for my return. I turn to face Giovanni, the worst manager and shop owner I've ever dealt with in the ten years I've worked on cars. "Couldn't you order any parts? We've had this car for a week now."

Giovanni looks at the car, then at me. The sneer is already in his eyes and on his mouth. "You tore the motor down when I told you not to. You can put it all back."

I know he thinks he's only screwing me over, but in reality, this affects all of us. "What about the axles, Giovanni?"

"What about 'em?"

I cross my arms. "The customer specifically asked for better axles. He's making this a race car. He needs them."

Giovanni snickers. "That's your problem, not mine."

"I'm doing what the customer asked," I say again. "And I've put most of the engine together already. I am not okay with sending out junkers to unsuspecting people. Nor do I like giving back vehicles I've had to install second-hand parts on because you're too cheap to order new ones. That the kind of reputation you like for this place? You want to destroy everything your pop and his family built?"

He points a fat, greaseless finger in my face. "Our reputation is just fine. Now get some work done."

After Giovanni stalks off, Ricardo laughs. "Man, you got the weasel all worked up today. Where you been?" He looks over at my scraped face. "Caught up in a fight?"

"Long story."

Ricardo's been at this shop several years longer than I have. He started at twenty-two, when Giovanni's dad still ran it. Sixteen years later, with the asshole having been here all those years, but in charge for three of them, I wonder how Ricardo hasn't tired of this garbage. "Let's just work on the A/C condenser and radiator," I say. "I'll scrounge up some axles from somewhere. Again."

"No can do on the A/C. Giovanni told me to take it from the Tahoe out back. One, it doesn't fit."

"Obviously." I feel a pain growing in my temple.

Ricardo nods. "Two, he left it out there so long it's rusted to nothing."

I run a hand through my beard. It's too early in the day for this shit. Tyler, one of the many other mechanics, tightens the lug nuts on an Elantra in the next bay over as I stand here and brainstorm. Because our cheapskate, son-of-a-bitch boss refuses to order new replacement parts, we're left holding the bag. "What about the G6 Giovanni's got?"

"His nephew's car?"

"Not since he bought that Subaru for him. The kid barely drove it. It's like new."

"Giovanni's gonna be pissed about us scavenging through his personal stash."

"Do you want that car out of here or not? Giovanni wants to get paid. We don't get paid unless he does. At this point, he won't care how. And maybe this will teach him a lesson about not ordering parts for us to use. We can't give our customers lemons because of him. It's our asses, too. He'd be more than happy to blame us. If he ran this shop like he's supposed to, we'd never have to worry about this mess."

Ricardo gathers everything we need for the A/C while I rummage through our "supplier" lists—aka junkyard contacts—to find someone who will deliver the bigger axles here today. By the time six o'clock rolls around, the Malibu and the Elantra are finished. I owe my buddy at the salvage yard a case of beer for his quick delivery. Thank God Spiros already had what I needed in a pile of other axles, and not still on the busted car in their yard. I also thank God that the damage to the broken vehicle is not on the end of the car I need for my repairs.

I scrub as much dirt and grease off my hands as possible with the gritty orange pumice soap, then dry them on some brown paper towels. Once I've chugged the last of my second cup of coffee, I grab my coat and head out the door. I'm in my truck before too much of the cold affects my body.

Reluctantly, I told Ricardo about Gwenn and the wreck during our lunch break.

"Damn, man. What the hell are you doing here?"

"Didn't know what else to do. I can't get this woman out of my head."

His response? "Your girl get her stuff out of your apartment yet?"

No. Not yet, but she will. I can't focus on that right now. I have something else I need to focus on first once I'm home.

Chapter 20

Rhett

I'M IN MY APARTMENT long enough to shower and crack open a beer when I hear the lock tumble from my spot on the sofa. I stand and walk toward the opening door.

"What are you doing here?" I ask, my voice hard.

Edin gives me a quick headshake and seems to be gesturing with her eyes, but I don't know what she means. She's holding a square box I recognize as a cake box from her bakery. Then the door opens again.

"Hi!" her two baking assistants exclaim as they come inside, then close the door behind them.

"What are y'all doing here?" I ask with a nicer tone than the one I used for Edin.

"Surprise engagement dinner!" Phoebe, one of the assistants, says.

"Edin told us you two have finally started planning the wedding. We're here to celebrate," Val, the other assistant, adds.

"It was nothing to be ashamed of, Rhett. We understand," Phoebe tells me.

Now I'm apparently ashamed of something? I wonder what the hell else Edin has been telling them.

"What do you mean?" I ask Phoebe.

Val looks at me and speaks first before Phoebe has a chance. "The real reason you held back on planning."

"You finally agreed to let Edin pay," Phoebe adds, as if reminding me of this.

"Not being able to fund a wedding is no big deal. Totally okay," Val says.

I force myself to look at Edin. She smiles demurely but doesn't speak.

"Is that what Edin said?" I ask the others. My voice is harsher out of my mouth than it was in my head.

The two women look a bit shocked. They've stopped smiling as much as they had been. Phoebe's mouth hangs open a little bit. Both of them stare at me in silence.

Edin laughs, I assume to calm the mood. "Of course," she says.

She's acting like there couldn't possibly be any other reason. Like Jill, perhaps. Or Gwenn. Edin's smile also doesn't falter as she eyes me, clearly waiting for me to agree with her.

I have no idea what to say to her. No, wait. I know exactly what to say, but chewing her out right now is not going to do any good.

"Excuse us for a moment," I tell Phoebe and Val. Then I put my hand on Edin's arm to pull her out of the room.

But she resists. "Before we arrived, we were just talking about your terrible accident," she says to me.

"Edin explained to us how it gave you a new look at your life," Val says.

"In a manner of speaking, I guess, but—" I begin, only to be interrupted.

"Oh. My. Gosh. Yes. And how scary it must have been all alone," Phoebe says.

"Alone?" I ask, then dart my eyes Edin's way. I think I just saw her flinch.

"Oh, did I say alone?" she asks them with what I guess is supposed to sound like an innocent tone. "I meant he was practically alone, but not the only survivor."

The women nod in understanding. I doubt it makes much difference to them, but it means the world to me, and Edin knows it.

It's only been one day since Gwenn and I found help. That's hard enough to deal with. It's been a day with Edin trying to pretend Gwenn doesn't exist. She didn't bother inviting anyone I know, meaning she's at least smart enough to realize none of them would believe this crap if I told them it wasn't true.

"Enough about sad things," Edin says breezily as she reaches to link one of her arms with mine. She holds on to me so tight, it's obvious she won't let go, physically or otherwise. The cake box hasn't hindered her movements in any way.

There is a knock at the door. None of us move for a second. Then I jump at the opportunity to release myself from Edin and walk over to open the door. A food delivery person stands in front of me holding white paper bags.

"Oh! Food's here," Val exclaims. "We ordered from your and Edin's fave restaurant. All the foods you'd love from a fully catered meal, pared down to serve four."

Edin knows I'm not into catered or any kind of fancy dinners. Not usually. I'd rather have a beer and steak with a ball game or a casual dinner outside. Now I can't recall what restaurant she likes enough to have asked for this meal, while the delivery guy stands there and waits. I can't bring myself to take the food from him.

"They were so gracious about it, too, when Phoebe and I ordered," Val adds. "They almost never do special delivery orders for regular customers."

And now I feel like an ass for being so angry. This, coupled with Edin's pouty lip, which I seem to be the only one who's noticed, has me unsure what to do. My hesitance to react in any way apparently gives Edin enough encouragement. She has a wide smile as Val takes the food bags from the delivery person. Phoebe taps her phone and tells him she sent a tip, then he walks away as she shuts the door, while I'm still awkwardly in the way.

"Our treat." She smiles at me. "You and Edin shouldn't have to pay for your engagement dinner."

The more she calls it an "engagement dinner," the more I think maybe our breakup hasn't registered in Edin's mind.

I was clear on that last night, wasn't I?

It was such a long night. Not to mention the day and night before.

In order to be as unambiguous as possible now, I have a plan. I gently take the cake from Edin's hands and hand it to Phoebe. Then I say, "Excuse us, please. You two mind setting everything out for us? Plates and silverware are all the way to the left when you walk into the kitchen. My, uh, fiancée and I will be in there in just a moment."

"Aww. They want alone time," Phoebe gushes to Val in a syrupy-sweet voice. They are both as bad as Edin.

"No worries." Val winks at us. "Edin said your terrible ordeal added new sparks to your relationship."

"There will be sparks all right," I say, trying not to grit my teeth.

They both actually giggle at this, then they head down the hall.

I feel a pang of guilt for having smiled at them in return before they walked away, but it isn't nearly as bad as the tightness from having called Edin my fiancée. Even when we were a couple, I rarely had to call her that to anyone.

"Are you crazy?" I ask Edin quietly once the other two are gone. "You and I are not together anymore."

"Last night, you said you weren't sure. That usually means you want the same thing I want. You almost never disagree with me."

"Well, I'm sure about this now. I want us to end right now."

She puts her hands up. "I know. I know, and I'm sorry. But honestly, this evening is the nicest you've been to me in days. Aren't I allowed to enjoy it?"

"Edin, I've barely seen you in days. I wasn't here. I almost died with Gwenn."

"Will you please stop saying that woman's name to me?" she snaps. Then she softens her tone and her facial expression. "Rhett Liam Mason, I'm in love with you. I want to plan a wedding to you, but if you genuinely want us to be over, we'll officially break up."

"That's exactly what I want."

She nods. "Okay. But first . . ."

I let a sharp breath out. "Here we go."

Edin ignores this. "But first, please, please just go one more night as my fiancé. I'll tell the girls the truth tomorrow at work."

"Your truth or the actual truth?"

"That we broke up. Please don't make me do it right now. It would be too awful. Too humiliating."

I don't say anything, but I do run a hand through my hair. "Edin . . ." I stop. I'm not a hundred percent sure how I was going to continue without sounding like an ass. There's no nice way to do this. I tried the way I thought would avoid any conflict, and that backfired.

Her eyes get all glossy and wet. "Please, Rhett."

I can't say no. I really wish I could. I know I should. I just can't.

Edin smiles, obviously aware she's won.

"I'll give you an hour. That's it. After an hour, we make up an excuse and you three leave. Got it?"

Now her smile grows. "Oh, Rhett Liam Mason, You are the best guy ever!" She pulls me into a hug. It's so fast, I don't have a chance to step away from her. She's just as quick when she kisses my lips. Then she puts a kiss on my neck just below my beard, the spot I always go weak for.

"Why did you do that?" I whisper-choke. I'm starting to sweat.

"To add the glow I adore to your face. The one you get before and just after," she tells me. "They already suspect we're being romantic in here. Might as well make a good show of it."

Which is exactly the problem with her. She makes a good show of everything.

Edin pinches her cheeks and a spot on her neck, and also gently bites her lips to pink everything up. I watch her in dismay and a bit of disgusted awe. In a flash, she's gone, down the hall to her gossipy assistants.

I feel so used and so stupid right now. Maybe I need to find a way out of this sooner than the hour I promised her. And the kiss on the neck . . . I mean . . . yeah, it got me. But not the way it did when Gwenn accidentally found that spot. I pull out my phone and call Ricardo. I need his help. He'd be willing to come up with any excuse for me, I just know it.

Except he doesn't answer.

No one else comes to mind who could rescue me from this mess.

"Rhett?" Edin calls out from the kitchen. "We can't start without you, sweetie."

If I leave, maybe they'll take the hint and be gone by the time I come back. Or maybe Edin would send the National Guard out to look for me the way she tried to over the weekend. That was probably the one time I wish she could have succeeded.

I try Ricardo again, to no avail. Reluctantly, I drag myself down the hall, hoping my car alarm will go off. I clutch my phone, praying someone will need me to come help them with a problem. I'd even love for Giovanni to call me back to the shop. I'd be there in a heartbeat.

Instead, I join the others at the kitchen table. We eat our meal of grilled shrimp, seared scallops, and something they called a big, fancy name for what are essentially tiny potato cakes.

The three women laugh and smile and chat about colors, fabrics, and I'm not sure what else. I don't listen. I just keep moving my eyes from my plate to my phone to the clock on the stove just beyond Edin's shoulder and back. Edin tries to encourage me to participate, but I'm not biting.

I catch the end of Phoebe's words and realize she's speaking to me. "Sorry?"

"How many groomsmen will you have? Preferably the same number of bridesmaids Edin's chosen."

"Edin has how many bridesmaids?" I have to ask.

"Eight."

"Eight?" I almost choke. How could she consider eight bridesmaids to stand up with her? She doesn't even have that many close friends.

"I might possibly raise that number to ten." Edin smiles to all of us. "I'd like a nice, even number. Perfectly symmetrical. Ten seems just right. Just think of all the beautiful photos we could stage with so large a bridal party. It would be amazing!"

"How many people would you invite to this thing?" I ask her. I can't call it "the wedding" since it isn't actually happening.

"At least two hundred," she replies innocently. There's that tone again.

I know better. Two hundred is more like four hundred. My chest thinks maybe my throat had the right idea and starts making it harder for me to breathe. Four hundred guests. I don't know half of four hundred people total, let alone people I'd want at what's supposed to be one of the best days of my life. I doubt Edin does, either.

"I just had the perfect idea," Phoebe says. "You two should have your engagement photos taken on Quill Bridge."

Edin takes in a breath. I look over at her and immediately see the sparkle in her eyes at that thought. She always wanted me to propose there. Though she never said, I know it bothered her when I didn't.

Of course, I didn't genuinely propose in the first place. Never got on one knee and begged her to be my wife. It was just one of those suggestions she gave me that I agreed to because I didn't care one way or the other at the time.

Then Edin finally acknowledges my scowl with a tiny, almost imperceptible nod. We are just beyond the hour now.

"We should go get some coffee and let Rhett rest. He had a rough weekend," Edin says to her friends.

"But we haven't cut into the cake yet," Val protests. "Besides, you said you wanted your fiancé involved in all this. We can't make any more wedding decisions without him."

Edin gives a small, sad smile. "We'll talk about it over coffee," she says to them. "You keep the cake," she adds to me.

"It's okay," I tell her. "I don't want it. Not anymore."

Her expression tells me she understands completely. And finally, it's done.

But then her eyes start to tear up again, and I hear myself say, "Or you can leave it. That's okay, too."

"Leave the cake?" Edin asks.

"Or stay. You can stay and eat cake here. We can all have dessert together."

Edin grins, but she also scrunches her eyebrows. Her eyes are still glossy. She looks like she's trying to figure out what to say.

"Can we talk in the other room for a minute?" I ask her after a few more moments of her silence.

She nods quietly.

Edin tries to speak just outside the kitchen, but I shake my head to silence her and lead her back to the living room.

"What's going on, Rhett? What are you doing to me?"

"I hate to see you cry."

"That's good. That should be how you feel. But you basically just pushed me out. You told me we were done. Not that I'm not grateful, but why the change of heart? Are you going to finally stop breaking up with me?"

"This isn't a change of heart. It's showing you I have a heart. I'm not the ass you make me out to be when you're angry, but I'm not the perfect guy you think I am when you're not. I'm just a regular guy. You and I are over. Nothing in that regard has changed."

Val walks into the room before Edin has a chance to respond. "Are we staying for cake, or no?" Val asks. She looks back and forth between us.

"You're staying," I tell them both.

Chapter 21

Gwenn

"I hate Tuesdays," Lourdes laments over speakerphone. "So much more than Mondays."

"That doesn't make any sense," I tell her as I see a listing for a mid-century modern house that would be great for a client couple of mine. It is about twenty miles from their current place, but also still close to both of their jobs. They already told me they're willing to relocate.

"Of course it does. At least Mondays are supposed to suck. We all know this. Tuesdays never know what they're supposed to be."

"Rough day?" I ask.

"I don't want to talk about it."

This makes me laugh. "You mentioned it."

"My top delivery guy called in sick. I just broke my best clippers. The blister on my thumb is getting worse. I lost an entire box of ribbon. And I was asked out by a man who came here to buy flowers for his girlfriend."

"Oof. That's a whopper," I agree. "All of them. How often do customers ask you out?"

"Almost never. And then he had me write out this dumb, lovey-dovey card to her expressing his undying love. I felt like I needed a shower after."

I send a link of this amazing listing to the midcentury modern couple. It's so perfect for them. It's also the sixth perfect listing I've found for a client in the past two hours. I am totally on a roll with no bumps or mishaps, like yesterday's awful catching up paid off despite keeping myself working nonstop until almost two in the morning. Things just couldn't be better than now.

For my work, anyway. Last night, I stood next to my open closet door for a good twenty minutes, unable to pick up the folder that potentially holds the keys I need to unlock my past. It was ironic how I had to keep myself balanced with a mobility aid, considering how much I needed one back then.

I've never gotten much further with the folder than I did last night. I stare at it, but don't open it. Bravery is not my forte.

But right now is about Lourdes.

"You never complain about clients hitting on you. Does that never happen to you, either?" she asks.

"Not really. Like your customers, my clients are usually committed to the person they're looking with."

"And if they're single? Or philandering?"

"I never think about dating, so I'm never aware of any flirting. No one's directly come out and asked me to dinner or drinks. Or more."

"Did you know Rhett was into you before the big make-out sesh? You talked about meeting him in the airport, but you didn't mention any flirting."

"There wasn't any," I tell her, trying to keep my intonation flat.

Then I see I have a new email from the midcentury modern couple. That was a lot faster than I'd expected. I can't help grinning before I even open it on my computer. The commission is going to be incredible, yes, but the joy of my clients just might be even better. These are the moments I adore my job. These are the moments which make up for all the struggles I endured learning this trade.

"Maybe I just have the bad luck of meeting more jerks than you do," Lourdes says.

I read the new email on my desktop. "Oh no," I say. "Damn it!"

"What? What happened?"

I don't answer yet. There's more in the message.

Lourdes waits.

When I reach the end, I say, "Not only was the listing I just sent a couple apparently not the right house for them, now they think I'm not good enough to be their broker anymore. They are going with someone else."

"Did they say why?"

I look it over again. "The letter they apparently co-wrote says I, quote, clearly don't know what mid-century modern is. They go on to say they want someone who gets them and their style, not someone who can't be bothered to imagine the houses from their point of view."

"Translation: They have no idea what they want and are just looking for a way to ditch you."

"Yeah. I'm sure you're right. I know it happens. It just sucks. This felt like an absolute guarantee. I never saw this coming."

"Hey, call you back." This is Lourdes's way of hanging up when a customer enters her flower shop. Though she has employees and spends the majority of her time designing, part of the work space is open to the showroom, giving it a more inviting atmosphere. It's the way Lourdes's grandma planned the shop when she first opened it, long before Lourdes took over.

While I wait for my bestie's call, I scan through all my messages again. Lo and behold, another client is ditching me. Well, clients. This time, the clients are co-owners of the historic Mackintosh estate in Syracuse Falls. The Mackintosh family is one of the oldest, and richest, in town. The siblings and cousins wanted me to help them sell the family farm and orchard as well as the winery, as they only wanted to keep the house in town in the family trust. According to their message, by the time I emailed them back yesterday, after no word from me since last week—Saturday, before the crash—they'd already decided to hold on to the farm for a few years and hope its value will increase.

I understand this to mean none of them want it, but perhaps one of them is hoping their children do. Or perhaps one of the children or grandchildren got upset at the idea of the farm and winery belonging to someone else, even if none of the Mackintoshes of my generation want to run it.

This is a huge loss for me. I was looking forward to the commission from that sale. It would have been a pretty big chunk of change.

I decide it's time to take a break. I don't want to read any more emails. I don't want to know if more clients are leaving me. I want to just stay in a bubble for a while. It's a rapidly eroding bubble, but if I cling to it, I might be able to keep it a little longer.

Of course, I never truly stop working while at the office. So instead of thinking about clients, I focus on properties. I look up a few listed last week that I'd like to see in person. Nevertheless, the loss of income nags at me.

Trying to convince them to change their minds would only come across as desperate. I don't know any of the younger Mackintoshes well enough to bring it up in conversation outside of the email exchange.

I answer my phone during the first ring when I see it's Lourdes calling.

"The last hour has genuinely made me thankful I am single," she says.

"Why's that?"

"I just had a bride cry to me that her soon-to-be mother-in-law suddenly hates all the flowers the bride chose for the wedding this coming weekend. Her fiancé believes it's best to let his mom get what she wants. Neither the fiancé nor the mom care how nearly impossible it is to change everything now. I did all I could to reassure the bride her wedding will be gorgeous with her original choices. What I honestly wanted to tell her was to run. Because who the hell wants to marry into that?"

"It's possible her fiancé does love her, despite this shortcoming. Though it is a pretty big one."

"I'll say. This shortcoming is always going to come between the bride and groom and will probably end up pitting all three of them against each other. Sounds like a nightmare. I've seen far too many couples where things are out of balance, usually when one loves the other much more or when one is in love but the other isn't. I sometimes wish maybe I could be a counselor as a side job to help people through wedding crises."

"Sounds like Rhett and his ex-fiancé. She was in love, but he wasn't, which is why he broke things off before the flight."

"He was smart enough to not go through with it. Sometimes I wonder how many couples ever make it to their first anniversary."

"How many repeat customers do you have?"

"Probably not as many as there should be. I can only hope they've moved away instead of divorced. I hate bumping into people somewhere and finding out the truth."

"At least you don't have to worry about that with me."

"Because you're not allowed to move away?"

I laugh. "Because I'm never getting married."

"I completely agree with you. I'm there, too. But sometimes I wonder."

"Wonder what?" I ask. A heat spreads through me. Not a good heat. Not a heat I ever want to feel. I fan my face with my hand.

She gives a wry laugh. "Oh, you know. Those same old what-ifs."

"Same."

"I mean, I know that in order to form a relationship—well, a healthy relationship—both people need to be able to compromise. I am unwilling to do that. Probably always will be."

"Same," I repeat. "Sometimes, those what-ifs have me questioning if maybe I should have given in a little more, but honestly, I know those answers wouldn't change my resolve."

"Even if you had excellent prospects for marriage? Or a steady relationship?" Lourdes knows the answers to these questions, but that never stops her from asking sometimes. I think she likes knowing she and I are on the same page when it comes to romance.

"Even then. Besides, I've never wanted to spend more than a week or so with any one man. As for marriage, my best prospect right now is a man I literally just almost died with, and I'm never going to see him again." I try to hide my changing disposition by keeping my tone light, but I fail. As it is, maybe Lourdes will listen to my words more than my voice.

"Are you sure about that?"

I want to chuckle if only to convince my brain that it's okay. "Positive. We don't even know how to contact each other. I didn't think it a good idea to exchange numbers or email addresses. I still stand by that. So he told me his whole life story. That doesn't mean we're destined for each other." Except I know I'm saying this out loud for my benefit, not Lourdes's.

It's harder to breathe normally. "Oh shit."

"What?"

I can't answer. I've put my phone on my desk to get ready for what I can never prepare for or anticipate.

No, no, no, no, no, I think. But this won't do any good. It won't help. It won't stop. I can't stop it.

Stop it. Stop it!

Though I sit at my desk in my office, there's a train heading right at me, and I can't get out of the way. Its light is in my eyes. I can't see anything else around me. I try to move my body away, but it instead shifts forward, backward, forward, backward. Only, I can't feel this.

Then the tears come.

They might be silent, but I am not. I weep to the point I'm blubbering, desperately and almost involuntarily suck in air, and weep some more. I squeeze my hands onto my thighs and my breath keeps hitching. Squeeze and release, squeeze and release, yet I don't feel this either.

I can't speak. I can't tell Lourdes what's wrong or what triggered me this time.

Still, I can hear her soft soothing voice, though it sounds a million miles away.

"You are safe," she says. "This will go away. Breathe, my friend. You are safe."

I am safe, I silently repeat with her though it's like I am a mile underwater.

And then, ever-so-slowly, I start rising to the surface.

Soon, the hitching stops. I can take deep breaths again, albeit sharp ones. I can finally lift my hands and wipe the tears off my cheeks. There's nothing I can do about the ones that fell to my sweater and slacks. My racing heart starts to return to its usual pace. I've stopped rocking myself.

I let out a loud exhale.

"You okay?" Lourdes asks. She's helped me through these before.

"Yeah."

"This was a big one."

"They haven't felt quite so 'out-of-body-experience' lately, until now."

Lourdes is quiet. Then she says softly, "You've mentioned that Rhett needs to face his past. What about you?"

"You think now is the right time to ask me that?"

"Actually, I do."

"Well, I'm way ahead of you, my friend," I reply, still teary and a little nasally from having cried.

"I know it's hard to push yourself into that arena."

"Clearly," I tell her with a sardonic laugh. I only have panic attacks because of the very thing I can't seem to confront. "But I have a plan this time."

"Care to share?"

"Not just yet." First, I want to see if my idea will pan out.

Once home at the end of another—intentionally—long work day, I stand in front of my teeny, tiny bedroom closet. Simply opening the door is difficult enough. Not physically, though it almost feels that way.

But I have to push through this. The only way to find closure of some kind is to do what I consider impossible. I've already survived so much. I can survive a simple internet search.

In the closet, I find the manila folder I'm looking for. It isn't as thick as maybe it should be. A lot of information I managed to take from the hospital is either missing pages or had redacted sections on the originals. I don't have much else.

My hand begins to quiver as I pick the folder up from the shelf. I carry it to the living room, hobbling much less than I did Sunday night, and place it on the table in front of me. I haven't looked in this thing since I moved to Syracuse and settled in. It was my first day here. I didn't have any furniture yet.

Slowly, I open the folder and pull out its contents.

There it is. My old name. Technically, it's currently still my legal name. Jaymie Jonas.

I am sure I could have easily done this search many, many times. But "easily" isn't the right word. I already know those people wiped any traces connecting me and them from the very beginning. I don't know how they did it, but I'm guessing their massive wealth helped.

Yet they still felt the need to pay all my hospital bills and leave me enough money to start over wherever I wanted.

I use search engines all the time for work. This will not be any different, I reassure myself. It's going to be okay.

Except it isn't. Well, not in the way I want it to be. Every keyword search ends in either too many unrelated results or none at all. Combination after combination. I sort through what must be thousands of pages. My eyes burn from staring at the screen, so I take a quick break and grab an orange out of the fridge for a snack. I'm not hungry for much else.

Is it possible Rhett is doing the same emotional work I am? I know how it goes avoiding the pain. I hope if he is, he's making better progress than I am. But then I remember I have to stop thinking about him. There's no point in allowing my thoughts to meander his way. I'm truly never going to see him again.

Chapter 22

Gwenn

MY CLIENTS TEND TO call at the most randomly early hours. I honestly wish I had the answer as to why, but I'll never complain if it lands me a sale. Two new clients, Kelby and Amaryllis, phoned me at four in a flurry of fear they were going to lose the brand-new penthouse in Syracuse they would like to lease for the next year. No matter how many times I assured them that since the contract was signed, no one else would be able to buy it, they wouldn't chill out.

It didn't help—in their eyes—when I went out of town and they couldn't get ahold of me for two days. I thought it wouldn't be professional of me to tell them I'd almost died, so unfounded fears were not that big of a deal.

The call from Kelby and Amaryllis was two hours ago. I'm already at my office in Syracuse Falls due to that conversation. There's no need to organize anything because I always leave things as tidy as possible. I check my emails, so thankful I haven't lost more clients since yesterday—though I did check three times last night before bed as well. The only email I have to send off right away is one from potential clients requesting the current market absorption rate for our area. The length of time it would take to sell all the houses currently listed if nothing else is added to the list is unfortunately longer than I'd like it to be. I'm sure my clients feel the same.

I also scan my long list of to-dos, open several web browser tabs of listings and potential "cold calls," and text Lourdes, knowing she is always awake this early. Running her own flower shop has her working crazy hours like me.

Ruby, an interior designer I often recommend to my clients, has emailed a few pictures of the finished job she did for a couple I sold a house to over a year ago. As always, her work is absolutely stunning. If I ever buy a house of my own, she's the only designer I'll work with.

Lourdes texts back that she is in the cooler but wants to talk to me later in the day. I reply in the affirmative and return to my work.

It isn't long before I receive a call from another client. She's also my only other best friend, Lucy—the one I mentioned to Rhett. Through the long process of apartment and house rental "shopping," Lucy and I grew close. I helped her and her roommate find their current rental a few months ago, before the owner unexpectedly sold the property. "I can't afford twice my current rent," Lucy moans to me. "I'm a teacher! Where do they think I'll get that kind of money? And I can't live with a roommate forever. I'm not in college anymore. I need to be a grownup in my own place. And as much as I adore my family, there is zero chance of my parents letting me move back in. Well, they probably would, but I need to be a grownup in my own place."

"Luce, fair or not, the new owners are allowed to charge as much as they want. Rent control was not part of the lease agreements."

"But my sister has a bigger place and pays less." She's quiet for a few seconds. "I have to go to school now, but can we start a new search soon? Maybe later this afternoon? We only have a half day today in the building. The rest of my work will keep until a later time."

I, of course, agree. Once we hang up, I move on to item number one: email. So. Many. Emails. Buyers, sellers, real estate lawyers, potential new clients, loan officers, and more people I have to keep in contact with, sometimes daily. I check who needs replies right away and who can wait. It also depends on who is in their office this early.

Ooh! This email tells me an offer has been accepted on a house that has been a trial to sell. The sellers—a couple with unmistakable animosity for each other—filed for divorce just after accepting a previous offer, which led to a lot of extra lawyers getting involved and the deal being called off. Those buyers wanted nothing to do with the drama they unintentionally walked into. I was the most disappointed for them because I could tell it was their dream house.

After all the emails are read and responded to, or drafts are drawn up for future responses, I begin rehearsing my "script" for cold calls. I have a trick for these cold calls and a particular way of doing them—always friendly, a little chipper, and never a hint of disappointment if told no. Some days, this is easy-peasy. Most days, I'm a total fake when it comes to being perky. I'm much more "in the zone" showing houses than I am making cold calls.

I also start my coffee pot in the little breakroom of my tiny, three-room office space. While the dark-roast coffee percolates, I return to the front, still role-playing my approach. "Randomly" contacting people to ask if they are looking to buy or sell does not make me nervous. However, I do sometimes wish there was an easier way. Occasionally, the hardest calls I have to do are the ones to those selling their houses FSBO—for sale by owner. A few of them have become pretty indignant or downright rude. But without trying, I never would have gotten at least eight new clients over the years.

After I've unlocked the main office door for the day, I receive a new text. I'm a little surprised to see it's from Lucy, since we just spoke.

> Whatever you do, do not look at the news.

I don't need to ask which news or why. There's a story some-where about the crash, most likely because it was a tragedy that didn't happen too far away. Also because the plane took off from the Syracuse airport, meaning at least some of the victims were from around here. Though the news won't mention Rhett and me by name, I'm having trouble finding comfort in this fact.

Maybe it's because I'm not quite sure they won't if they do figure out who we are.

Adelaide isn't the kind of person who would spill all the gory details to a reporter, but what about the hospital staff or someone at the police station? What if the reporters discover that not only did Rhett and I survive the crash, but we also spent a harrowing night on our own in a frozen shed during a blizzard? This would easily be deemed newsworthy to a journalist. Add to the humanistic side of the story.

I never could stomach the thought of strangers knowing all about my last brush with death. That's clearly the case this time as well. It's so upsetting, I need to sit back down, close my eyes, and take a few slow breaths in and out. My throat tightens at the idea of other people being privy to my ordeal out in the snowstorm.

A loud, echoing buzz tells me someone has opened the outer door and is inside the building. They could be going to any of the other offices in this shared structure, but I decide to stay alert in case. It's probably a little early for any clients to be here, but that four in the morning phone call proves my clients in particular don't run on any sort of schedule. Having never sat down, I pause at my desk, eying the hall through my frosted glass door. The person is in the long corridor leading from the front door to my office. Then I see him.

Rhett is here.

It's only been three days, but my heart races at the sight of him.

I am in so much trouble.

Chapter 23

Rhett

THERE SHE IS.

Finally.

It feels like it's been way too long since I saw Gwenn. I can't tell if she's happy I'm here. Her facial expressions give nothing away. No creased brows or anything.

Gwenn stands near her desk, still using her crutch, as I step closer to her, gripping the flowers I stopped at the grocery store to buy her. I open my mouth and say the first thing that's on my mind.

"I just can't stay away from you. I took the day off to come see you. I needed to see you."

She's the only person in the world who I blurt things out to.

Shit.

Chapter 24

Gwenn

RHETT PUTS HIS EMPTY hand up. "I'm not a stalker. I swear I'm not."

I believe him but don't say this. Not yet.

"I found your real estate office in an online search, and I'm glad I did. I hate the way we left things."

He pauses, and I let the silence linger.

"But it's more than that. I just feel this pull to you. I don't know what it is."

"My eyes. Like Jill's."

He opens his mouth, but I don't give him the chance to speak.

"You aren't desperate to find an easy substitute for Jill?"

His face grows red at my question, but he doesn't reply.

I continue. "Edin. Me. That's what it seems like." And as cruel as this sounds, I need to hear his answer. I wait.

"That's not what I'm doing. At all. I'm sorry if it seems like it is. This has more to it than you think. It's more than just the color of your eyes. It's more than what I felt when I saw you in the airport."

"Well, we aren't facing the possibility of death anymore, so I know it can't be that."

"It wasn't that before, either. You're special. I've never met anyone else like you. I . . . Dang, I sound like such a cliché right now."

I mean, he kind of is. He showed up at my work with flowers and the intention of pouring out his feelings for me.

Thing is, I like clichés. I like sweet and romantic, even if it did take him three days to find me.

I kind of hate myself right now, though. I'm letting my weaknesses get to me. Rhett might be my biggest weakness. No one has looked at me and made my heart palpitate the way he does.

It isn't fair.

Part of me wishes I could be cold and unfeeling. Just enough to clear him from my thoughts. I've done this easily enough in the past. Keeping to myself has protected me from the attention of most men. The rest who showed an interest ended up with nothing or a few nights with me before I shut them out, at most.

Then Rhett and I make eye contact again.

"It's okay, Rhett. It's nice to see you, too." I reach for the bouquet of pink and purple blooms. He tilts them toward me with a grin, but he also looks uneasy.

Before I have the flowers in hand, I stop my movements and ask, "What's going on?"

Rhett hesitates, and in doing so, doesn't answer.

Then it dawns on me. "Edin."

"Yeah," he says with a slight nod.

Is he kidding me with this right now? I was just hating me instead of him, and for what? "You're back together?"

"No. Nothing like that."

"I told you at the hospital you had to be done with her before you could contact me. I was very clear."

"You were. I was just as clear with her when I told her she and I are over."

"But?"

"Gwenn, I can't just drop her from my life. She's been a great friend to me. But that's it. Just friends. I swear it isn't anything more.

I told her in no uncertain terms that she and I are not a couple anymore, engaged or otherwise."

I can't say I'm happy about Edin still hanging around. At least they are still broken up. He kept his word. "Okay. I understand. I guess. But if that changes—"

"It won't."

I finally take the bouquet from his hand. There's a little cabinet in the break room where I keep a green-frosted vase Lourdes gave me a while ago. Rhett follows me from my desk to the other room. I grab the empty vase and fill it with the flower food and water, balancing my crutch under my arm without my hands. As I busy myself with floral-related tasks, I try to keep my back to Rhett. He's making me nervous and also a bit warm. I'd splash some of the cold water on my face and neck if I thought he wouldn't notice.

"Clients aren't usually allowed back here," I say.

"Good thing I'm not a client."

I give a long, hard look at him. "Good thing." If he were anyone else except Lourdes and Lucy, I would have forced him back into the reception area by this point.

Then he smiles, and I figure it couldn't hurt to let him hang out with me. He did come all the way here. But only for a little while. Anything longer than a few minutes is far too dangerous. I turn away from him, and when I look back, he's still wearing a sexy half-smile. Time to distract him with something else.

"So, what brings you—" I begin at the same moment Rhett says, "What are you—" We stop and give short chuckles.

I don't have time to ask him to continue. He does, anyway. "What are you doing for lunch?"

"It isn't even seven o' clock," I reply.

He grins. "Breakfast?"

"I'm working," I protest. Weakly.

The smile falters, but the glow in his eyes does not. He takes a step closer, then seems to reconsider and returns to his original spot. "You're the boss. Your name's on the door. I'm guessing you make your own hours."

"I am and I do, but I still have to work. Plus, I've been without an assistant for a few weeks."

"Dinner, then. As friends." He scrutinizes my face. I wish I could know what he sees. "No pressure. If you don't want to, I can leave. I don't want to make you uncomfortable." His phone beeps, but he ignores it.

I'm surprised he broached the subject of leaving. Now I smile. I'm so far from uncomfortable, it isn't funny. And after my teletherapy sessions both Monday and Tuesday, my anxiety is at a reasonable level—apart from the panic attack that I try not to think about. I've already picked up my prescription meds from the pharmacy here in town. Florence, the pharmacist, had already heard about the crash when I saw her Tuesday evening and told me a new website she found that might be a great add-on to my current meditation techniques.

"Lunch. Today," I tell Rhett. "I planned to do some research and make a few phone calls during my lunch hour, but that can wait until later. I also have to stop at the pharmacy here in town and pick up my anxiety-med refill, but I'm pretty sure I can squeeze that in."

"Would you like me to come back?"

"Do you want to leave, then come back?" I slowly ask. I make it sound like I'm asking for clarity, but I'm still shocked he's even considering this. Maybe all I've said to him really has sunk in. I'm not sure how I feel if that's true.

"No. I don't. Can I stay?" His optimistic eyes watch mine.

"How would you like some on-the-job real-estate training?"

"What's first, boss? Would you like me to be your temporary assistant?"

I have him push the extra desk over to mine, mindful of the long power cords that are still plugged in. He moves the chair as I start the second computer.

"I was just getting ready to do some cold calls, but there are a lot of other tasks requiring attention. I check current listings. I need to know what's available in the areas I typically sell and how much those properties are going for. I also look for potential listings."

Rhett scrunches up his face in confusion. "How do you find those?" he asks as I seat myself in my own chair.

With my left hand, I turn my monitor screen so he can see what I pull up. "It's a lot of just asking people if they want to sell or if they know anyone who does. Sometimes I guess that former clients might be ready to move on to their next house. It took me a while to develop enough connections. The beginning, back when I first started in real estate, was so much harder and way more nerve-wracking."

He still has not sat down at the assistant's desk. Instead, he moves closer to mine. And to me. Oh. My.

I clear my throat, fighting the urge to fan myself. "I mainly work with first-time home buyers and some renters."

"Does it make a difference?"

"Oh yes. The markets vary widely depending on not only budget, but also life stage and how much or how little work they need to do or are willing to consider."

I hear the beep of a new email and check it on my phone. There are five emails, actually.

"Oh! Two offers on one of my properties. One rejection from a seller. And an inspection report just came in." My phone beeps again. Yet another email. "Huh. And an issue one of my clients is having with securing their earnest money. I need to make a few calls. I'll have to leave you on your own for a few minutes, to give them some privacy. Especially this one in particular. She has a tendency to loudly rehash all the gory details of why she's selling her house to buy one for her daughter so she can move in with said daughter and the daughter's husband and five kids, and on it goes."

He doesn't look particularly happy, but the frown quickly disappears.

"How are you at social media?"

Rhett laughs. "Oh, you're serious. I'm sorry. No, I don't know the first thing about it."

"Right." I quickly pull up my spreadsheet for home prices and values. "Can you search these areas, please? Write down the ones that are different."

"No problem."

I'm beginning to sense he knows how alluring his half-smile is.

When I return, the smile has faded.

"I'm sorry I took so long," I say.

"Figure something out the down payment money?"

"Mostly." I'm impressed he knows what "earnest money" means without me having had to give a synonym for it. Not everyone can do that.

"She have new gory details to share?"

"Always something new to add to all the stuff I unfortunately already know." But I think it's cute he asked.

"Have you seen the local news?" Rhett asks now.

"I've been warned off it."

He doesn't say any more.

· ♥ · ♥ · ♥ · ♥ · ♥ ·

Four hours later, Rhett and I stop at our fifth house of the morning. We are here to take pictures for listings, same as we did for the other houses. Every agent does the best they can to make properties not only presentable, but "I must live here" incredible.

He seems pretty acclimated to the process I have with these properties, but it took some work to reach this point. The first question he asked at the first house was why I bothered fixing anything before shooting a series of photos.

"Because staging means value. It's to present the ideal. To sell the ideal. People sometimes can't imagine the potential of a place when it's empty."

"So why not take the pictures when the other people still live here? They left their furniture, but everything else is empty. Shouldn't it look lived in?"

I laughed. "Yes and no. Some people, unfortunately, don't have the best eye for décor, some never bother, and some have amazing houses I do photo shoots in before they leave if they give permission. Often, though, I suggest they put their stuff in storage and use the staging furniture until the house sells if they can't leave before then. Not everyone wants strangers scrutinizing their personal items at showings. All this furniture here is rented."

He makes a sound like he's choking before breathing out and shaking his head. "You paid money to borrow this stuff?"

"Sometimes I do, and sometimes the sellers do. It's more common than you might suppose."

Rhett's actually more gifted with a camera than he led me to believe. He's also pretty helpful with some of the extra staging I need to do, especially with my limited ability to move the heavier stuff around at the moment.

Well, he's better at taking orders than he is at coming up with his own ideas of design and décor.

"I can design vehicles no problem," he tells me as I fix a set of ruby-red canisters on a gray, faux-marble kitchen counter. Potential house buyers need not know these canisters are empty. Unless someone decides to look in one of them. Oh well. I can't fill them with anything that could spoil, and this place is pretty much vacant, anyway, except for the staging furniture.

"Houses are out of my league," Rhett continues. "Far too many variables and vernacular I don't even care to know."

I wipe away a smudge from the backsplash, then step back for a better view.

There's something missing.

I pull a small tote out of the pantry and dig for the glass bowl. I often mix a few types of fresh fruit with fake wax ones, but didn't have time to shop for any fresh produce this week. It just doesn't look or smell right with only fake ones. I put it all back in the tote and pull out my phone. I send a text to Lourdes, asking her to put together a few small arrangements for this kitchen in complementary tones. She calls me back almost immediately.

I've already moved on to the table settings. Rhett puts the dishes out onto each spot as I talk to Lourdes.

"You need them today? I'm not sure I can, but I'll try."

"It's okay if you don't have time," I tell her while straightening a navy-blue charger. I glance up and catch Rhett watching me.

"Gwenn?" Lourdes says.

"Yeah. Sorry." I turn away from Rhett so as to not be distracted again. "If you don't have time, it's okay." I adjust the phone in my hand before realizing I already told her that. "I'll just pick up some flowers at the store."

"What?" Lourdes's voice screeches through the phone. "Don't even think of buying grocery store flowers. Same goes for gas station flowers. That's just gross. And rude. And heartless. If they aren't from me, they aren't the best. I will make time. I will have them delivered to you by the end of the day."

In jostling the phone, I accidentally hit the speaker icon. Lourdes speaks again before I have time to fix it. "Grocery store flowers. How dare you. Seriously—"

I fumble with my phone, but it's too late. Rhett already heard her. And now I'm pretty sure he thinks I think those lovely flowers he gave me are crap.

Once Lourdes and I hang up, I tell him, "Sorry. That was Lourdes. She owns a flower shop. Total flower snob." If he made me less nervous, I might be able to fix it better than this. As it is, I can only offer what truth I have without embellishments. Not that this in any way erases any hurt he might have incurred.

It suddenly occurs to me that I haven't replied to his last statement. I'm not used to having someone work along with me like this, and my bestie already potentially offended him. This is not going well. "It's the same with me and vehicles. A car is a car is a car, right?"

"Hardly." Rhett shakes his head with a laugh when I turn to look at him. He doesn't give off an air of being upset in any way. "There are huge differences between sedans, convertibles, wagons, SUVs, and vans. Two-wheel drive versus four-wheel drive. That's only the beginning. I haven't mentioned trucks and all that pertains to them. Gas versus diesel versus electric versus hybrid."

"My point exactly. Too complicated. Real estate is easier." He looked as if he won the "debate," but his triumphant expression is now floundering.

"Though not nearly as affordable."

The broker in me cannot let his words slide without a counter. "What I represent is. Approximately half of the properties I handle cost below the national average. I like staging rentals just as I would one that's for sale."

I hear a sound. This is the fourth time he's ignored his phone beeping at him. "Is Edin going to be a problem?" I ask. I have to assume it's her Rhett is avoiding. Why else would he not answer?

He doesn't seem surprised I've figured this out. "Not at all," he replies. "What kind of rentals do you deal with?"

"Apartments, townhouses, and single-family homes." I turn to face the kitchen again and appreciate all the work it took to make it this beautiful.

"So, about me not being a client."

He has my full attention now. I move my body toward him but stop several feet short. "What about it?"

"Maybe you can help me find a new apartment."

"You live in Auburn. You're already better off there with lower costs. Are you considering relocating to the Syracuse area?"

I almost see the answer in his eyes, and it sends a tingle through my body. Then he says, "Not just yet."

"I don't know as much about the market in Auburn, but I'm sure I can find a broker there who will help you."

"What if I don't want anyone but you?"

I smile, but I also scoff. "Rhett, like I said, I don't know the market well in Auburn. I deal more in Syracuse Falls, Syracuse, Lyndon, Fairmount, Nedrow, East Syracuse, Camillus, Fayetteville, Onondaga. All these local areas. Rarely in Auburn. I can't possibly help you as much as another agent could."

"You underestimate your abilities."

This makes my cheeks hot as I smile. "Well, first, some rentals are handled by the management company of the complex, which would make it slightly more difficult for me to help."

"I'm sure you'd find a way."

My blushing intensifies. "Are you going to compliment me the rest of the day like you have since you showed up in my office?"

"I'll stop if it makes you uncomfortable. Do you want me to?"

Chapter 25

Rhett

I CAN'T HELP BUT laugh as Gwenn squeaks out an uncertain, "No . . ." Then she shakes her head and starts using her professional voice again. "If—if—I agree, you need to know what your budget is and the area you want."

"Two thousand," I say without thinking.

"Two thousand a month?" she asks for clarification.

Shit. That's more than twice what I pay now. I nod. "Yep."

"Okay, honestly, such a high budget will make the search so much easier. More available the higher we go."

"We? Does this mean you'll help me?"

She doesn't reply right away.

"How about this: You consider it, and we go eat. It's almost noon."

"Okay," she agrees. "We can find something in Syracuse if you want."

I sense the tone in her voice. "Or?"

"There's this great diner here in Syracuse Falls. Just down the street."

"Is it truly great, or is it great only because this town has all of two places to choose from?"

"Both. I promise, you'll like it. I've heard the apple pie is to die for."

"What do you normally order?"

"Chocolate cherry, of course."

I chuckle. "Of course."

Gwenn locks up the house we are in, deposits her bags and boxes in her car with my help, and motions in the area we need to head. We set off down the sidewalk. Nearly everything is covered in a dusting of snow, but not nearly as bad as things were down in Lake George. Still, I wish I had a way to hold her hand as we go. She's refused my help even though the walkways look a little too slippery for her.

Storefronts have banners and signs advertising seasonal sales for the upcoming spring. A couple snowpeople stand watch over a grassy area down the way. All the sidewalks here have been shoveled and salted. The few people who are outside have all waved and greeted each other.

"This looks like a nice little town," I say as we cross one of the only main streets here.

"It really is. It's technically a village and a town. I've sold several houses here. Just recently, I sold this adorable eighty-year-old Cape Cod to the sweetest first-time home buyer for only two hundred twenty thousand, which was well under asking price. Quinn sent me a fancy bottle of champagne in celebration. I've also helped quite a few renters here in town, including Lucy."

"So you like it here."

"I love it. It's so charming. All the neighbors treat each other like family. There are enough retail locations to keep this town from feeling too small. Enough people visit or commute through, so it isn't isolated. Lourdes's flower shop is here. Lucy teaches at the public school here."

I think Gwenn realizes she's been gushing.

She clears her throat as we pass an arched doorway still covered in Christmas lights. It highlights the brightness in her cheeks. "They have two main apartment complexes, on the small side, as well as several rooms for rent above the shops in the older part of downtown." She glances over at me.

I hope she doesn't catch on to the fact that I've watched her talk this whole time. I've been watching her all day. There's something about the glow on her face when she speaks. It doesn't matter the subject.

"Are you reconsidering adding Syracuse Falls in your search?" she asks.

"Maybe." Her attachment makes me want to spend more time here. This is also exactly the kind of place Jill would have loved.

"If you do, let me know. I'll make a call to Jenni Jo."

"Who's that?"

"Jenni Jo Holley. She's the manager of the Apple Lane apartments. It's the small complex over by the dollar store and the farmers' market."

I gesture in a way I hope shows her I don't know where the area is she's talking about.

"Not too far from the new gas station. The apartment building is old but updated. Not as modern as you can afford but very clean."

I nearly choke at her words of what I can afford. I can't pay what she thinks I can. There has to be a way to let her know this without looking like an idiot or a loser for lying. Gwenn is still talking.

"If she likes you, you're golden."

She must mean Jenni Jo. "What happens if she doesn't?"

"Don't be late on your rent. I'd be safe and pay it a few days early just in case."

"That sounds bad."

"It does, I know, but she's extremely fair. She just doesn't have the patience for accommodating those who try to screw her over.

That's actually happened before. I don't blame her, honestly. She has a job to do. Not like she can make up the difference for everyone who doesn't pay their rent."

As we cross a second intersection, Gwenn looks over at me with a sweet grin. "Based on what I know about you, she'll love you."

Damn. I can't help but smile in return. Despite the cold, I'm feeling a little warmer. She slows her steps, and I don't know what to expect next. Then she nods her head at something behind me. I turn and notice the sign for the diner.

"Or would you rather walk the whole town first?" she asks.

I'll go anywhere she wants me to, but it would be nice to be warm with her for a while. That, and I don't like how wobbly she is on these slick sidewalks.

"Lunch first is good," I say.

We step inside the diner. The door has a bell hanging from it that rings, signaling our entrance. A woman much older than us comes over and greets us with a genuine smile. "Gwenn, sweetie! I heard about your accident. So glad you're okay. Two?"

"Yes, please. And thanks, Dottie," Gwenn replies with a smile.

"The booth you like by the window is available." Dottie motions to the right side of the restaurant, facing the street.

Gwenn thanks her again, then leads me over to the table.

"Is this 'your' booth?" I ask as we sit, Gwenn directly across from me.

After adjusting the crutch she leaned against the end of the booth, she replies, "Usually. I told you it was a great place."

"Does she call everyone sweetie?"

"Only those who don't mind. She asks first," Gwenn adds.

I love how important that part is to her.

She smiles and pulls out a menu from a small silver holder at the end of the table. After handing the menu to me, she grabs one for herself. Then a younger woman, maybe seven or eight years older than us, comes by.

"Hey, Gwenn!"

"Hey, Kenzie! This is Rhett." She motions to me.

Kenzie and I greet each other.

"Wait a minute," Kenzie says, moving her eyes back and forth between my companion and me. "Is this the guy who rescued you?"

"Word travels fast," I say. First Dottie, now Kenzie. "Does everyone in this town know?"

"She's Lucy's sister," Gwenn tells me by way of an answer.

Kenzie gives me a once-over. "Cute. So, what can I get you two started with?"

"Coffee," Gwenn tells her.

"Same," I add, trying not to be embarrassed by Kenzie's "cute" comment. Jill's voice tells me this must be how Gwenn has felt all day, and I'm even more embarrassed.

"Sure thing. Be right back."

Gwenn starts reading her menu. I don't bother looking at mine. I'm not hungry, even though I suggested this meal. I was afraid she'd come up with a good reason for me to leave. But if I don't order something, she'll know I'm not hungry. She might say she can eat later and suggest we go back to work or her office. She's already given me the vibe that she postpones meals like this sometimes.

Gwenn moves her eyes back up to me.

"Do you always stare at your friends?"

This is different, and I know she knows that. Still, I can't say it. Not now. "I was wondering if you've decided to help me tomorrow."

Kenzie leaves our coffees on the table. Gwenn reaches for one individual creamer cup and two packets of sugar. I only go for one sugar.

"Not yet. For one thing, we not only need to find the right apartment, but also the right building or complex and the right location, including town or city. We might not find all three at the same time. And since I don't often work in Auburn, I won't have places in mind right off the bat to start the search. I also don't know of any currently unlisted units that may be on the market soon."

I nod in understanding. "You know all of this information for Syracuse Falls?"

"Absolutely."

Which makes my desire to live here much stronger. "I'll keep that in mind."

"Do you have pets?"

"Never wanted one."

"Okay. If you think you may want a dog or a cat in the future, let me know now. That way, I can try to negotiate with the landlords about allowing pets if their policy is to say no. Some aren't as firm about it as others. I'm pretty good at negotiating bad credit, but it doesn't sound like you'll need me to."

This is the moment I should tell her the truth about my budget. She's dealt with things like this in the past, I'm sure. I take in a breath and glance around the restaurant to steel myself for what I'm about to say. But before I speak, I notice that Gwenn is watching something on the other side of the diner that seems to amuse her. I follow her gaze to see Kenzie chatting with a guy around her age.

"Is that her boyfriend?" I ask.

Gwenn laughs for a moment or two. "Oh, no. She's still hung up on her ex, even though he left her years ago."

It makes me sad that Edin immediately comes to mind when hearing this story. I don't want to be the man Edin still hasn't gotten over years from now. "So, who's the guy?"

"Trevor? They're just friends."

"Sure they are."

Gwenn moves her eyes to me, her mouth now in a straight line. "Men and women can be friends and flirt with each other and not have it mean anything."

"They can. But if that conversation over there doesn't mean anything, why was it making you smile? Because that tells me you know they should probably be together. You at least see that he's crazy about her. I don't even know them, and I see it."

Of course, now this has me wondering if I've been as googly-eyed staring at Gwenn as that guy has been while staring at Kenzie. It's probably just as obvious to everyone else.

"See that guy with Trevor?"

I answer with a yes.

"He's his brother, and Dottie is their aunt. They have reasons for being here that don't involve romance."

"But that doesn't mean it can't or won't happen anyway."

Gwenn makes no reply.

Kenzie stops over at our table. "Ready to order, or do you need more time?"

I still have yet to glance at my menu. Flustered, I mumble out a few incoherent words.

Kenzie gives a mysterious smile to Gwenn before winking at me. "Take your time. I'll come back."

Once she's gone, I focus my eyes on the menu. Or I try to. I pretend the pictures of fried chicken sandwiches and whipped cream-topped pies are the only things I want to look at while the person I do actually want to look at puts her menu back in the silver stand. She leans across the table to read my menu upside down.

"Do you like the idea of breakfast more or lunch? They make both very well here."

"What would you suggest?"

Every dish she points out sounds amazing. That, or it sounds amazing because she's the one describing it—even the ham and cheese omelet, even though I'm not a big fan of ham. I want to try her favorites and see if maybe I'd like them as much as she does. I never cared about this stuff with Edin, the little things that she might have wanted to share with me. The only times I experienced something Edin loved were when she outright asked me to, and I figured it couldn't hurt to try. It wasn't done with this driving feeling I have now of wanting a particular food because it could give me the same joy as it gives Gwenn.

Although I finally decide on what to eat, I chicken out on telling Gwenn the whole truth about my budget for a new apartment that I'm not even sure I need or want. She really is the only person I ever blurt things out to, but why couldn't I have kept that dumb idea inside?

I hate myself for not fixing this. Gwenn happily and breezily moves on to her next point about rental leases and real estate attorneys while I squirm. I wish it was my padded seat making me uncomfortable, not the guy in it.

Chapter 26

Rhett

It's been a while since Gwenn dropped me off at my truck and went back out to meet a client. I'm home now, but I really don't want to be.

"Maybe I should leave this here," Edin says as she holds up her favorite fleece blanket. "I do get cold easily and might need to cover up."

She called three times while I was with Gwenn and once after I left Gwenn at her office, and she also sent at least five texts. I still avoided her, until her text arrived telling me she should probably pick up all her stuff from my apartment. I couldn't say no and make her think I changed my mind. Now that Edin and I are doing this, I'm struggling to hold on to the high I felt while with Gwenn.

"I have blankets here," I tell Edin, wondering why it matters.

She rolls her eyes. "Yes, but I hate your blankets. Too old and too scratchy. I like soft and fluffy and new. I shouldn't have to remind you."

When she thinks she'll ever be here long enough to curl up with a blanket, I don't know, but I won't say this.

Nodding, I turn away to tape up a box of the clothes she kept in the top half of my dresser. It'll be nice when everything is my own again. I never wanted her to move in. She said we couldn't very well be married if we didn't know what it was like to live together. While I was okay with not knowing, I didn't argue the point with her.

I wish I had.

The box I'm taping is a little too small, but I doubt Edin thought it would be. Or maybe she knew and brought it, anyway, hoping I'd let her use it as an excuse to keep more stuff here than we originally agreed on, which was none.

She agreed to "let" me keep the wooden chess set she gave me for my birthday. I hadn't realized birthday gifts were up for grabs in the "what stays, what goes" conversation. Edin was the one to bring it up first. Of course, with her gone, I'll be able to unpack the pewter set Jill gave me when we graduated high school. Edin was always too jealous for me to be able to leave it out. It's the only reason she bought me one, too.

"What about this?"

I have to swivel to face Edin again. She holds up her gold engagement ring.

I was not expecting this, but I should have. Actually, I should have known better than to think it would all be so easy. Edin's hand trembles as she holds up her ring. She and I both understand what's happening here. This is the end of us and our engagement. That ring is the only thing left.

"Who keeps this?" she asks.

Chapter 27

Gwenn

"Lourdes, if you listen to this within the hour, please call me back."

Ever since my brunch/lunch with Rhett earlier today, I haven't been able to force a certain thought out of my mind. Though it's quickly changing from evening into night, I need advice. Helping Rhett sounds like a great idea, but what if it's too much? What if I can't suppress my attraction to him? It was already difficult spending all day today doing just that. I flirted and accepted his flirting more than I'd wanted to. He had to have noticed.

We are only supposed to be friends. I was clear to both of us. I can't go back on my decision now. But lunch was so wonderful. I've never had the kind of connection Rhett and I share with anyone else. The way he looks at me melts my defenses, even if only temporarily.

Must focus. I have an important phone call that I can only make on my own. I've put it off since Rhett left, but if I don't do it soon, it'll have to wait until tomorrow. That isn't something I am willing to risk.

After making it through the automated menu, I finally get a real person on the line.

"Hi, my name is Gwenn Rhys. I'm calling on behalf of a former patient."

"I cannot give any information to anyone who is not the patient," she immediately tells me.

Instead of arguing the point, I thank her, hang up, and call back. This time when a real person answers, I choke down the massive lump in my throat and say, "Hi. My name is Jaymie Jonas."

I explain in simple terms how I need information regarding whoever paid my hospital bills. My call is then transferred from department to department. Each time I give an explanation of what I need and whom I'm searching for, I am told slightly different versions of the same thing. It's a total runaround.

"I'm sorry. I don't have any of those records in my computer," says the most recent "helpful" person.

"How long does your hospital usually keep records for?" I ask this same assistant I've been transferred to for the third time.

"I can't really answer that," is his reply.

"Certainly for a lot longer than it's been since I was a patient."

"I could have a nurse contact you with your chart information," he tells me.

"I have a copy of my chart. I don't need medical info. I explained this to billing before they sent me back to you. I need my family history."

"Family history should be part of the information your chart contains, and—"

"Not that kind of history," I correct. "I need names of family members, last known address, telephone numbers. Information relating to who I was and who they are. Can't you tell me anything?"

"You're asking for information that's currently unavailable to me." There is silence for a few moments before he speaks again. "I'm sorry. Is there anything else I can help you with?"

So that's that. An hour on the phone, and nothing productive to show for it. I tell him no and am not at all surprised when he doesn't ask me to complete the survey at the end of our call.

There is only one other option I have available to me. My finger hovers over the number to one of my nurses from back in the day. She was so kind in a friendly, almost motherly way, though she's only six years older than me.

"Gwenn! How are you?" she greets me.

I don't need to explain the Jaymie/Gwenn aspect. It's only been three years since Francesca and I last spoke. "I'm not doing so well," I reply.

I hear her suck in a breath and immediately know what she's afraid of. My injuries. She always worried I'd suffer a setback at some point despite the excellent surgeries and difficult yet tremendously effective therapies.

It's time I told her about the plane crash.

"Oh no. Oh, that's terrible," Francesca says after I finish my story. "It must have been absolutely frightening for you."

"That's an understatement."

Then I explain the reason I'm calling. It's the first time I've ever been brave enough to explicitly ask her for this information since I left the hospital. Before, she either skirted around the answer or simply changed the subject, and I never pushed for more.

"I wish I could help, but I don't know much about them. I never saw them at the hospital. Dr. Mitchall instructed us to not focus on your parents in order to help you heal since they never came back."

I flinch at the words "your parents."

It's still physically painful. Almost as painful as my other injuries. In some ways, more so. I don't even have the luxury of missing them because I have zero memories of them. I have zero memories of anything in my life before waking up in an unfamiliar hospital all those years ago.

Hot tears steadily flow from my eyes. They drop onto my sweater and my desk. They blur my vision. Not only can I not see clearly,

I can't think clearly, either. I have no idea where to go from here. Francesca was my last hope for answers.

I would love to sit and talk with her for hours like we used to, but this isn't the right moment. She wishes me luck before we end our call. I wish I could be as hopeful as she is about my prospects. But then, I think she's more hopeful I will forget all about my family and move on completely without ever looking back again.

Someone knocks on the inner office door, and it opens enough for me to see Lucy walk in. I wipe at my eyes, but there is no hiding the fact that I'm crying. Especially not from her.

"I'm so glad you're still here. My entire grade had 'emergency' strategizing for the coming month. Again. Even though we've been over and over this and know exactly what we need to teach and when and also when to be more flexible. And they never take into account the lessons we might have to reteach when the kids just don't understand the concepts they need in order to move on. I swear, sometimes certain co-workers act like we're all newbies instead of well-qualified educators."

"Maybe you need a new job in addition to a new house." I try not to sniffle.

"If I could hire into a different district right now, I would." She drops down into one of my chairs for clients and puts her small bag on my desk. "Of course, I don't really mean it. I love our little district. I don't want it to change. I'll fight against our school being swallowed up by a larger district anytime it's necessary." Then she looks at me more carefully. "Whoa. You okay?"

"Yeah." I nod. In addition to my now red, puffy eyes, I know how awful the rest of my face looks. Makeup only covers so much, at least without airbrushing. I did the best I could to mask the scrapes and bruises.

"You okay?" she asks again, not convinced.

I don't blame her. While I am not sobbing, I'm not nearly as settled as I'd like to be.

We've already talked about the crash once, but I know it's possible she rightly suspects there is more bothering me. I just don't think I am ready to tell her this part yet.

"I'm all right. Could be worse."

"Could be better."

All I can do is nod. "So, I was able to compile a list of possible rental options. Some are smaller than you'd like. There's a good mix of houses and apartments. It's all in the email I sent, but we can look at some now that you're here. Let me just pull the first one up."

I click a few buttons on different tabs on my computer. Then the first house listing finishes loading. I turn the screen toward Lucy.

"This one's a little far from town," she says almost instantly.

"It is," I say, "but the drive into Syracuse Falls shouldn't be too bad. Would you like to look at it a bit more or move on to the next one?"

"Next one, please. I won't be able to tour rentals when spring break comes. I'm going to spend the week up at the lake. Need to find as many options as possible before then, if that's okay."

"Of course."

Lourdes calls.

I put her on speaker and explain the story of Rhett showing up at my office to both of them.

"Why didn't you say something sooner?" Lucy asks. "You let me come in here and complain without a word. You told me you were okay."

"I am," I assure her. "It wasn't because of Rhett."

"Tell him to come to me for flowers next time he needs to buy some. I'll hook him up."

I notice she doesn't mention him buying flowers specifically for me but choose to gloss over it for the moment. "I'm sure he would. He heard you being a flower snob on the phone today."

"It's no secret I'm a flower snob," Lourdes says.

Lucy agrees.

"Lourdes, is that all you have to say?"

"You want me to comment on how he had to have woken up before the sun in order to reach your office while it was still early?"

"Yes!"

"Mm. No can do. It isn't really out of the ordinary."

"Oh, not at all," Lucy adds with a laugh.

"Come on, Lourdes. Please tell me what you honestly think."

She takes a breath in and lets it back out. "Showing up unannounced doesn't necessarily take a lot of thought," Lourdes tells us.

"I disagree. It takes a huge amount of thought. There are a lot of logistics involved. It also takes time and effort," Lucy adds. "He was willing to wake up early and drive all the way out here. I'm assuming he called off work to do this. It's Wednesday, after all."

I nod in agreement, trying to absorb and understand their words.

"Obviously, he cares enough to have kept you alive," Lucy says.

"But nearly every person would have done the same, or tried to," Lourdes counters. "It's a crucial part of humanity."

"He also cares enough to have found Gwenn after they were released from the hospital," Lucy tells her.

"True." I nod again, though only Lucy can see me.

"He wants to date you," Lourdes says matter-of-factly.

"Yes."

"How you didn't straddle him then and there, I'll never understand," Lucy says. "You already made out. Why not go a little extra?"

"The bashed leg would have made that difficult," Lourdes tells her. "You want to be friends with Rhett," she adds to me in the same matter-of-fact tone as before.

"Yes."

"Are you questioning this decision now?"

I let out a sigh. "I am. I really am. I mean, it's so fast. Like, Lucy falling in love fast."

Lucy laughs. "I should be offended by that!"

"But you're not," Lourdes tells her.

"So not." Lucy laughs again.

After giving her a smile, I continue. "But there's no other way. It wouldn't work between us. I just know it. With my history, my mental health issues, with—"

"Stop," Lucy interrupts me. "You cannot give your anxiety the power to control your love life. Certainly not your life. Just because other men couldn't deal doesn't mean Rhett can't."

"Well, I never gave those other men a chance, though I get what you're saying. You might be right about Rhett. But maybe both of our pasts are too complicated to be dealt with together. My accident. Jill and Edin. It's so much. Maybe it's what makes us incompatible."

Lucy is aghast. "Gwenn, you seriously think you and Rhett are incompatible? After all that alone time in the shed? All you learned about each other?"

"Why do you guys have all the right answers and questions?"

"It's a gift." I hear the smile in Lourdes's voice.

"He could fall in love with you," Lucy says.

I can't help but audibly scoff. "Luce, you think everyone is going to fall in love."

"I wish I could fall in love."

Lourdes and I both laugh.

"What are you talking about?" Lourdes asks her. "You fall in love all the time. I have the flower receipts to prove it."

"I mean with the right guy." Lucy rolls her eyes for my benefit, as if it's so obvious what she meant.

I stifle a giggle.

Lucy continues. "Why can't I find the one? When will it be my turn?"

"I'm sure it won't be long," I say, doubtful of whether it's the truth, but fully aware it's what she wants to hear. "You never know."

"You just want a diamond on your hand," Lourdes says.

An outsider might consider this harsh, but Lucy and I know better. We all laugh.

Lucy grins. I can practically see floating hearts in her eyes. "That's just the frosting on the love cake."

"I don't suggest meeting him the way Gwenn met Rhett. Not a great introduction," Lourdes says.

"Exactly," I reply. "Not romantic or sweet in any way. It was about survival and grief and loneliness."

"Lots of people survive harrowing experiences together, but few, if any, end up with the kind of connection you two developed," Lucy tells me.

Lourdes makes a sound like she's trying not to scoff again.

"Oh, speaking of connections, we really need to set my brother up with someone new," Lucy adds. "He's been moping around town for months now."

"We can't make him date," I tell her.

"That's not a good idea," Lourdes says at the same time. "Isn't he off dating right now?"

"Dom swears he'll never date again, but I don't see why. He was only with that woman for a few weeks. There's bound to be someone else who could catch his eye. We just need to help him find her."

"We can't all believe in a happy ending the way you do," Lourdes tells her.

I agree.

Lucy shakes her head in disbelief. "You guys are such spoilsports when it comes to romance. Yes, I fall in love easily. Yes, I believe there is a true love out there for me. I enjoy looking for him. Why shouldn't we help someone else find their true love? I don't believe Dom is meant to be alone no matter what he says. And Rhett shouldn't have to be alone either if you're the one for him." She gives me a pointed look.

"So, are you going to help Rhett?" Lourdes asks.

She knows it's a terrible idea, and I have to agree with her. I don't think I can help him. I don't think I should.

But when Rhett shows up again in the morning, I agree to act as his real estate broker.

"Really?" he asks. I'm not sure if he means to sound so giddy.

"I had a chance to look at a few properties last night."

"Even though you were going to tell me no?"

My cheeks feel a little warmer. "I hadn't decided."

"Is that what you're going with?"

All I can do is sheepishly smile in return. I suggest it's time to leave before we lose too much of the day. Despite it not making any sense at all, we drive to Auburn in my car.

"You didn't have to come all the way out to Syracuse Falls," I tell Rhett for the fifth time as I maneuver around a slushy pothole. "I would have met you. And now you'll be close to home without your vehicle."

"It's all right," he says, also for the fifth time. "I have things to do over in Syracuse when we get back."

"How did you take off from work two days in a row?"

"I'm technically on a mental health day. And it isn't a lie. I couldn't take another day of my boss's crap. Being back after the crash, it's worse than ever."

"I'm sorry to hear that." I almost feel guilty now for initially not wanting to help him in his search. Of course, I hope things won't be as bad for him when he returns to work.

I try not to smile at the realization I care about him more than I ever intended to. But hey, friends are allowed to care.

Then there's something else I feel that moves this far beyond friendship.

While I easily could have shown him each apartment online and saved the gas money, that idea didn't set my heart and stomach aflutter like the idea of a road trip alone with him.

We tour each property slowly, carefully. Before I even open the lockboxes, I find myself torn between hoping he will love the place and hoping he'll hate it so we can keep searching. As we wander down hallways and into bright bedrooms, cozy bathrooms, and sleek kitchens, Rhett asks the appropriate questions. Size, price, neighbors, distance to work.

With each apartment he decides against, my stomach flutters return. More time together. More time alone, just the two of us.

My assumption of Rhett in regards to home design was spot on. Most units we tour have a clean, timeless look, which I think he appreciates. Beyond that, he truly does not care about styles, decades, flow, and the like. The hardwood previously hidden under hideous laminate is no big deal. The all-white and stainless-steel, professional-grade chef's kitchen generates the same reaction as the hardwood. Many of these homes have quartz or granite counters, which are usually easy selling points, but not this time.

All he wants, in addition to a good price, is a place to park his pickup truck every day. Unfortunately, more of these buildings are lacking parking than I expected.

I try a different tactic. "There's usually a lot of linoleum in buildings as old as this one, but the owners here did a full custom renovation a few years back. Nothing will need updated or replaced for a long time."

"You're more comfortable doing this than anything else," Rhett says in response.

My cheeks grow warm. "I am. This is pretty much my life." Both the way he looks at me and the glow on his face as I reply intensify the heat to the point I am now, where my complexion must match a poinsettia plant. "So, thoughts?"

It takes him a moment to reply. "You mean, about the apartment?"

"Yes." But he's piqued my curiosity. Now I do want to know his other thoughts.

"I'm not sure it's for me."

So we move on again.

I'm growing selfishly thankful he didn't hire a local broker or real estate agent for his apartment search. I don't care about having to drive out here. The joy of doing my job well along with the thrill of being with him are enough. I'll learn anything I have to about Auburn's real estate market if it means I'll have more days like this.

In more than one moment, I find myself wishing he would kiss me again.

Chapter 28

"I WASN'T ABLE TO see good pictures of this one, or even very many at all," Gwenn says as she begins unlocking the door to an apartment. She perfectly balances her weight on her crutch.

We step into what looks like a closet. Well, it's the size of one, anyway.

As I watch her glance around, I can see she clearly hates it here already. It doesn't seem to be as updated as she expected, but it also seems to be well within my true budget. We've only walked beyond the long but tiny kitchen into the living room that's apparently also the dining room, office, and bedroom, when she turns to face me with her broker smile.

"What do you think?"

"Not sure. What would you tell me to do?"

"As your agent, I'd advise you to compare this unit and what it contains with the units you liked, and also to think about which place best fits your life."

"And as my friend?"

She hesitates, but only for a second. "Don't pick this one."

I agree with my friend's choice.

We slowly walk across the street to a different apartment complex. The sidewalks have been shoveled, but it still isn't as easy to maneuver on them as Gwenn assumed since they don't appear to have been salted. Just enough liquid from the slowly melting snow was enough to add some ice where it shouldn't be.

"This complex has several types of units," Gwenn tells me as we reach the first building. "I have two for you to see here, one in one building and one in another."

Luckily, this place has an elevator, as the last one only had stairs. Of course, that wasn't so bad having Gwenn lean her body against me when she needed help after a while—not that she really asked. It was more that I had to put myself close to her and let her do the rest.

"Now, this apartment is exactly like the one you'd be renting, only flipped. So the kitchen sink would be on the east wall instead of the west, and so on."

It's much ritzier here. I'm a little scared.

Gwenn acts as a guide through each room, highlighting not only the biggest selling points but also what she, as my friend, thinks I should know. "I obviously have to tell prospective buyers and renters any key issues with the houses or apartments, but I'd hate for you to choose something you'll regret. Remorse often happens when someone is in a rush or doesn't know as much about the property as they should."

"And when did you decide to tell me about all the flaws?" I ask, not meaning to put her on the spot, but also understanding that she didn't do this with the first few we saw.

She blushes. "When you made it clear that you care about what I think."

There isn't anything else for me to say. She said exactly what I wanted to hear. I leave it at that, content with this knowledge. I'd be happy as hell if not for the lie that started this all.

Her eyes light up as we enter the large bedroom. Or, as she puts it, "the grand en suite, with double vanities, separate shower and soaking tub, and heated floors. This entire complex has underfloor heating, no matter the unit size or layout."

Heated floors?

I don't even want to think about how much those would cost every month.

"How much is this place again?" I ask. I think I was too distracted by watching her to listen the first time she said it.

"Just slightly over budget."

"How slight?"

"This unit is twenty-three hundred a month."

I don't answer. I'm too busy trying to hide the shock from showing in my expression.

"You did say you were comfortable going a little over."

I did, didn't I? That was when she had a hold of my arm when I helped her into her car.

It's so difficult to muster up the courage to tell her it's a lot over my limit. I don't think I can right now. I want to see her eyes shine like that every day. I want to make love to her on the small enclosed balcony and make her breakfast in the fancy chef's kitchen she about salivated over. But I'd have to sell everything I own, including body parts, in order to make this a reality. I tell her I'll think about this one, and we move on.

It's doubtful I'll think about this apartment, but I won't be able to stop thinking about her. The more time we've spent together today, the more she's relaxed around me. She hasn't used the kind but disinterested professional tone of voice in at least two hours. When we stand close to each other, surveying one element or another, she almost uses the same soft voice she had in the shed. Even when we separate to go next door, I can't stop hoping she whisper like that to me again.

I quickly move my eyes to look around this kitchen in this next apartment I also can't afford. I know she wants me to find things I like, but that's difficult when I can't even guess at the price of anything here. The rent is even higher than the last one. That two-thousand-dollar stainless-steel oven Gwenn raved about mocks me as I wonder how in the hell I'm going to tell her the truth. Will she forgive me? Will she feel like I deserve forgiveness? How bad have I screwed this up?

"What's the verdict?" Gwenn asks. She's without her crutch now. After the last apartment, she decided the last lingering pain didn't warrant its use anymore. I think she just doesn't want to use me as support and is trying to hide how difficult walking without it really is. She still has to carry it around, though, because her car is across the road.

"Not really my taste." I motion to the glittery backsplash.

As Gwenn explained earlier, it isn't actually glitter; it's some kind of stone. And I don't mind it, to be honest. I doubt I'd ever pay attention to it. But I need a reason to look at yet another place with her. I need a reason to extend this trip as long as possible.

"That's okay. I just don't have anything else for you today. I'm sorry."

"Oh." I didn't expect this.

"I promise I'll do more research back at the office. There are a lot more properties available, I'm sure. I just need to find them. Plus, I might be able to make some connections on currently unlisted ones. Some of the agents I spoke with to gain access into a few of these units sounded like they would be helpful."

"Don't worry about it," I tell her.

"We should go back to Syracuse Falls," she says to me.

Not what I wanted to hear. "Yeah. Probably should."

Gwenn locks the door with the key code given to her by a local real estate agent. We haven't even reached the elevator when I stop her.

"Wait. I'm sorry."

"What's wrong?" She looks at me with such trusting eyes. I worked so hard to convince her to help me. She's going to hate me.

"I lied."

Her eyes go wide, but she doesn't say anything. I watch her face, watch her breathe, watch her freeze every other muscle and focus solely on me. She searches my face with her eyes, probably hoping she heard me wrong. At the very least, probably hoping I mean it in any way other than I wasn't honest with her about something. Honesty seems so important to her, and I feel like I failed this test.

"I didn't mean to, I swear. But yeah, I lied. I'm sorry."

"What?" she asks slowly.

"I can't afford the place here. I can't afford any place you showed me today."

She's again quiet for a few moments. "Why did you lie?"

I blow out the air from my lungs. "I don't know. I guess I was trying to impress you. It just slipped out."

And now's the moment she's gonna tell me she can't help me anymore. That I betrayed her trust. I know how it works with her.

"Rhett, I'm a broker who lives in possibly one of the smallest apartments in Syracuse. You don't need to impress me. I already like you. I would have helped you, anyway."

I'm blown away by this. So much so, I don't have a reply.

Her phone rings. She answers it and begins walking toward the elevator again. I follow. The ride down all three floors, she stays on her call, even as we head to her parked car.

Gwenn already likes me. She finally said it out loud. And she isn't avoiding eye contact with me, which is a good sign. When we reach her car, she stands next to the driver's side, still on the phone. Her free hand pulls out her keys, and she unlocks the doors. Then she motions for me to get in. When we are seated and she's ended her call, I wait for her to put the key in the ignition.

She doesn't. Instead, her eyes watch me. Her whole body is turned toward me. I don't know if I should say something or not. I don't know what she's thinking or waiting for. It feels like it's been over a minute of her staring at me. And that's now the second time she's looked at my mouth. I'm desperate to ask her on a date but cannot figure out how without it being too complicated. I did just admit my dishonesty.

I decide to speak without really knowing what I'll say. "What do—?"

"Did you like—?"

Talking at the same time again.

I motion for her to go first. But then she chooses to fasten her seat belt. I do the same. She starts the car, puts it into drive, and pulls out of the parking spot.

"Did you prefer the one-bedroom places or the two-bedroom ones?" she asks. No mention of what I told her in the hallway.

Does this mean I'm forgiven? Or is she simply trying to find decent conversation for the drive back? "I don't have enough guests to need two. No one stays with me." Well, except Edin, but I don't want Gwenn thinking about her. She won't be staying over anymore, anyway. Not now that we've broken up.

"Right." She smiles without taking her eyes off the road. "That third apartment we saw was in a nicer area, so maybe there are other buildings I didn't see before."

Now's the time to finish the awkward conversation that got interrupted. It's also time to eat more humble pie. "So, my rent is half as much as those places we saw. You asked for a budget, and I blurted out an answer."

"You can't afford close to two thousand a month?"

"No. I'm sorry," I say again.

She takes a breath in and lets it out. "Okay. This changes things, for sure."

But her tone tells me things aren't as bad as her words imply. It also tells me this isn't going end as awfully as I'd feared.

"Rhett, I still don't know why you didn't just tell me earlier. A lower budget is nothing to be ashamed of."

I apologize once more. "I've been accused of not having enough money before, and I guess I didn't want you to look down on me."

"It's too bad you didn't realize I'm not like that. I am sorry I didn't get to show you places you'd actually consider. This could have been a much better day for both of us."

"Was it not a good day for you?"

She takes a moment before replying. When she does speak, there's a hint of a smile on her lips. "It would have been a more productive day. So, what is your real budget, and what, if anything, from today could help salvage a new search?"

Though she seems to have easily forgiven me, our conversation steadily remains on the topic of apartment hunting the entire rest of the drive to her office building. It never leads anywhere personal. Of course, I don't tell her I also lied about having errands in Syracuse so I could return with her instead of staying in Auburn. Gwenn clearly expects me to head to my truck once we are in front of the glass door.

"I don't have any explanation for my behavior today," I say.

She nods in silence.

"I was nervous, and that was and is not your fault."

Gwenn still doesn't say anything.

She might be pissed after all, but I have to take a shot. I need to inch closer to where she might be more receptive, but I have to do it carefully. "It felt like I made you a little nervous today, too. In a good way."

A smile begins to grow across her face. I wait for her to straighten it back into apparent indifference, but she doesn't.

This is the moment.

I work up the courage and ask.

Chapter 29

Gwenn

"Yes." I answer without thinking.

"Yes?"

He lied to me. I know. Lourdes would call that a red flag. Maybe I'm naïve, but I believe it isn't. I think I also know at least part of the "too poor for us" history he's talking about, and it makes me ache for him. I hate that he's been judged for not having "enough" money to make others happy. What's worse is he's been nervous around me from the beginning. He doubted himself so much, he thought it better to fib instead of give me the honesty he's given me from the very beginning, harsh as it sometimes is.

Besides, I know I am not being as honest with him as I could be. For good reason, yes, but then the same could be said of him.

I nod in reply to his question. I'm not sure I know how to give "come hither" eyes, but I hope he gets it all the same. My mouth has spread out into a giddy smile.

Rhett steps closer and places his hands on my waist. He almost touches a kiss onto my lips. "Sorry," he tells me, stepping back before we've had a chance to make contact. "I'm just—"

"It's okay. Don't be sorry. I'm excited, too." We've come a long way in just a few short days. I didn't expect any of this, but I'd like to fully embrace it.

"Tomorrow?"

"Yes," I say again, understanding exactly what he means. Our date. I don't need details in order to know how happy I am. Everything else is superfluous.

He turns to leave, but I'm not ready for him to go yet. I don't care that it's four thirty in the afternoon, and we spent six hours in Auburn. I need an excuse for him to stay.

"Would you like to help me find places online you can afford? Preferably with no glitter grout, I assume." Then a thought hits me. "Or do you need to do your other errands?" The best answer he can give to my last question is an absolute no.

Rhett's face scrunches up. "Oh. No, that can all wait. There isn't much at all. I don't need to go home yet, either."

I sigh with relief. I don't even care if he knows I was holding my breath in worried anticipation.

So we settle in at my desk and search all different areas in his lower-than-he-first-told-me price range in and around Auburn. After a while, sitting at the desk becomes tiresome. My chair is super comfy, but I know from experience the chairs from the other side, one of which Rhett is currently using, are not as comfortable as I expected they'd be when I ordered them. Lourdes complains about those chairs all the time, but I don't have the funds I need to replace them.

I told him he could use the chair from the assistant's desk, the one he used earlier, but he turned it down. It's like he refuses to complain.

It's been two hours since we started. Two hours of shifting my hip so as to keep my leg comfortable and two hours of discomfort and possible back pain for Rhett, though I know he won't admit it. He has already refused to switch seats with me.

I take a moment to send a text to Lucy with a picture of the glitter grout apartment, telling her if she ever wants more sparkle in her life, this might be the way to go.

She sends a laughing emoji in reply, as I expected her to. Lucy's style is bright and bohemian, definitely not sparkle and shine.

"You hungry?" I ask Rhett. "Are you able to have dinner with me?" And again, I silently suck in air and hope he gives me the answer I want.

His eyes light up as he replies a happy yes.

Chapter 30

Rhett

IT FEELS LIKE WE are on our first date before our first date, except this restaurant isn't exactly romantic. It's the only restaurant in Syracuse Falls, apart from the diner. Gwenn did say it "lacks ambiance," although she doesn't seem to mind. She and I are next to each other, and that is enough for me. She voluntarily sat in the chair closest to me rather than across from me. Good thing the server didn't have any two seaters to put us at. It's also a good thing the restaurant isn't crowded, it being a Thursday night.

Gwenn starts on the topic of the plane crash. "When will we get our stuff?"

"Not sure. They'll probably release it soon, as it isn't related to the cause of the accident."

"Has the investigator called you?"

I nod. "With all the data I suspect they'll have, looks like they'll officially declare it weather-related. Eventually."

"Eventually?"

"Could take a year or two."

"What?" she asks almost breathlessly.

"It isn't a fast investigation. They inspect every literal shred of evidence and piece together what they can. There is no rushing that kind of thing. They might even need to speak to us again in the future."

She pales for a moment. "You think it's weather-related and not pilot-related?"

"I don't know. The guy seemed like he was doing okay, at least for a while."

"We were in a tiny, low-flying, non-pressurized plane. We were never going to escape the blizzard. All of us were still trapped, just in the wrong place. We belonged at the airport, and that asshole—"

"He was just trying to help us," I quickly remind her.

"Which got him and all the rest of the passengers killed." Her eyes darken, and her mouth curves downward even more. "Why couldn't they have waited at the airport? Why were they in such a hurry to get out of there? Why couldn't things have been different for them? For all of us?"

"I don't know," I say again. "I ask myself that question about the pilot and the other passengers and Jill all the time."

"I'm sorry," Gwenn says, then she sniffles. "I shouldn't have brought it up. It must be so painful for you to think of her. Then you saw all those people die. That had to have forced so many sad memories to the forefront of your mind. Oh, gosh. I'm so sorry." She starts to cry harder.

I reach over and take her right hand in my left. "It's all right. Probably better if we talk about it. Can't be avoided forever."

She squeezes my hand as I stroke hers with my thumb. "You're right."

And yet I think I know better. "New topic?"

"Yes, please." She wipes at her eyes, then asks me my favorite part about living up here.

"I'd have to say how different it is from home. There's the temperature differences, sure, but it's more than that. So much here is nothing like Georgia. Home will always be home, but it couldn't give me the change I desperately needed." Then I tell her about my job and my dream build, a truck I've wanted for a long time. I also tell her my dream of running my own shop one day.

"That's amazing!" she tells me. "How long have you wanted to be a business owner?"

"Years."

"Are you close?"

I chuckle. "Not yet."

"Speaking from experience, running your own business isn't always easy or fun, but it's totally worth it." Gwenn gives me a bright, radiant smile. It makes her face pink up and almost glow. "You'd be a great business owner. You're kind, intelligent, and you handle crises well."

"Right now, it's more the lack of money that keeps me from it."

"I wish I could help you."

"Nah. I'll get there one day," I say, grateful for the offer, no matter how unrealistic it is.

I love this with her right now. I love hearing her talk and laugh. I love seeing her smile all the way up to her eyes. Those eyes still captivate me. I watch them, and her, more than I watch anything else.

Gwenn is also the first woman I haven't actively compared to Jill. That's a big step, and one in the right direction.

Gwenn fans her face. Then she tries to take a sip from her iced tea, but it's empty. She fans her face again. "A bit warm in here," she tells me. She's already removed her thick blue sweater, revealing a lace-trimmed top underneath. Our legs have been up against each other's for several minutes now. We gave up moving them away.

Her phone beeps, and she quickly silences it. After checking the screen, she sets the phone back down and turns her body to face me a little more. "So, this shop you want to open. How long will it take before you can start things up?"

"Oh gosh. Years, I'm sure. I don't have that kind of capital."

"You can't get a loan?"

"Need to be able to pay it off. The interest alone is a bitch. It's hard to promise payments on something that, right now, I can't guarantee."

"I hope it works out for you." There isn't much else she can say in reply. She doesn't have it in her power to find me a loan or make the payments for me. Even if she did, I'd never want her to, or anyone else for that matter.

I watch her face in silence for a few moments. "I hope a lot of things work out for me."

"Like me?" she asks.

Whew. She was right. It is warm in here. And is she blushing? Damn. I move to drink the rest of my Coke.

The waitress comes over with a fresh glass of tea for Gwenn. Just as she sets it down, another customer accidentally bumps into her, and she knocks into the cup, spilling cold tea all over Gwenn, who shrieks and jumps. Then she and the waitress both grab at the cup to stand it up again.

"I'm so sorry," the lady says over and over.

I signal to another server and ask them to bring a bunch of napkins over. I've already handed Gwenn mine, and she has hers in hand.

"It's all right," Gwenn tells her in the meantime.

The mess is quickly cleaned up, but Gwenn is still wet. I don't think she has anything except a bra under her lace top. As it is, she dabs at the fabric, trying to soak as much liquid out of it as possible into some paper napkins.

"Not exactly how I expected to cool off," she tells me once it's just the two of us at our table again. "I'm sorry," she adds as her phone rings.

She looks at it and pushes her chair out to stand up. "I have to take this." She walks away in a rush, saying, "This is Gwenn," into the phone.

I pull my wallet out when I can't see her in the distance.

When she comes back, she no longer wears a happy face. I know it's time to go. But I don't want to leave Gwenn, and I don't want her to leave me.

"A buyer needs to give me the escrow money before the end of the night. And he somehow misplaced the number for the real estate attorney, so I need to find that for him. For some reason, it doesn't seem to be in my phone. I wouldn't go otherwise."

Yet neither of us moves. I paid the bill and tipped the waitress while Gwenn was on her call, so all we have to do is exit the restaurant. Gwenn reaches for her bag, her sweater, and her coat. I stand from the table, put my coat on, and reluctantly guide her to the exit.

We walk out to our vehicles. I couldn't very well use the excuse of needing to ride with her anymore. Then we stand in between the cars in the parking lot despite the cold. Only a few inches separate us.

"About our date tomorrow," I start.

"Yes?" She looks at me with raised eyebrows and wide eyes. She parts her lips but doesn't say anything else.

I smile to put her at ease. "Dinner at my place? I'm not a very good cook, but I'm sure I can whip up something edible."

She grins. "I'll be there at seven."

I start to lean toward her but stop, afraid she might think I'm being too forward. She bridges the gap and leans into me, but she stops as well.

"I really do have to go now," she says before we have a chance to kiss. "I can't make this client wait any longer."

"I guess I'm the one who's going to be left waiting now."

Gwenn smiles at me. "Yeah, but you can handle it." She winks, and then she's in her car and gone before I know it.

Chapter 31

Gwenn

"Okay. My dress is on. My hair is done. Makeup is on. Skipping nails because I don't feel like doing them. Did I miss anything?"

"Sexy heels," Lucy says. "No boots."

Like I would really wear boots with this dress, but I see where she's coming from with the whole "Gwenn only knows how to dress comfy" idea.

"I have strappy heels," I tell her. "They're at the door." Thankfully, I can walk almost like normal now. Nothing was actually torn, as the ER staff first suspected. This gives me hope that it shouldn't hurt tonight. Just in case, I put some ibuprofen in my bag. I'm tempted to bring those boots, but Lucy would freak out if she saw me do that. "Anything else?"

"Breathing," Lucy reminds me. So does Lourdes.

I invited them both here to help me get ready for this date, hoping I'd be calmer with them around. I was wrong. I'm still a bundle of nerves.

"Charisma is really good at getting people pumped up and still relaxed," Lucy tells us. "She's seriously the queen of cool on first dates. Never nervous. I always try to emulate her."

"Too bad she's with Dom and some of their other friends tonight," I lament. I really did want her help because I've never had this apprehension for a date before. It isn't entirely fear, but something I can't quite name.

"She's Kenzie's bestie and yet she spends all her time with our brother," Lucy continues with a laugh. "Charisma and Dom's friendship should seriously be friend goals."

"We don't have that problem," Lourdes reminds her. "We are friend goals, too. And Gwenn, you're usually the queen of cool on dates, too. Don't forget that."

Leave it to Lourdes to get us refocused on the task at hand.

I start to move but can't remember why. "What am I doing?"

"Deep breaths," Lucy says. She starts dramatically acting out breathing techniques that sound borderline orgasmic before bursting into a giggle.

I laugh. "Got it." Well, not really. I am breathing, but not as slow and steady as I should be. "Is it normal to be this nervous?"

"Nervous about spending the night with a guy you like?" Lourdes asks. "If you weren't at least a little excited, I'd tell you not to bother."

"You already did that, remember?"

"I just don't want you to get hurt."

"If I'm going to take a chance on having a real relationship with a man, Rhett is probably the best candidate." Then I realize what she said before. "What makes you think I'll spend the night there?"

"For one, you traded in your chunky sweaters for a tighter outfit."

This is true. I know exactly what I was thinking when I put this on. The dress barely skims the middle of my thighs. That's more skin than I ever show, even in summer. I pull at the fabric around my midsection. "It honestly isn't as comfortable as it looks. And it's only dinner at his place. Maybe he expects casual, like my comfy sweaters. I should go change."

"Comfy? Yes. Sexy? Not even close. Unless you wear only a sweater and nothing else, which you and I both know you are not planning on doing. Trust me. And Lourdes. And yourself. You are the one who asked for help. And trust Jade. She is our friend and an expert at fashion. She had an entire boutique at her disposal and picked the perfect thing for you to wear. You said you were okay with stepping outside your comfort zone. This is no time for doubts," Lucy says.

I glance down at the cream-colored satin dress covered in printed fuchsia rosettes. The spaghetti straps are just barely keeping the top up enough to avoid an early wardrobe malfunction. As it is, the low-cut neckline and push-up strapless bra have my cleavage almost unrestricted. I'll be making payments on this dress for months, but at least Jade gave me a discount. She told me she couldn't resist treating me, and since I never buy anything as glamorous as this dress, the occasion was sure to be a special one.

"Trust. Okay. Right. I can do that. Sure. Anything else?"

"Remember to breathe when you see him."

Rhett comes to mind, and this makes me smile. "I will. It was so worth closing the office early and putting my phone on silent, even with all the headaches some of my clients might give me. I cannot wait to see him. And for him to see me." My smile grows wider.

"Good. Grab your coat, bag, and shoes." Lourdes smiles at me. "Have a great time."

"You'll lock up?" I ask, though I don't know why. I gave her a key ages ago. Lucy doesn't have one, but I think she understands. Trusting people is so much harder than it sounds.

"Of course," Lourdes tells me.

"Go have fun!" Lucy adds.

We all three share a group hug before I'm in my shoes and coat, out the door, and on my way to my plucky Fusion.

I have a date. And I mean, it isn't like this is only a date or only the first date I've had in a long time. It's with Rhett. I never thought I'd allow myself the joy of this, yet here I am. Even scraping snow and ice off my windshield doesn't bother me.

I'm at Rhett's apartment a little early, but this is far better to me than being late. I'm sure he won't mind me arriving at six-thirty instead of seven.

When the door opens after I've knocked, Rhett looks at me in surprise. "Hey!"

His eyes scan my body, stopping at a few key places he hasn't seen so exposed before. I grin, happy he likes the look of them. It makes me feel so much better about trading in my sweater and leggings for this dress.

He pulls me in for a tight embrace, which I gladly return. I missed being in his arms. The fact that this doesn't alarm me is both surprising and electrifying. So is the sensation of his hands and arms around my back.

Once we finally pull back, he motions for me to step inside. He takes my coat from me and goes to walk away. Before he makes it too far, though, he comes back and plants a quick kiss on my hand. The tingles from this kiss definitely do not stop at my wrist. He lingers, his hand still holding mine, his face only inches away from mine. He's so close that the smell of his shampoo immediately hits my nose. "So happy you're here."

"Me too." I smile. "Sorry I'm early."

"Never apologize for me getting to see more of you," he says.

Lucy and Lourdes are right. I'm absolutely going to straddle him when I get the chance. It shouldn't be too long, either. Then I smell smoke coming from down the tiny hall and what I assume is the kitchen. "Is something burning?"

Rhett looks confused, then his eyes grow wide. The smoke alarm starts blaring. "Oh, shit!" He turns to walk away again, then stops once more. "Um, why don't you wait here? I'll be right back." He gently places my coat on the chair nearest us in the living area and rushes to whatever is burning.

"Do you need help?" I call down to him.

"Nope. I'm good," he replies.

I drop my purse with my coat and sit over on the sofa. His apartment doesn't appear to have anything wrong with it, and he has designated parking for his Tacoma outside. This confirms my suspicion, from admittedly late in the day yesterday, that he needed an excuse to spend time with me. I love this thought so much, I smile even though I'm alone at the moment. I don't care that it led to the budget debacle. Rhett wants me and only me and isn't afraid of showing it.

I hear a couple of metallic-sounding clicks nearby, then the front door opens. I can't help but move back a bit in surprise.

Edin walks in.

My presence startles her as well. She almost jumps at the sight of me but quickly recovers.

"Oh. Hi. I didn't expect anyone else to be here. It's Gwenn, right?"

She steps the five feet over to me to shake my hand. I don't bother standing. I also don't know why she is being so friendly. I can't possibly be the only uncomfortable one. Then she eyes my risqué dress, including the one strap that refuses to stay up on my shoulder. Every time it falls, a little more cleavage is revealed. My choice of outfit, obviously appalling to Edin, I see, as she narrows her eyes, seems to have her even more flustered than my presence. It doesn't help that she's wearing a sweater and jeans and seems to have no discomfort about her own outfit.

"Nice to officially meet you, Edin," I say as she confidently settles her body on the sofa as if she owns it.

She's staying?

"I didn't realize you kept a key," I tell her.

She laughs like it's just so funny and so cute. Of course, there's nothing funny or cute about this to me. "I forgot to give it back to Rhett. Since I still had it, I figured it couldn't hurt to use it just one last time instead of knocking." She gives me a tiny smile then her expression changes to curiosity. "I'm sorry. I didn't know you were going to be here. Rhett didn't tell me he made plans."

Edin doesn't say the word date, but she has to know that's what this is. She also keeps apologizing, only it doesn't strike me as genuine or authentic in any way. "Well, it happens—"

"Edin?" Rhett interrupts me.

I look up.

He stands in the entrance to the living area. "What are you doing here?"

Edin rises to her feet and gives him a sheepish grin. I'm surprised she isn't batting her huge eyelashes. "I came to talk to you about important things that I don't think should be discussed over the phone. Or with anyone else here." She gives me a side-eye glance.

Rhett gives his head a shake of disbelief. "Edin, can this wait?"

"No." She softens her voice. "It really can't." Her lip just quivered.

She's serious, isn't she? Damn. I can't help feeling sorry for her, and if I can't, I know how likely it is that Rhett is having the same reaction. I look to him to see if he's going to give in to her.

"Right. Well, as you can see, Gwenn and I—"

A timer goes off in the kitchen.

"That will be the pork loin. Granny has high hopes for me this time with her special recipe she messaged me. And the smoke was from a towel on fire," Rhett tells me. His eyes never leave mine. "Dinner is going to be perfect. I'll be right back. I promise. Don't go anywhere."

I reluctantly turn back to my unwelcome companion. As much as I don't want her here and don't understand why she hasn't left yet, I don't want to be rude. After all, she is still Rhett's friend, though he just told her to go.

He didn't use those words, however, did he? He never said, "Edin, leave now." Then again, he really didn't have a chance to. But I believe in him. I know as soon as he comes back, she's going to be on her way. Then, he and I can start our much-needed, and anticipated, alone time. Maybe I'll put this slipping spaghetti strap to good use.

Edin and I share an awkward, silent smile before something catches my eye. The glint of light on a small diamond. Diamond engagement ring, to be exact, on her left ring finger.

She moves her eyes to the same ring it feels like I've been clobbered by.

"Gwenn, I'm . . . well, I wish I could say I'm sorry, but I'm not. We did break up. Honest. We haven't even talked much in three days. Well, except for when I came here to get my things. Move out, so to speak."

"When was that?" I manage to ask, though my voice still makes it sound like I'm being strangled.

"Oh, two days ago." She speaks in a laughing, breezy way.

"You were here two days ago?" My tone gives away the fact that Rhett never told me.

Edin clearly catches on to this. There's a smile in her eyes, but she keeps her face mostly expressionless. "After the engagement dinner, of course."

I almost run out right now. "The what?"

Rhett had plenty of opportunities to mention this to me. We spent all of yesterday together, from early morning until after dark. Why did he not say anything? Is this a pattern of dishonesty, like lying about his budget? It seemed so innocent at the time, but this conversation with Edin has given me major doubts.

Edin continues. "Oh, it was no big deal. My friends didn't know we broke up, and Rhett and I didn't have the heart to tell them. Afterward, he said I could keep the ring."

Which is also news to me.

I try to not let this show. It's challenging keeping my facial muscles as still as possible. Edin seems to notice this, too. The glow in her eyes brightens, then she sniffles without even crying. Yet. I brace myself for what's to come.

"He's the best person I know. The best one I've ever been in love with. Do you know about Jill?"

I nod.

Edin flinches like I've smacked her with this answer. "I know I will never live up to Jill's legacy, but I also know I have the best shot of ever doing so out of anyone. Rhett loves me the best he could love anyone, such as it is." She wipes at the tears now spilling out of her eyes.

I am stupefied. How can I possibly reply to that? I feel sorry for both of us at this point. It's all too ridiculous for me to feel any other way.

"No, I'm sorry, Edin. Honestly. I don't think I'm in the right position to say if Rhett knows what he wants, but if it is you—" My breath catches. "I need to remove myself from this situation."

She doesn't say anything to contradict me. She actually doesn't say anything at all.

I stand and grab my coat and purse. I'm only a few steps away from the chair when Rhett comes back. Edin, still crying, excuses herself to the bathroom and rushes down the hall.

"What happened in here?" Rhett asks. He looks at the things in my arms. His brows furrow. "Where are you going?"

"I'm only going to say this one more time. I said you had to be done with Edin if you wanted to contact me. Correct?"

"Yes. And I am."

"Then why is she here? Why is she still comfortable enough to just show up without calling? To enter your apartment with the key she never gave back? To wear the symbol of an engagement that is supposedly over?"

"I told her she could keep the ring, but I never gave her a reason to still wear it."

"Did you explicitly say it or just hope she'd figure it out, like you did the whole rest of your relationship?"

He winces. "We broke up. You know we did. I can't just drop her out of my life completely. You know that, too."

I nod. "I do. I know. But I also know other things about you. Nothing ever seems to be completely over for you. That's why I have to leave."

"Please don't go. As soon as she comes out, I'll send her home. I promise."

But it's too late.

It really sucks walking back down the stairs to my car in the parking lot. I had such high hopes for my dinner with Rhett. I let myself believe things could be happy and fun with him, giving in to the growing feelings I knew I should have ignored.

Edin was right. I will never live up to Jill. Hearing all those stories about her that Rhett told me compelled me to question whether this might be true, but Edin's words solidified my fears. Perhaps she won't live up to Jill's memory, either. That isn't for me to decide.

Maybe I would have fought for my date if it hadn't been for that damn ring. Any man who is serious about not marrying someone either wants the ring back or, at the very least, wants it off the hand of his ex. He still hasn't found the courage to stand up for what he wants, which tells me he'd never stand up and fight for me if it came down to it.

I'm such a fool.

Chapter 32

Rhett

I stare at the closed door, willing Gwenn to come back through it. But she won't. I think I understand her enough to know chasing her down the hall is a bad idea. I turn around and storm down the length of my apartment in quick footsteps, meeting Edin outside the bathroom door.

"What the hell did you say to her? And why are you still wearing that ring?"

She appears to have dried her face of all remaining tears. "I told her the truth."

"Your truth or the actual truth? I mean, shit, Edin, we aren't together anymore. We can be friends, but not if you're going to ruin what I have with Gwenn."

"Rhett, I don't just want to be friends. You know I want you back. I won't hide my feelings. I'm not sorry for them."

She steps closer to me in order to reach out to my arm. I take a step back, but she moves forward a little. Her hand doesn't make it all the way before she drops it back down. "Giving up on our relationship feels like giving up on so much more," she says.

"I know." I nod.

Jill and I once got into a fight over my inability to say what I wanted. We were eight at the time. I never disagreed with her. My mama had called me a people-pleaser. Jill's dad called me weak.

"There's nothing wrong with making other people happy," Jill said one day while we were on the double slide at school. "But you have to be happy, too." She was wise even back then.

She was right, of course. It wasn't easy, especially when she'd intentionally choose games or toys or snacks she knew weren't exactly my favorites or even hers. Such was the case of the bologna, mustard, and marshmallow cream sandwich.

"If you aren't happy, you need to say so," she told me after seeing the disgusted expression on my face.

I know she'd hate to see what I've become with Edin. Jill would want me to say what I feel.

"We aren't giving up as much as you think we are, Edin. How many times have I honestly been the man you want to marry? Not the man pretending to be the one you want to marry?"

"I don't have an answer," Edin says after a short while. Then she looks over at the front door. "Did Gwenn leave?"

"Yep." I sigh and run a hand through my hair. "I need to make this right with her. Because of you, she thinks I don't want her."

"Maybe it's more that she believes you don't know how to let go. Which you don't. Not of me, and certainly not of Jill."

I pretend Edin doesn't use herself in this example. Though I already have Jill at the forefront of my thoughts, as usual, I still ask Edin, "What does Jill have to do with this?"

"Oh, come on, Rhett. We all know she is the ideal. I can live with that. I've proven this. I'm not so sure Gwenn can. She ran at the first obstacle you two faced." She puts her hands up. "My fault, yes. Fine. But still."

I go to speak, but Edin continues. "Why is she so important to you, anyway? Other than her eyes being the same color as Jill's. And yes, I noticed."

"It's more than just her eyes. What I feel for her began before I ever paid much attention to her eyes. Besides, we were in the dark most of the time in the shed."

Edin sucks in air.

"No, no. Not like that. Nothing happened. We didn't have sex," I correct myself. "There just wasn't any light." I take a breath. "Look, Gwenn and I connected. It was how comfortable she was with me and me with her. I told her about Jill and our years growing up together. I also told her about my relationship with Jill and what happened when she died."

Edin doesn't reply right away. I force myself to look her way. Her eyes are teary again and her pale skin has pinked. "You waited six months before telling me anything about Jill."

"I know."

She slowly nods. "Okay, Rhett."

"Okay?"

"Yes. Let's go eat. You can tell me all about this plan you have to get Gwenn back."

"How did you guess?"

Edin gives me a sad smile. "Because I know you."

I start to turn, then stop. "No. Edin, I'm sorry. I promised Gwenn I would ask you to leave."

She huffs. "But she's gone now."

"I promised her," I repeat with emphasis.

"Your promise to a woman you just met means more than all your promises to me?"

"Yes, it does."

Edin gets quiet, then licks her lips. After taking a few steps closer to me, she reaches out for my shirt at my chest like she usually does when she wants something. "Rhett Liam Mason, I know what you need. A warm dinner. Cold beers. A warm body. I'll give you all those things and more. I also happen to be madly in love with you."

Tempting.

So damn tempting.

Like every other time before now, it would be so easy to agree with her, and—physically speaking—it would feel damn amazing. At first. Then I would feel like the crummiest guy in the world.

I slowly remove her hands from the front of my T-shirt. "Edin, I need you to go."

She doesn't move. "If you one-hundred percent want me to leave, I'll leave. If even the tiniest bit of you wants me to stay, whatever part that might be," she adds with a smirk, "I'm staying."

Chapter 33

Gwenn

I SHOVE ANOTHER FRY in my mouth, ignoring the searing of hot oil on my tongue. Greasy takeout burgers and fries are always my go-to in these situations: the debacles of ruined dates or the miseries of me letting myself grow attached to a man. I added sorbet and wine to the mix this time. Lourdes watches me from her spot on my sofa, Lucy from the carpeted floor. If I hadn't already called them on my way home from Auburn, they'd be asking a thousand questions right now.

"I'm such an idiot!" I yell out with a full mouth. The bite of burger gets washed down by my favorite Pinot noir.

"You trusted him. That's what people do in relationships. You are not stupid for doing so," Lucy tells me.

I glare at her, my eyes narrowing to almost closure. "He left me before we were even a thing for the fiancée he may or may not have broken up with." I point to myself. "Idiot!"

"He screwed up. Not you," Lucy is quick to reply.

"Oh gosh. I know." I start crying for the third time tonight. "Just when I thought it was going to be okay. Just when I thought he had finally moved on from the past, there she suddenly was."

I'm not sure if I only mean Edin.

"This is why I don't let people in," I say in a loud burst then cry harder.

"But we're close," Lucy says. "And you've been friends with Lourdes for several years now."

"Yeah, because she forced her way in."

Lourdes moves a little closer to me. "You didn't have anyone. That was easy enough to understand. I'd see you showing clients around Syracuse Falls, then you'd eat all by yourself in the diner or even in your car. You never bothered going back to your office when you didn't have an assistant. I knew you were lonely. Besides, I haven't fully converted you yet. You still live alone here in the city." She gestures vaguely at my apartment.

"I plan on living alone, too, but at least my sister is never far from me," Lucy says to us.

"It's difficult to find new clients in a small town," I reply. "I love my office there, and I love the affordable rent, but it isn't always practical. I need to be available early in the morning and late into the night. When I'm not at the office, it makes sense to be more localized here in the city."

"It seems like it's getting easier for you to open up to others," Lourdes says.

"But neither of you are threatening," I tell them.

They immediately freeze, faces in alarm. "He threatened you? Or she did?"

"What happened? What did they say?"

"Why didn't you tell us sooner?"

My friends start to spiral even more with worry.

I put my hands up for a second to stop them. "No, no, no. Neither threatened me, physically or otherwise. I just don't feel at ease with Rhett when it comes to explaining my life and my past. He hasn't been entirely forthcoming. I'm not sure I could ever open up the way he wants, or wanted, me to."

"So don't," Lourdes tells me. "No one said you owe him anything. If somehow this mess gets cleared up and you and he are friends, well, you can be friends and not have to go too deep. You decide what, if anything, to share. He has to respect that. If he doesn't, he's not the right friend for you."

"If things clear up and he is actually still single, would you be open to another date with him?" Lucy asks.

Lourdes cringes at her words but says nothing.

"What?" Lucy presses her.

Lourdes turns to me. "His belief that you two share a connection is just a hunch, a hypothesis at most, not even necessarily a gut instinct."

"But Gwenn feels it, too," Lucy tells her.

"It's based on the thrill of life-or-death circumstances in the mountains," Lourdes continues. "If it's this distressing for you, this entire situation, it's not worth it."

"What isn't?" Lucy asks.

"Rhett."

Lucy makes a sort of shocked, gasping sound at Lourdes's suggestion.

"There's already too much baggage for both of them," Lourdes tells her. "Why add to that?"

Lucy looks at her like she can't quite find the words to voice just how horrified she is at the idea of me giving up on Rhett. Finally, Lucy turns to me, without having said anything else to our friend. "When he calls—because, if he's a smart man, he will call—will you talk to him?"

"What is there to say? I told him everything he needs to know in order for us to move ahead with forging a relationship."

"At least he texted," Lucy says.

"Yeah. Two words. 'I'm sorry.' Is that all I get? Don't I deserve more?"

Lourdes swallows her mouthful of wine, then clears her throat. "What are you going to do about you?"

I take a bite of cheeseburger large enough to fill my whole mouth. "What about me?"

She ignores the fact that I'm talking with my mouth full and gives me a look of furrowed eyebrow cynicism.

I understand her completely. "What, my abandonment issues? Yep. Experiencing this full force right now. Abandoned and disappointed."

Lucy gives a sympathetic "aww" sound. I think she relates to this more than anything else. She feels abandoned and disappointed in love much deeper than Lourdes or I ever do at the end of a growing romantic relationship.

I continue. "Jill was taken from Rhett. No one had a choice. The people who raised me chose to desert me in the hospital with nothing and no one. They put up no fight at all to stay in my life or keep me in theirs. They provided money and nothing more. They stole my freaking driver's license from the hospital and anything else that could identify them. Lourdes, you were the first person who chose to love me as I am. The hospital staff, as wonderful as they were, could only do that to a point. I couldn't stay there forever."

"What made you come up here?" Lucy asks. She's never broached this subject in the three months I've known her, and I haven't been willing to volunteer much info. It's never been easy for me to talk about, but with my current mood—and current disgust—I no longer wish to avoid this topic anymore.

"New York was about as far as I could get from everything I knew out west. Thousands of miles, different climate, and most importantly, nothing familiar."

"It must be sad to not have any family."

"Not everyone is as close to their family as you are to yours and Lourdes is to hers," I remind her. "Not that I have any relatives to miss." To say the least.

"Then Rhett comes along, saves your life, appears to be the greatest guy ever, and then abandons you for his past," Lucy says. "So close to bliss then bam!"

"Bingo."

"Whatever he chooses to do now doesn't matter much. What does matter is what you decide," Lourdes says. "You've already started looking into your history."

"With zero luck."

"What about the plan you and I came up with a while ago?"

"You mean find and bitch out my so-called family?"

"Why not? It would be cathartic. You need healing from their hurt."

"You make it sound so simple."

"Not simple, but necessary."

"I'm sure her therapist already discussed this with her," Lucy half-whispers to Lourdes.

"Thank you!" I cry out. Then I turn to Lourdes as well. "Why do you always have to use your psychology degree on me?"

"Since taking over the shop for Gam-Gam, I need to use it on someone."

"All your hopeless-romantic customers aren't enough?"

"Never." Lourdes laughs.

"Hey, I take offense to that," Lucy says.

"Maybe you should use your degree on Rhett," I tell Lourdes.

"Or me," Lucy offers.

"I can't help Rhett," Lourdes says. "No one could unless he was ready for them to. And Luce, you don't need therapy. You just need to be pickier about the guys you fall in love with."

Now Lucy laughs. "I wish it was possible to be picky. There aren't a lot of choices out there. I find a guy with potential and start from there."

"Except he stays the same, and you end up miserable," Lourdes replies.

We've talked about Lucy wanting to "create" the perfect guy before. She adamantly denies this is her goal in each relationship. I wonder sometimes, because she's immediately fallen in love with some men I'd never give a second look to without a personality and/or lifestyle change.

Lourdes sets her empty wine-glass down on the coffee table and picks up her phone. "Since your searches haven't led anywhere, let's go at this a different way. We can start by finding a program or agency that might be helpful with the search."

"I bet your Uncle Sal would know. He's seriously into all that genealogy stuff, right?" Lucy says to her.

"Great idea," Lourdes replies. "I should have thought of that before. Uncle Sal is a whiz with history. This won't be too difficult for him."

Lourdes sends off a text while I finish my food binge.

Lucy's phone dings. She looks at it, and her face falls into a concerned frown. "Oh. My sister needs me to meet her at my parents' house. Something about a family discussion." She looks over at me. "I'm sorry your date was a flop."

"Thanks, Luce. I'll have more listings for you tomorrow, okay?"

After she leaves, Lourdes checks her phone. "Okay, so I was wrong. Uncle Sal says he doesn't know for sure what may help find living people. He only knows how to find records of dead ones."

"That's a little morbid."

After a laugh, Lourdes continues. "He asked Pippa, and she's going to send me a link."

Uh-oh. "You okay with Pippa helping?"

"For you? Anything. Even that." She grimaces.

"Even make nice with the woman your high school boyfriend cheated on you with?"

"Let's stop focusing on those assholes and focus on you."

"Lourdes, You won't watch Rent with me because you overheard Pippa telling Florence it's her favorite musical. You also won't watch anything with an actor or character named Spencer."

"I would do anything and deal with anything to help you with something this important," she tells me. "You still have all your paperwork?"

"Of course."

I wipe my greasy hands on a paper napkin from the takeout bag, stand, and make my way to my bedroom where I left my folder, wanting it somewhere I wouldn't pay much attention to it. It doesn't take me long to reach my room. My might-as-well-be-considered-a-studio apartment is smaller than my rented office. I simultaneously envy my clients with large budgets looking for large houses and hope they never find out my own home is probably smaller than their pantries.

As one of my clients, Lucy is so lucky I ever let her see where I live. At least it's always extremely clean. I keep my apartment as organized as my office. And really, though I sometimes complain about how small my place is, I like my minimal, decluttered life here. It helps to keep my anxiety at bay. It's a lesson I learned after my first accident.

I return to my best friend, useless, unhelpful folder in hand.

Lourdes gives my empty hand a quick squeeze. "Are you ready for this?"

I nod. "Yep. As ready as I'll ever be, I suppose."

"Okay. For now, let's skip the programs you've already used. Probably won't get much more out of them. Pippa says this search engine costs forty-five dollars a month, but she sent her username and password for us to borrow."

"Why would she do that?"

Neither of us speaks.

"Lourdes? You hate this woman. Why would she be so generous?"

Still, Lourdes is quiet.

"You had to tell her my history, didn't you?"

"I'm sorry. I thought it was the best way to find results. Believe me, I hated having to act like her friend and betray your confidence. If it helps, I don't think she'll tell anyone. She's good about keeping secrets, I'll give her that."

Lourdes logs in and begins search number one. It will take more than a few tries to find what we need. I have zero hopes for this.

"There are no results with the exact name we checked," Lourdes says, turning the phone's screen my way. She is careful to avoid the word "your" in association with Jaymie. This is what she's always done as a way to protect me.

I shuffle through the pages. "Try that name in Lake Havasu, Arizona. Or Gomez Memorial Trauma Center, where I was treated."

"You couldn't access the hospital's online portal?"

"It's all the same info I have here. Nothing about any previous conditions or visits before the accident."

Lourdes taps on her phone. "No. Nope. Oh wait. There is a Jaymie Jonas here but no sign of parents or anyone else."

"Does it look like this?" I hold up a piece of paper.

"Oh. Yeah. That sucks." Lourdes's hopeful expression falls.

"It's okay. Let's keep going. And let me try. I'm a pro at programs like this. Real estate or hospital records, it's all the same kind of search in the end. Though I still don't think it'll do any good."

Desperate to have results, anyway, I take Lourdes's proffered phone and type in a phrase using keywords from the hospital forms I have. I've tried these in other searches to no avail.

As I scan what pops up, Lourdes says, "We know no one told you the parents' names because none of them knew. Except that isn't entirely true. The doctors must have known. Even though you were an adult, they had to consult or try to consult with someone, at least for the initial tests."

"I asked, and they wouldn't tell me. I asked back then, I asked through the years of therapy and testing, and I asked this week, including a different nurse I was really close to who I hoped might have heard something. It's no use."

"Did you make friends with the billing staff?"

"Everything was paid anonymously online." I sigh.

Then I remember something I have yet to show her. Frantically, I flip through pages until I find the one I haven't been able to read without having a panic attack. But I have to risk it. "Here. These are the notes one of the nurses took for me describing the people who came to visit me. She was one of only three people to see them and know why they were there."

Lourdes reverently takes the paper, as if it might disintegrate if she's too rough with it. It honestly is as irreplaceable as she's treating it, so I appreciate the effort.

"Okay. Can you call her and ask her more about this?"

"Unfortunately, no. She moved out of state, and obviously, no one can or will give me her contact info. These notes were also written days after seeing them, once they knew for sure my memories were gone and I'd start asking questions as soon as I was able."

"Right. Well, this is a start. So let's look for newspaper announcements or articles. People with that kind of money have a hell of a time keeping to themselves. They most likely are pillars of their community, or at least they think so or like to pretend to be," she says.

She types "Jonas" and "Lake Havasu City, Arizona" into another search engine Pippa mentioned. Several results pop up. "Holy crap, there's a doctor there." She pauses. "Who looks nothing like the description from the nurse. Damn."

"If my father were a doctor, I highly doubt he would give up on me so easily. He would know what ER staff and specialists are capable of."

"True. And that's the first time you've called him your father to me. How does it feel?"

I take a moment to let it sink in. "It feels a little scary and a lot heartbreaking."

"Understandable."

I start rubbing at my chest muscles, hoping to relax them, yet I know anxiety doesn't work that way. "I think I need to call and ask Florence to refill my other prescription a week early. I don't want to run out." I look to Lourdes, who glances back with kind eyes.

"You want to keep looking?" she asks softly.

"Definitely." I close my eyes. "Maybe they don't live there." This is the first time that particular idea has occurred to me.

"Like you all were just visiting?"

"Yeah, maybe. If they were so rich and prominent in Lake Havasu, wouldn't someone have recognized them?" I give Lourdes her phone back, pick up mine, and look up a map of Arizona, hoping to pinpoint where we might have lived back then. "We could have lived in a different state. I mean, it's right near the West Coast. Or we could have been from a frostier climate. Maybe that's why I was so drawn to up here. I didn't know I was used to the cold."

"Possibly." Lourdes grows quiet while typing different things into the search engine. "Wait. You see right here? This area of Arizona looks promising," she says, pointing to the page.

Chapter 34

Rhett

I DIDN'T CALL GWENN after she left last night. Thought it best to let her feel her feelings without being hassled. I did text her, but I can't find my phone to check if she replied. I have a plan to help me apologize, but I'm not sure how she'll take it. The worry of it was enough to keep me up all night. I couldn't bear to eat the dinner I'd worked so hard on for her, either. It wouldn't have been the same without Gwenn.

Somehow, I still couldn't find my phone by the time I left for work. It's hard to put the plan into action without it.

While it may be Saturday, the shop I work at is still open. Ricardo and I silently change the timing belt on a 2013 Fiesta. I won't tell him about my mess of a date, and he won't ask. He knows something went wrong based on my attitude. I've snapped at him twice already today, more than I have in months. We usually work well together. Out of all my coworkers, Ricardo is my favorite. He's easy-going, knowledgeable, and oftentimes flat-out hilarious, unlike most of the others.

At least I've managed to avoid Giovanni. The last thing I need is that weasel harassing me. What I need most is Jill's guidance. I know it's impossible to bring her back, but being able to talk to her would help.

I move on to a brake change for a Mini Cooper while Ricardo and the other guys break for lunch. Still no appetite. I hate not knowing Gwenn's standpoint right now. Her interpretation of all this might be changing by the minute. I write her texts in my head, full of apologies and how much I already miss her, but obviously, I can't send them. I really wish I could.

This is new territory for me. Jill and Edin both always just took control and quickly forgave. Gwenn told me she hasn't trusted any guy enough to have a committed relationship. I want to be worthy of her trust, and I need her to know that. No matter what, if I can't find my phone tonight, I'm in big trouble.

Chapter 35

Gwenn

RHETT AND I WERE supposed to be together now. Last night was our ruined date, but it feels like it happened ages ago. He still hasn't contacted me other than that quick "I'm sorry" text. What good does a two-word text do without anything else to back it up? Granted, I didn't respond, only because I didn't know what to say or what else needed to be said. I'd made myself clear in his apartment.

Researching my disaster of a previous life has been fruitful in some ways, but Rhett is still there in the back of my mind. I can't believe I let myself think he could be over her. Edin was and is essentially Jill's replacement. There's no way he would ever truly let her go.

I receive a call on my phone. It's from an unknown number. Of course I have to answer it. New or potential clients call all the time, even on the weekends. I haven't had my phone silenced since my would-be date with Rhett, when I actually missed two important calls. "This is Gwenn."

"Hi, Gwenn. It's Edin."

"Are you kidding me?" Oops. Didn't mean to say this out loud. I'm totally caught off guard right now. "What do you want, Edin? I mean, what's going on? Is Rhett okay?" I have a difficult time keeping my tone out of the fiery, ill-tempered zone.

"He's fine. Well, in most ways. Perfectly healthy, so don't worry. Can you and I meet up for coffee? Would that be all right?"

I want to say no, but I need more information first. "What's wrong with him?"

"Do you really need to ask?"

Memories of last night come to the forefront of my mind. "I guess not."

"You and I need to talk. I'd rather not do it on the phone. Please." She adds this last word as I take in a breath to reply.

"Fine. Do you know the On the Corner Café in Camillus?"

· ♥ · ♥ · ♥ · ♥ · ♥ ·

"Is this a good idea?" Lourdes asks, her voice coming out of the speakers in my car.

"What else can I do? Let her keep calling me? Besides, she said it's important."

"Yeah, right. She just wants to rub her reconciled relationship in your face."

"That would be cruel."

"And that word doesn't immediately make you think of her?"

"No. Should it?"

"Gwenn, she owns a bakery. She could have easily asked you there if she was sincere about making nice."

"Maybe not asking me there is her way of being considerate."

"Maybe she doesn't want you near her territory, including Rhett. She wants to make sure she was clear enough last night. Rhett is hers. She has no other reason to see you. If I'm wrong, why hasn't Rhett called you?"

"Be that as it may, I can grin and bear it for a few minutes."

"But you shouldn't have to. Why not tell her to talk to her fiancé about her concerns and leave you out of it?"

"Hey, Lourdes, I have to go," I say as I pull into an empty parking spot along the street. "Tell you all about it later."

"You should leave now," she replies just as I am about to end the call. I stop and listen. "It's too complicated of a situation. You didn't want to be involved with him in the first place. It can't be worth all this. And I know it's fun to think of how arousing it was in the shed and all the attention he gives you, but you need light in your life, not lies and cover-ups and psycho ex-fiancées."

"I seriously have to go now," I say by way of reply.

Once inside, I'm immediately aware I have arrived at the café before Edin. A worker grinds coffee beans, the wonderful aroma filling the air. Another swirls caramel onto a foam-topped beverage. I choose a table and am instantly greeted by a server. He hands me a menu and leaves the table to collect a glass of ice water for me. When he returns after a minute or so, I order a cold brew coffee and panini. A customer walks by with a steaming mug of lemon tea. The scent makes my stomach grumble. I haven't had time to eat lunch today, even though it's after two.

Edin actually arrives before I thought she would, but she's still half an hour late. She sits down with the flush of cold still on her cheeks. I set my remaining half-sandwich down, wipe my hands on my napkin, and force myself to look into her eyes.

Edin smiles and casually says hello. She doesn't give me any reason or excuse for her tardiness. I say hello in reply, then we are silent. After the server comes to greet her, she orders a chai latte. It only takes the waiter a few minutes to bring Edin's drink. We don't talk the entire time. She doesn't even bother sipping it once it's on the table.

I finally speak again. "What is this all about?"

Edin closes her eyes for a moment before replying. "Gwenn, about last night—"

I put up a hand. "No. What happened happened. It's clear you and Rhett can't stay away from each other. I understand."

"But you don't understand."

"Look, I have things in my life. Something truly horrific happened, and I almost died. Way before the plane crash." She hasn't earned details, so I give her none. "I know how spectacular and yet excruciating it can be to survive those kinds of events."

She nods. "So that's why you've held on to Rhett."

This statement makes me want to cry. "No. That's why I tried to let him go. To get him to let me go. We can't form a relationship or even a friendship based solely on having been there for each other when no one else was."

"Is that what you think it's based on?" She asks this with a tilted head.

I don't answer her.

"Gwenn, it seems to me you two have formed some kind of connection already."

I don't know how to answer this. She's right. It's what Rhett is always saying. Telling Edin anything else would be a disservice to both of us. "Deeper than I ever thought was possible," I finally reply.

"My kind-of fiancé prefers his new friend to me. There's no other way of looking at it." She now takes a sip of coffee. "Rhett and I had a long talk after you left."

Did I hear her right? "You stayed?"

"Not overnight. I admit I ruined things for you. I knew what I was doing as I did it. I'm not even sorry."

My voice crackles despite my best efforts to keep it emotionless. "Are you back together?"

She smiles again. This expression is cryptic. "We're not."

This woman sure knows how to mess with someone's mind.

"You know, Rhett has opened up to you in ways he never did with me."

"Jill," I say in comprehension.

"Yeah. He showed me pictures. He told me stories. But he never talks about losing her and how he deals with that. He waited months to mention her to me, but he told you about her right away."

"Wait. You said you were the only one who could help him mourn her and move on from her."

"And I still believe that's true. He's not obsessive, and he's not obsessed. Not with her. Not with you."

I can't tell if she intentionally avoids Jill's name. "You're going to keep wearing that?" I point to her ring. "Act like things are fine between you and Rhett even though he told you that you were over?"

"Have you ever been in love?"

I won't give the detailed answer this question demands, but I also can't refuse her a reply. "No, I haven't."

"Then I don't expect you to comprehend how difficult this all is for me."

"Just because I've never been in love doesn't mean I don't know how it works or what happens when it ends or how any of it feels."

Edin avoids my gaze. She doesn't say anything.

"You think you and Rhett had or have this one great love. This fantastic bond between the two of you because you assume you're helping him get over Jill. Let me ask you this. Has he ever told you he loves you? The actual words. Has he ever said how he can't wait to marry you or spend the rest of his life with you? I know you never set a date for the wedding."

"Because of Jill! Not because of me. He never gave me a fair chance. That's all I'm asking for." She doesn't say this last part with anger or jealousy. She states it without added emotion. "Since you've already been trying to let him go, isn't this a better incentive? Giving two people a second chance to fall in love?"

Wow. She's good. And I don't mean it in an insulting way. She really knows how to get what she wants. But a voice keeps telling me

I'm what, or rather who, Rhett wants. I can't ignore that, much as I'd like to.

"Edin, I'm not in charge of Rhett, and neither are you. If he told you it's over, you need to believe it."

"I think Rhett and I know more about what I need than you do." Then she gives me one of her mysterious smiles. "I'm a baker. Say I create dazzling strawberry shortcakes, but the customers don't want those. If the people want chocolate, give them chocolate. Give them all you've got."

"What exactly are you saying?"

She looks like she's trying not to roll her eyes. "He's the people, I'm the chocolate. Any more questions?"

I have no reply. It was hard enough trying to keep my voice from shaking before this.

When she speaks again, her voice has a playful yet seductive tone to it. "Rhett's an expert at knowing just what I need."

I can't finish my coffee, my panini, or this conversation with this growing queasiness. I have just one more thing to say to her. "If Rhett truly loves you, why was he so interested in me?" I leave more than enough cash on the table for the server and head out the door.

The tears don't spill until I'm already on the road. I drive straight to Lourdes's shop with blurry eyes. The bell dings as I step inside. The sweet fragrances of lilies, lavender, and roses immediately greet me.

"Be there in a second," my bestie calls. She doesn't know it's me.

I walk over to the main counter where she takes orders. It's the tidiest one in the whole shop, though still a little messy today. It has four spools of ribbon and a pair of shears needing to be returned to their drawers. Everything else she has is always so cluttered with full vases and example/display arrangements and little extra goodies to include in flower deliveries if the customer so chooses. This layout was chosen when her grandma was still in charge, before her health declined and Lourdes decided to give up her psychology career in order to keep the shop going. Lourdes has updated but will never change the core of her grandmother's essence in the shop.

"Lourdes?" I call to her. My voice is thick and heavy.

She rushes out from the back, wiping her hands on the green half apron she wears when arranging floral designs. "What happened?"

I lean against the counter facing her, put my head in my hands, and tell her the whole story.

"How. Dare. She." This isn't a question.

After wiping my eyes with a tissue from my bag, I look to Lourdes again. "But why shouldn't she? If they're back together, it's on him for pursuing me."

"Do you think that's what's going on?"

"I don't know. He still hasn't called me."

She gets a text alert. "Oh, shoot. I'm supposed to finish an arrangement for Lucy. One of her co-workers is retiring, and she wants flowers for the surprise party."

I let out a long breath and wipe my eyes. "You want me to help?"

Lourdes shows me how to snip the stems on the last two yellow roses that need added. Everything else is done, apart from the card she includes with every order, containing a message from the sender. This is always added with some ribbon in a coordinating color. She has hundreds of spools of ribbon at any one time, so her choices are almost limitless.

Her phone beeps again. It's a different sound from her texts. I know this to be an order alert. She picks up her phone and looks at it.

"Um . . . Gwenn?"

"What's wrong?"

She turns the phone my way.

Rhett ordered flowers?

Chapter 36

Rhett

"THANKS FOR LETTIN' ME use your phone, man," I say by way of apology to Ricardo.

"Don't mention it. All good?"

"Yep."

I just wish I could find my own phone. At least I had the ability to add a note to the order explaining to Lourdes what happened last night, though I'm sure she knows, and how I hope she'll help me out. I also hope it's a good plan buying flowers for Gwenn, in colors she loves, from her best friend. Might make her more inclined to listen to my side of the story.

"Hey, Mason!" Giovanni growls from the other side of the shop.

I groan.

I don't want to deal with that asshole right now. I don't bother coming out from under the wrecked Camaro I've been checking the driveshaft on. Ricardo remains sitting nearby.

Then Giovanni adds, "You got a visitor."

This time, I crawl out and see Edin standing there. I wipe my greasy hands on a rag as best I can, then head over to her.

"Make it fast," Giovanni tells me before I reach Edin, then he stomps off.

Whatever it is she wants, it can't be good. She's never visited me at work unless we were having some kind of crisis. Of course, everything is a crisis to her. Anything to draw sympathy from people, especially me.

"What's up?" I ask her when I'm close enough.

"Oh, nothing. I just wanted to come visit you."

"Hey, Edin," Ricardo says as he walks by.

"Hey," she replies while not really looking at him.

He moves to where she can't see him and gives me a look that says I'm about to have a whole lot more trouble in my life. I'd bet anything he's right, too. Not that there's much I can do to stop it, I'm sure. I usher her to the break room.

"Will you have lunch with me?" she asks.

"Lunch is over," I tell her.

"Oh. Okay." She pauses, clearly wanting to say more.

Edin is much better at convincing people to talk when they don't want to, but I have to try. There has to be a reason why she's here. "What's up?" I ask again, this time with a more serious tone.

"Nothing. Really." She again stops talking for a moment. "When do you get off work?"

"Six. Same as every Saturday."

"Two hours?"

"I guess. I don't have my phone on me."

"Can you come over tonight?"

I shake my head. "No."

"Right." She gives me a big, fake grin. It's the one she uses to manipulate me when she wants something. It usually works. "Then can I come to your place?"

"That's not a good idea. Not right now."

"Okay. I understand."

She actually leaves, too. Not once did she call me my full name, which is new for her. Maybe she finally accepts that we are over. Gwenn will be happy. Or she would be if I could call her.

Chapter 37

Gwenn

"You're kidding." I almost shove Lourdes out of the way of her own phone so I can see the screen. "Is this a joke?" I ask her once I've seen it.

I call Rhett, but it goes straight to voicemail, so I leave a message for him to call me as soon as he can. After I hang up, I add to Lourdes, "What does this mean?"

"No idea."

"Do I just wait to hear from him? I mean, I can't exactly ask Edin. I can't just show up at his place."

Lourdes grimaces. "Yeah. Don't do anything his ex always does."

"I won't. Believe me. But now what do I do?"

Chapter 38

Rhett

I'm home for only fifteen minutes or so when I hear someone at the door. I'm in the middle of tearing my living room apart in search of my phone. After swinging the door open, I find Edin standing there with a smile and a plateful of caramel pecan shortbread cookies. At least she couldn't use the key I remembered to take back from her.

"What did you do?" I ask.

She gives me an expression that's innocent but still a bit caught off-guard. "What do you mean?"

I gesture to the plate in her hands. "Those are your apology cookies."

"Rhett Liam Mason, I have no idea what you are talking about. Now, are you going to let me in or just make me stand out here?"

I press on. "You only make those cookies when you have something to apologize for. They're your specialty. You don't just have them lying around at home or the bakery. It's not going to work this time. So, what did you do?"

"Let me in, please?" This time, the smile is hopeful.

Feeling like I have no other choice if I want an answer from her, I step aside, and Edin walks in.

"Oh!" She sets the plate on the end table. "By the way, I found this in my purse." She opens her bag and pulls out my phone.

I don't believe this.

"I must have accidentally taken it last night."

"How do you accidentally take someone's phone? I've been looking for this." My voice is so loud, it echoes down my short hallway.

She doesn't reply.

"Edin, why did you take my phone? Gwenn's probably waiting for me to call her, or she's trying to call me. I might not have a chance with her anymore because of you."

"Rhett Liam Mason, you have no idea how hard this all is for me!" She sniffles like she's crying, only she isn't. I think she wants to, though. "And it really was a mistake. I'm not sure how I took it. I didn't even take it, per se. I just . . . I found it and thought you might want it back." She stops, again with a hint of something else on her mind.

"There's more," I say. "Isn't there?"

Edin looks like she wants to deny this.

I finally grab my phone out of her hand and turn it back on, hoping it isn't off because of a dead battery. It isn't. Gwenn did reply to my text after all. She sent several texts and also a voice message, all at different times last night and today. I check the texts first.

> It's going to take more than that.

> Just sorry isn't enough.

> Are you sure your ex knows she is an ex?

> You need to talk to Edin

I look up at Edin again. "What happened? What did you do?"

Her tears start to come. "It isn't fair how you've chosen her over me."

"But I have," I say as gently as I can. "Edin, I broke things off with you before I met her."

"The same day," she replies. "It couldn't have been more than an hour before you two met. Maybe you didn't call until after you saw her. How will I ever know?"

"You and I weren't going to marry, anyway. We both know that. You have no say in my relationship with Gwenn."

"Relationship?" she asks in a sharp tone. "You hardly know her."

"You and I were a couple for a long time, and I know Gwenn better than you know me."

It looks like hearing this is physically painful to Edin. This is exactly what I never meant to do. Things have never gotten this bad before. We would have been making up by this point. But not now and not ever again. I can't say sorry this time. I can't get over how mad I am, and I can't take her back. I won't. There's someone else now who quickly became more important.

"I need to fix things with Gwenn. She has no idea."

"And we will. Have patience, Rhett. If she's as interested in you as think she is, we have to be careful. You and I both ran her away. Give her a chance to cool off." Edin comes close enough to kiss my cheek. I step back before she's done.

Like hell I'm going to give Gwenn more time not hearing from me.

As soon as Edin heads out the door in a flurry of tears, I call Gwenn.

"You bought me flowers?" she asks as she answers her phone.

"I wanted to find a way to make it right."

"It is better than a two-word text," she concedes.

Then she tells me about her conversation with Edin. Smoke will start coming out of my ears soon, I know it.

"I swear I didn't know she was doing that. And I told her to leave last night, just like I promised you I would. Honest. I need you to know it's over with her."

"I believe you. But." She stops, but it doesn't sound like there's any hesitation.

"But?" I ask.

"I don't want to keep going through this. How many times is she going to come back and try to tear us apart?"

"None," I say without hesitation. "It will not happen again."

"I'm just leaving Lourdes's now. I have to run to my office for an hour or so, then head home. Can I call you later?"

"Please. I'm home. I'll be home all night."

I guess I have to give her time after all.

Chapter 39

Gwenn

ONCE I'VE MADE IT back to my office, I open the files Lourdes sent me, the ones she saved from our search.

The Jonases. They are out there somewhere. I can't stop searching.

The bell on the door dings, reminding me that I forgot to lock it. In walks Edin.

"You have got to be kidding. Twice in one day? To what do I owe the pleasure?" Sarcasm drips from my words. I don't bother sympathizing with her drive out here. Whatever she wants, she is the one who should be making the effort.

"I did something I'm not proud of, out of desperation."

"Other than telling me to stay away from Rhett?"

She nods. "It's my fault he didn't call or text you. I, um . . . well, I stole his phone."

I suck in a breath of surprise without meaning to. He didn't tell me this. "Why?" is all I manage to say.

"First it was Jill, and now it's you. It has never been nor will it ever be me. I get it."

"You get that now," I tell her. But still, I'm a lot less indignant than I was a few moments ago. Something tells me I can trust she's being sincere, which almost feels like a whole new concept.

"You mean a lot more to him than I ever could. I stupidly tried to take him from you like a child whose toy had been snatched away."

"I'm sure he means more to you than that," I can't help but tell her.

She wipes at her teary eye. "I thought if I could just convince him to have dinner with me—the dinner he made for you—I could seduce him and make him forget you ever existed. That was easy to do in the past. He never put up a fight about anything. He'd rather shut out the world than live with its pain." Edin begins to cry harder.

I offer her a tissue box, which she accepts. I also motion for her to sit in one of the client chairs, but she refuses.

"If I'd told him I'd called you and you were no longer interested, he probably would have believed me. That's part of why I took his phone."

I have no doubt she wanted to try that line on him, but somehow, something kept her from doing so.

"This is super weird to say, but I'm glad it was you trapped with him in the blizzard. I was wrong about, well, everything." She laughs through her tears but the smile is fleeting. Heavy drops of tears keep falling. "He trusts you more than he trusts me."

What is going on right now? When she walked in here, I expected animosity. I've ended up both receiving and giving her compassion.

"Does Rhett know you're here?"

"No. He will know I was here, though, when I give this back to him. Finally." She looks down at her engagement ring. "I never thought I would take this off. But I knew better. Or I should have. I knew Rhett didn't love me as much as I loved him, but I was okay with the situation. Rhett told you all about it, didn't he?"

I nod.

She nods in return. I'm guessing it feels like a gut punch, but she doesn't flinch. "I'm going to be fine. Great, even. You and Rhett could be fine without each other, too, but why would you choose that?" She gives me one more smile, then turns and walks out the door.

That does it. If Edin can face her life truths, so can I.

I'd planned on cold calls and emails for this afternoon but never got to them. It's too late for the calls now, and the emails will have to wait. I have other work to do.

Although the idea Lourdes had last night didn't pan out, I will not give up. I search the last remaining cities she and I haven't yet gotten to. Nothing and more nothing. After typing yet another town and Jonas into the search bar, the results pop up.

There they are.

OH MY GOSH THERE THEY ARE.

Delaney and Vara Jonas. They are the right ages, have the right position in their city, and have accumulated the right amount of wealth. There isn't a doubt in my mind these are the people I have been looking for.

To be sure, however, I search their names against Jaymie Jonas.

This is incredible! It's a photo from when Delaney was given a key to the city. There they are, all three of them. Rather, all three of us.

So weird.

I don't see myself in her. The reconstructive surgery changed a lot of her/my facial features. Jaymie was picture perfect in every way. I have keloid scars that developed after my accident, which were treated but still remain. There's a silvery hint of them, but then, I know exactly where to look. I wonder if these people would spot the scars, too.

I can't decide if I'd rather they would or wouldn't. Seeing my scars might mean they'd continue judging me. They might still consider me to be not good enough for them. Not spotting the scars, on the other hand, could mean they didn't know the me I was then well enough to see such differences.

Now I just need a way to contact them. I'm on a roll now and can't give up after reaching this point. I have to see them in person. I have to meet them and speak to them and ask them what the heck they were thinking abandoning me like that. Their position couldn't possibly have dropped any from having a daughter like me. And if they were worried about me being paralyzed or disfigured, I mean, how much lower could you go from there? Yet they managed to.

I send a quick three-word text to Lourdes.

> I found them.

> I'll close up and be right there.

"Hey, sweetie," she says as she rushes through the open door twenty-five minutes later. She walks over to me and gives me a hug. "Where are your emotions right now, about this?"

"I feel amazing! I need to meet them."

"Like, fly to them?"

"Why not? It would be easy for them to ignore my phone calls. How could they possibly ignore me if I'm in the same city? You've already told me a million times that I should go if I ever found them."

"Okay. Just wanted to be sure you were serious. I'm with you no matter what. I'll go with you, too, if you'd like."

"Lourdes, you're the best!" I wrap my arms around her in a hug. Then I hear the ringtone I already set for Rhett. I check the time. It's eight-thirty. He must have been waiting a while for me.

While clutching the ringing phone, I ask Lourdes, "Why am I suddenly so nervous?"

"Because you're about to embark on a momentous journey. Perhaps two."

I still don't answer. It stops ringing.

"Rhett will understand if you don't return his call right away."

"You're right, and that's exactly why I want to get back to him now." Then the phone beeps with a new voicemail notification. I enter the passcode and hear his voice right away.

"What's he saying?" Lourdes asks.

I start his message over and put it on speaker.

"Hey, Gwenn. I'm sorry again. So sorry. I should have handled things better."

"He's right," Lourdes says as Rhett continues the message.

I shush her and start it over again since I missed what else he said.

"I'll be home all night, like I told you before. Please call me back." He pauses. This is where I know he wants to say he misses me but won't. "Just say the word. I'll be out there as soon as I can."

"You should call him," Lourdes says once Rhett's message is over.

I laugh. "You just told me he could wait. You've been against the idea of him since the beginning. Why the change?"

"Because I see it now. I hear it in his voice. He can wait, but do you want him to? I've never known a guy to be so sincere. Honesty is hard to come by."

"I'm a lucky woman." I smile. While I don't call, I do send off a text just to let him know I heard his message and haven't pushed him out of my mind this time.

> Can't call you yet, but I promise we're good. Talk to you soon

I return to my computer and look up a way to find the Jonases' phone number. Even an office number would be okay right now. I just need some way to contact them.

Vara and Delaney aren't listed in any free directories, but Delaney's business number is. This is exactly what I wanted. Then I realize I need to dial down my desperation. If I call the corporate number, I'll never get through to anyone of importance. Besides, how could I possibly explain who I am? I have to find at least a home number.

"Cell would be better," Lourdes corrects me when I tell her this.

"My only choice right now is to pay for a background check. We aren't getting anywhere with just searches."

"How long do those usually take before they send the results?"

After a few clicks, I discover some findings are near instantaneous, which I didn't expect. I choose the most comprehensive, detailed search that will give me answers today. The cost really isn't much, especially considering this is going to give me the most information I have on "them." I'd give all my money for this if I had to. The irony of some of it being their money is not lost on me. A report comes back to me within minutes.

I stare at the electronic file, as afraid of it as I would be a shark or Bigfoot. I open it, anyway, and read its contents.

"What do I do now?"

"Are you seriously asking me that question?" Lourdes replies.

With wobbly hands and rapid breathing, I press the numbers on my phone's screen for the Jonases' home phone and put it on speaker.

A woman answers.

Not wanting to make assumptions, I say, "Hi! I'd like to speak to Vara or Delaney please."

"I'm sorry. There isn't anyone here."

I so badly want to correct her, because she is, in fact, currently in that home, but refrain. Lourdes must have had the same thought because she stifled a laugh at the woman's words. I say goodbye and hang up. No use wasting my time with who is most likely the housekeeper, paid to screen calls. Next, I try a cell number.

Disconnected. Must be an old number. I try another.

My call is answered after three rings.

"Who is this?" a woman asks right away.

"Vara Jonas?" I ask, hoping for confirmation.

Lourdes comes over to me and holds my free hand. I needed that more than I realized.

The woman on the phone is silent. I'm sure she is debating on whether she should lie or not. After all, I am calling from a strange number. "Yes. Who is this?"

I blow out a breath.

This is her. After all these years, I'm on the phone with my mother. It's too surreal to fully grasp. "Gwenn Rhys. Also known as Jaymie Jonas. And no," I add, "this is not a joke."

Again, Vara says nothing.

I'm so tense, I accidentally start to squeeze Lourdes's hand a little too hard. Once I mouth I'm sorry to her and let it go, she gives it a shake with a nod that says it's okay and for me to focus on Vara. "I got your number from a background check. I had to buy a background check to find the people who gave me up."

"We did not give you up," Vara finally says. "You weren't adopted out." Her words are crisp and cold.

Maybe I should have been. But I can't say this. She'll never agree to meet me if I start a fight with her. "I was hoping I could come see you. How about next week?"

"Next week isn't a good time. In fact, I'm swamped until the middle of May. You can come by then," she replies with an air of supreme disinterest.

"May?"

Lourdes scrunches up her face in similar disgust as mine.

"Why would we have to wait all the way until May? That's two months away."

"As I said, it's the best I have available. Take it or leave it." Her tone implies that I should consider myself lucky she's deigning to meet with me at all.

My friend tugs on my hand and nods her head at me. I start nodding back. "Yeah. Fine. May. I'll contact you then."

After I end the call, I say, "What was that about? Why did I just agree to wait two months?"

"To pacify her. But we aren't waiting until then, I promise you. We're packing as soon as we book plane tickets."

That is genius! "Thank you, thank you, thank you! Let's try to leave tomorrow." We both pull up airlines on our phones. "Got it! Two tickets at four thirty-five in the morning. Unless you can't close up the shop."

"I own it. I can close whenever I want." Lourdes leans over and presses on the "Book Now" button on my phone. "All set."

We share nervous smiles.

"So, you're facing your past. What about Rhett?"

"What about him?"

"Make him face his. It's the only way you two stand a chance."

I nod. She's right. He should have spoken to Edin by now about our second conversation. Despite the whole ordeal, I do want to be with him.

"Ready to make another call?"

I take a deep breath and click on Rhett's name in my phone. Lourdes and I wait in silence as it rings.

"Would you like me to go?" she whispers.

I shake my head no at her. "Not yet."

She nods in understanding. If for some reason things don't go well during this conversation, I will definitely need my bestie here with me.

"Hey, Gwenn," Rhett answers after only one ring. "Thank you for calling me back. Does this mean you're willing to give me another chance?"

I choose a question rather than an answer. "What do you think?"

"Edin took advantage of me and us and the situation, but I let her." He pauses. "I have so many things to say to you. I'm sorry I didn't call you last night. I thought I was doing the right thing by texting. Then I wasn't sure, but didn't have my phone to fix it. How can I make it up to you?"

"I think you're done apologizing now."

He blows out what sounds like a sigh of relief. Can't blame him. I did, too.

"It's okay, Rhett. Things have worked out in the end."

Lourdes grins at me as he replies, "Can I see you tonight?"

"Meet me at my office? Then we can go over to my apartment. If you'd like." I hope he hears the smile in my voice.

"I'll go anywhere as long as I can see you. Would you like me to grab dinner on the way?"

"That sounds great."

"Be there soon."

When we're done talking, I look at Lourdes again.

"He's got it bad," she says.

"Is this real? Because I literally don't remember being this happy. Or this hopeful."

Lourdes and I discuss her plan for our trip at length while we wait for Rhett to arrive. Then she tells me, "You should have a date on Quill Bridge."

"People are always doing that. What's the big deal about Quill Bridge?"

"You've never heard this one?"

I tell her no.

"The story goes that a porcupine family inhabited the same area where the bridge was built for a hundred generations, no matter the hardships. The bridge is thought to embody this staunch survival of love and determination."

"You want me to have a date at an actual bridge?" I laugh.

"It's a covered bridge next to a waterfall, if that helps make it more romantic."

I consider this. "Might be a bit too cold, but it sounds like it'd be perfect for summer."

"Huh."

"What?"

"You just made plans for a date with a guy further than one week out. That's progress."

"It is, isn't it?" I grin. "And you know what? It feels great."

When he shows up, I jump into his arms. It's a good minute or two before we move back far enough to be eye-to-eye. "Hey." He smiles at me.

With my arms still around Rhett, I turn to our companion. "This is Lourdes, my best friend."

"The flower snob," she says, laughing at the description neither Rhett nor I were brave enough to mention.

Lourdes and Rhett greet each other.

"We sort of met through email," she says, alluding to his flower order. The vase of them is on my desk.

Rhett almost looks like he's blushing.

"You did the right thing coming to me," she adds to him. Then she turns to me. "I'm going now," Lourdes says before winking. She starts to walk away but stops. "Oh, by the way, Rhett. No more gas station flowers."

"Grocery store," I correct her.

"How did you know?" Rhett asks me.

"My bestie is a florist," I reply with a shrug.

She waves a hand. "Gas station, grocery store, flea market. Whatever. Come to my shop. I know what our girl likes." Her phone beeps. This sound has her glowing. She hasn't even looked at it yet.

Come to think of it, I've never heard that particular sound on her phone before. She rarely changes her phone's settings. "Expecting a call?" I ask. "Who is he?"

"I really need to go now," she replies, only she can't stop smiling long enough to be serious despite her best effort. Rarely has she ever liked a guy so much to go through all this trouble.

I'm as happy for her prospects as I am for my own. "I want details!" I call after her as she leaves. It isn't long before she's out the main door to the outside.

"Our girl," Rhett repeats once we are alone.

We turn to face each other. He places his hands on my waist. I feel plenty of heat coming off them despite the fact that I'm in a super-thick cable-knit sweater. Rhett still wears his black coat. I unzip it enough to slide my hands inside and around to his back, where I caress him with my fingers.

He pulls me a little closer, then continues. "That means you're my girl. I like the sound of that."

"Me too."

"I have dinner waiting in my truck. Barbecue. If you don't like it, it's okay. I wasn't sure. Want me to bring it in?" Then he takes a moment to look at my lips before returning his gaze to my eyes. "Or is that other offer still available?"

I resist the urge to fan my face. "We can head to my place anytime you're ready."

"I'm always ready for you."

Oh my. It is the hardest thing to remove my arms from his body so I can lock up and we can leave. I'd rather take hold of him and not let go. While I have had sex in my office before, I want Rhett to have me here now. I know what would be the most comfortable, what positions work best in the not-so-comfortable spots, and the places where there's a bigger risk of us being heard by my office neighbors.

So long as we avoid anything in front of the frosted door, and so long as I remember to close all my blinds, any spot is good.

But there's something just as thrilling about making both of us wait. We didn't do it in the shed—for obvious reasons. We didn't do it when I wore my skimpy dress. Having to put it off just a little while longer could only make things better.

I don't touch him again before we get into our separate vehicles. I'd never be able to pull myself away otherwise.

Once I unlock and open my apartment door, I take the food bags from him and lead him all three steps into my atrociously small living room/foyer/home office. Whether he is surprised by my tiny abode, I'm sure I'll never know. He doesn't let on. Instead of dining at my tiny table in the kitchen, I decide to let romance guide this date, not practicality. I grab a blanket from the sofa and lay it out on the carpeted floor.

"Indoor picnic. I like it." Rhett grins at me.

I ask him to help me find the two wooden trays that came with my upholstered ottoman. Once the trays are on the blanket, we fill them with all the goodies from our takeout bags.

We sit cross-legged next to each other behind the trays and begin to eat our meal. We even feed each other a few bites every so often. I lick barbecue sauce off one finger of mine and cheese sauce from the mac and cheese off another. Rhett eyes me.

"I'm so glad you gave me another chance," he says.

After wiping my hands off as best I can, I swallow a sip of the tea he got me. It's sweeter than I'm used to, but I don't hate it. While I drink, I give myself time to think. I want to word what I need to say just right.

"I know what you told me about your relationship with Edin and how over it all you were, but then last night happened. I was face-to-face with the woman you said you didn't love. She was there in your apartment because of her key, engagement ring and all. On her freaking hand. I couldn't deal with it."

"Do you understand now?"

"I do." I lean over and kiss his cheek with a quick peck. I'm still holding off on too much contact. Every time I barely touch him, his eyes grow wider. I want to see how much teasing we both can take before we give in to the arousal. "Edin was to blame for a lot of it, but you weren't faultless. I'm glad you're working on facing your truths and your past."

He nods.

This is the moment I should tell him about facing my own past. It's the best chance I'll ever have. I'm pretty sure of this. But how? I told him I have no family. No one I used to know. How can I explain without knowing all the facts myself? "So, Lourdes and I are actually going out of town for a few days. Maybe a week. Could be two if we decide to stay longer. To the Grand Canyon." I ignore the sharp pang I feel as I almost choke on the lie I came up with when Lourdes and I booked the tickets. At the time, I'd figured if the initial research led us to Arizona, the lie should lead us there, too.

And right now, I just don't trust myself enough to tell him the truth. I can't tell Rhett what location we are actually flying to and why.

He stiffens. "When?"

"Tomorrow, actually. Early."

"Oh." His tone of voice says he's disappointed. The happy glow starts to leave his face.

I'm quick to respond. "I know this is terrible timing. I understand that. It's been so difficult for you and I just reaching this place, and our official, full, no-one-leaves-early date is long overdue. To go away now sucks. But this is something she and I can't change."

"You don't know how long you'll be gone?"

"It depends on all we find to do nearby. She travels like that a lot. Just going until she decides to come back, no set schedule for anything. And she's a rock climber, so she's super thrilled about all the places she can climb out there. And you know I never take vacations. Of course I'll have my phone on me. And I'm sure I'll love being out of this cold." I bite my lip to stop myself from rambling any more. These lies come to me a hell of a lot easier than I thought they would. I'm not even sure if where we are going will be warm. Haven't been brave enough to look.

He nods in apparent understanding, holding his forkful of baked beans just above his takeout bowl. "I'll miss you."

I put my fork down on the tray. "I'll miss you, too. More than you know."

Rhett gives me a grin and sets his utensil down as well. He slides the trays off to the side of the sofa, far to our left. Then he turns toward me, scoots closer, and kisses my jawline. It's the best tease yet.

"More," I whisper.

He complies, his mouth moving along the contours of my face. Then he returns to center himself at my mouth and kisses me. Like really kisses me. I'd expected it to be quick pecks, continuing his tantalizing, hands-off seduction, but it's like the kisses we shared in the shed and in the snow. Almost desperate and rough, but still gentle and heated and sexy as hell.

I don't know how much time passes. I've never made out with anyone for as long as Rhett and I do. I've also never wanted anyone to strip my clothes off me as much as I want him to.

I go for his shirt, which he happily gives up. He raises his arms and lets me slip it up over his head. I'm down to only my bra and jeans. Our socks are scattered around my living room floor from being thrown.

I put my legs around his like I've wanted to for so long now. Carefully, he puts his hands on my hips and lowers my body closer to his. Our temperatures intermingle despite so much denim between us. His gaze catches mine as I run my fingers through his beard. Rhett shifts our bodies together, just like he did in the shed, and it feels so good, I accidentally give his beard a tug. We force ourselves apart for a few beats, then connect our lips and bodies again and seem to never part, even once our remaining clothes start coming off.

Time moves too fast and too slow and not at all and exactly when it should. We turn off all the lights to give us the same kind of atmosphere that lead to us being pretty out of control in the shed, only now the wildness is more than welcome. And oh my, wow, does it intensify everything we do afterward. Every single thing we'd hoped to and things that hadn't occurred to us beforehand.

We eventually finish our cold dinner, sweaty, famished, and both completely satisfied. I can't say I've eaten a meal in the nude before, albeit wrapped in a blanket. It's new and thrilling and so much the better because it's with Rhett.

He refused a blanket on the grounds of being too warm. Smoking hot is more like it. Every time my eyes wander, I get a little too warm as well.

Once we gather up the dinner things and return them to the side of the sofa where they stayed safe during our naked fun time, we curl up in the same blanket together, bare skin on bare skin, and talk about all the fun things Lourdes and I should do while in "Arizona." It's nice to pretend we will just be ordinary tourists doing touristy things. He can't stop raving about the Grand Canyon, so much so that I wish I could ask him to take me there one day. I'm actually planning future vacations with him, too, though it's still just in my head, and it's the best feeling ever.

Rhett leans to kiss my neck, and we start rolling around on the floor again. Never did I doubt before, but now I know for sure the vacation-planning is the second-best feeling ever.

<h1 style="text-align:center">Chapter 40</h1>

Rhett

I HATE THAT GWENN is leaving so soon, but I know she'll be back before too long. Something she mentioned last night stuck with me. She said I'm now facing my past. In a way, she's right, but not completely. While she's gone, I'm going to use this opportunity to face my history for real.

I called from the terminal and put in a few vacation days at work, much to Giovanni's chagrin, especially since I took a couple days off last week. But he owes me. I've worked so hard these past several months that he is making much more profit than normal, and honestly, I have to get away from there. I already booked a flight down to Georgia. I'll stay with Mama and Granny. They insisted, though I wouldn't have argued back, anyway.

I'm still in the terminal when I receive a text from Edin.

> I know I told you I'll be fine on my own, and I will, but Rhett . . .

> I still love you.

> I can't be your friend anymore. Not right now.

Damn. Gwenn was right. Letting go is never easy. I'm sorry for Edin, but I can't say I feel the same for her as she did for me. I decide to not answer her.

While boarding my flight, I wonder if Gwenn is as nervous on hers. If her breathing is as fast as mine. If she is shaking as hard as I am. She wouldn't let me take them to the airport. Gwenn didn't want me driving them in since their flight was several hours earlier mine. I'm not sure she slept much before she got out of bed in the middle of the night to shower again, dress, and pack. She just laughed and kissed me when I asked her to do it all in a different order.

I reluctantly left when she asked me to. She said she couldn't concentrate on packing with me looking at her the way I was.

"That's what led to the first round," she said. "And the third."

"What was the second?" I asked, knowing full well what she would reply.

"You were naked and strutting around my apartment. My hands wouldn't control themselves."

"What about the rest of you?"

"There was no controlling the rest of me either."

"I wouldn't say I was strutting," I told her. "Can I help it if I walk a certain way?"

"You mean walk a certain way only when you have no clothes on and know how irresistible you are anyway, with or without them? As if that half-smile wasn't hard enough to not give in to."

I laughed.

"It is on purpose! I knew it. You have intentionally made my knees weak as long as I've known you."

"Only as long as I suspected it was already working. The first few were just me being me. A couple of them were directed at your heart on purpose."

Gwenn walked over to me, still lying in her bed, and wrapped herself around me. Her leggings and stretchy tank top were soft against me, but not nearly as soft as her skin. I placed my arms around her body and pulled her a little tighter. She nuzzled her head into my neck, her sweet-smelling hair covering hers. I gently moved a bit of it to the side in order to give her neck a kiss. But I let her go when she pulled away and sat up.

I was up to having a fourth round, but figured she'd turned me down for that once already for a good reason. Didn't want to push her. I needed to leave in order to be out of her way. I also had to do my own packing at my apartment.

Once I'm finally home in Georgia—and relieved to know Gwenn landed safely as well thanks to her text—I greet Granny with a hug. Mama picked me up from the airport. I tell them my plans while I'm down here.

"Are you sure that's what you want to do?" Mama asks. She has always worried about me where this subject is concerned.

"Yep. This is what I need to do. For me. For my relationship with Gwenn, new as it is. This is how things need to proceed."

"We will support you no matter what," Granny tells me with a smile.

Mama nods in agreement.

"Thank you," I tell them both.

Now it's time to get started.

Chapter 41

Gwenn

"Hi, Vara. This is Gwenn. I'm hoping we can meet up today. I'm here in town."

There is silence. Icy, terrifying silence. The kind she seems to excel at. Then I hear, "I'm surprised you came here so quickly."

"Are you? You shouldn't be," I tell her.

"I don't believe it's May."

If I weren't so angry, her tone would probably have me in tears. "I don't believe I should have to wait too long. Where would you like to meet? Or what would you like to do? Lunch? Coffee?"

"No," Vara replies. "No. We can't meet anywhere like that."

Oh yeah. I would absolutely be in tears. No question. I know this is about what she did and not about me, but my knee-jerk reaction to her words has me choked up and growing more despondent. "Heaven forbid anyone spots you with me, right? In case someone recognizes me? Or figures it out? Geez, Vara. I mean, seriously?"

"All right. All right," she says. I detect a hint of sadness in her voice. This somehow lessens my own. "There's a park over on Chestnut which isn't usually crowded. Let's meet there in one hour."

"You got it," I tell her.

Lourdes and I already have a rental car. She agrees to drive, giving me time to calm my nerves. We stop for coffee on the way. I buy one for me for the ride and one for after the meeting, just in case I need something sweet and comforting. I have a feeling I won't find any of that with this woman who is my biological mother.

I wait in the park by the bench Vara suggested. She originally wanted to meet by some tree, but there are so many trees in parks, I was afraid I'd never find it. Now I know that worry was absurd. This is probably one of the tiniest parks I've ever seen. It has a medium-ish grassy area and a couple benches, but that's about it. There isn't even a walking path or play area or flower beds. It must be the crappiest park in the city. Lourdes is over by the tree I assume Vara wanted. It's so close, I see her with no problem.

I didn't tell Vara I would have someone here with me. Better to catch her off guard, if need be. If she thinks we are being watched, she might not open up like I need her to.

A tall, thin, fake-tanned-to-an-orange-color woman resembling the one in that old picture walks up to me. Vara stopped for coffee as well, holding a disposable cup in her right hand. She sits, then stands again.

"What would you like to say?" she asks.

What would I like to say? Goodness. I have so, so many things I want to say to her, and yet she starts this all with such a cold opening.

If she were anything like a real mom, I could tell her about my company, my best friend, my budding relationship with Rhett. I could tell her how I almost died again and how terrifying the ordeal was and how I have flashbacks nearly every day because of it. But she isn't a real mom. Not even the apparition of one.

She gazes at me with eyes that have obviously never witnessed love.

I don't speak. I can't.

"I haven't got all day," Vara grumbles. "Your fa—my husband is waiting for me to come home. I told him I wouldn't be long."

"Then go," I hear myself say.

Why the hell did I just do that?

Vara looks surprised as well, although no one would know it by her almost plastic, clearly Botoxed face. This shock doesn't stop her from walking away and leaving the park without a word.

Lourdes runs over. "What happened? You barely spoke to each other."

"I choked," I cry. Tears tumble down my cheeks. "She wanted to leave, so I told her to go. I didn't even get to talk to her about anything." My body shudders. I wipe my face with my hands.

Lourdes leans over to give me a short hug. "This isn't over. Okay? You hear me?"

I nod. "What do we do now?"

"If she won't come back to you, we go to her."

"Right now?"

"Drink your coffee. Breathe. Give yourself time to calm down. You deserve to have the upper hand, and you're going to secure it."

Chapter 42

Gwenn

NOW THAT I'M HERE, I am not at all surprised by how enormous this house is. After all, these people paid thousands upon thousands of dollars for my surgeries and recovery and business and everything else until I started making my own money.

These people.

My parents.

I loathe that word. Parents. I despise it. I despise them with so much fury, my body quivers as I deliberately make my way up each of the twelve steps to the veranda. This house is so grand, no other description seems to fit. "Porch" or "terrace" would be like a slap in the face to it.

Was my room up in the tower? Did I ever pretend to be Rapunzel? Or Juliet at the uppermost window? Was there a maid or housekeeper who always answered the door? Did she spend more time with me than Vara and Delaney did?

Lourdes is beside me like always. She looks like she's full of the same trepidation and indignation I'm consumed with. When I pause and catch her eye, she nods at me as if to say, "Keep going. Don't stop now."

In front of the ornate double doors, I raise my fisted hand to knock. But the moment my knuckles reach the wood, I halt. Just for a moment. Just to breathe and tell myself this is going to be okay. If I leave here with no answers, I'll be no worse off than I am now. Then I can go home and tell Rhett the truth of how I almost died the first time and let him hold me and kiss me until I feel better.

I tap my knuckles on the door hard enough to make noise.

We stand and wait in silence.

Then the door opens.

I jump, though I saw her through the glass. Under all that blush and bronzer, her cheeks still change color from rosy to ashen. For several seconds, none of us speak. Then I push my way into the house. I dare her to call the police. What a story that would be!

Lourdes follows me in. That woman closes the door behind us and heads down a long, tiled hall toward the back. She doesn't say a word. We pass closed pocket doors and a cream-colored side table.

Okay, this is just weird. "Where are you going, Mother?"

She startles but keeps moving.

"Or should she call you Mrs. Jonas?" Lourdes adds.

"Don't be ridiculous," Vara calls over her shoulder without actually turning to look at us.

It's difficult to keep up with her brisk pace since I'd like to let my eyes wander around this place. I know I'll never remember it from my previous life.

We enter an expansive study in the rear of the house. A man—my father—rises from what appears to be a suede wingback chair. He's just as orange-tanned as Vara. His hair is thinning a lot more than it was in the pictures. He's put on a bit of weight as well.

"Delaney."

I'd hoped for shock when I said his first name, but he expresses nothing. He is tall and stoic and silent.

Neither Delaney nor Vara offers us a seat.

"Is this all we're going to do?" I ask. "Stand around staring at each other without speaking? Is this the best you've got for me?" I turn to Delaney. "I assume your wife told you who I am."

"Stop being absurd, sweetheart," Vara scoffs.

"Sweetheart? Seriously, Vara? After you told everyone I died?"

"We had no choice," Delaney snaps. He quickly regains his composure.

I narrow my eyes at both of them, standing so close together, as if one against many. "Yes. You did. You thought it better to lie than to deal with reality."

Vara fans her face and drops onto what I notice is actually a rather dreary-looking loveseat.

Delaney speaks, and I can tell he's flipped a switch. He's completely emotionless. "You were so different. You weren't you."

"And that somehow validates your choice?"

"Seeing you all broken, lying in a hospital bed, so vulnerable, was just—" Vara pauses to take a breath in.

Delaney is content with ignoring Lourdes and me and has taken to staring at the wall behind us. He doesn't bother comforting his wife, either.

"It was too much," Vara continues. "You didn't recognize us. We were told you'd never remember. You were nothing but bandages. You couldn't even talk."

"I was told you left me there before ever speaking to me. Is that true?"

"Of course not," Delaney finally responds. It's been a good ten or so seconds.

"You had a conversation with me?" I look at them both, but neither answers right away.

"Yes," Vara finally says. "Yes, we did, and you didn't know us."

"The first time you saw me there? The first day I was in the ER?"

She looks as though she doesn't understand the question. "Yes, of course. We went straight to you when we were first notified."

"I was intubated. On a ventilator. I couldn't talk," I tell them. "I stayed on that vent for a couple days before my lungs were ready to work on their own. There's no possible way you had a conversation with me the day of the accident."

They don't respond.

"Explain why you walked out on her," Lourdes speaks up, as affronted as I am.

Vara ignores her and maintains a steady gaze on me. "You weren't our little girl anymore. You never would be again. She died in that accident."

"No." I shake my head. "I wasn't a little girl, but I still needed my parents. You abandoned me."

They don't answer me.

"My goodness. You couldn't even be bothered enough to sue the guy who was operating the boat or the company who made the boat or the boat's engine. Aren't lawyers part of your world?"

Still, they say nothing. They don't really look at me either.

I push on with a harder tone. "I'm sure you have several attorney friends. Couldn't you have done something? Found someone to lash out at?"

"Don't be absurd," Vara says again, dismissively waving a hand.

"No," I respond to her. "Instead, you decided to take it out on me." And still—*still*—no reaction. "Do you have any clue how much I hurt? How much pain I was in, through surgery after surgery? How many times I wished I really had died?" My voice cracks at the end.

"Then I guess we did you a favor." Delaney shrugs. His tone again gives no hint of emotion.

Vara gasps and swivels her head toward him. "Del."

I realize this is supposed to sound like a scolding. However, the expressions on their faces tell a different story.

They were ready with these replies. This act. This fake concern on Vara's part. They assumed at some point I'd find them, even with all their work trying to hide from me. Here we are, a "family" with nothing but disdain for each other.

Chapter 43

Rhett

I REACH THE DOOR and am about to knock, but there's yelling inside, unusual for this house. The voices grow louder and louder. Something has to be wrong. I try the door handle. It's unlocked.

In the tiled hallway, I hear someone shout, "How dare you leave me all alone in that hospital?"

"Jaymie, honey." Vara.

"She doesn't want your fake pet names and lame-ass excuses. Give her an answer. A real one."

"We don't need your attitude, Jaymie, or this girl's, whoever she is."

"Seriously? She's my best friend. She's been there for me through so much, unlike you people."

A forced sigh.

"Stop being such a bitch, Mother."

My feet have finally unfrozen and start running toward the sounds. My heart rate increases every step of the way. I don't know how I'm able to move, but I keep going. My eyes have to see what my brain now knows.

"If you had just played tennis with that nice Whitson girl instead of going on that damn boat, none of this would have happened." Delaney's calm, controlled voice.

"No." This comes out as a growl. "It was not my fault. Don't ever say it was."

Then silence.

Shit.

I can't figure out what room they are in without voices echoing out to me. I decide to search room by room. The dining room is empty, as is the front living space. I'm afraid if I call out, I might spook them. My only choice is to keep looking.

"What do you have to say now?" That voice. That beautiful, perplexing voice. It almost has me on my knees. I follow it. I have to see her.

"Jaymie Lyn Jonas, don't you dare speak to us that way. Just calm down, sweetheart."

And there she is.

Gwenn.

My body stiffens at the sight of her here.

But she doesn't notice me. None of them do.

"Don't you dare call me sweetheart," Gwenn shouts in answer to Vara. "You lost the right to call me that the moment you and Dad told all my loved ones I died!"

"What's going on?" I manage to choke out.

My heart thumps around in my chest.

All four of them turn toward me.

"What are you doing here?" I mean for this to be a question, but it comes out like a demand. This can't be happening right now. It isn't real. It can't be.

"Why are you here?" Gwenn counters.

"I came to get answers. Where's Jaymie?" I search all their faces. No one answers me. They just stare, mouths agape. I focus on Delaney and Vara. "Where is Jaymie?" My voice thunders down the hall.

I think I already know. I need to hear them say it.

"Rhett, just hold on a minute, son." Typical Delaney. Always deflecting.

I ignore him. "Where is Jaymie?"

Gwenn's face is flushed. She clenches her hand like she does sometimes when she can't breathe well. She looks at Vara and Delaney. "You know Rhett?"

They remain silent.

"How do you know Jaymie?" Lourdes speaks up, eyes on me.

"She was my girlfriend. My fiancée, actually."

Gwenn falters. Lourdes grabs hold of her to help her stay on her feet, then guides her to a chair. "Jaymie Lyn. J. L.," Gwenn whispers.

She blinks really fast, but doesn't appear to see anything.

After a few shallow breaths in and out, her hand in a white-knuckled grip on Lourdes's, finally she looks at me. "I am Jill," she whispers.

<h1 style="text-align:center">Chapter 44</h1>

Gwenn

RHETT SLOWLY, CLUMSILY MOVES his feet and drops into the other shabby chair across from me. He won't look at me as he rubs the back of his neck. He won't look at anyone. "It . . . it can't be true," he whispers.

No one answers him.

"Why did I not know?" This is another whisper.

Again, he receives no response. I can't even breathe, let alone speak. Lourdes probably doesn't know what to say. Vara and Delaney are the ones who should be speaking up. Instead, they coolly look about the room, avoiding eye contact with all of us.

Rhett finally moves his head to face them. "You never believed in her." This he says in a louder, clearer voice. He moves his eyes back and forth from Delaney to Vara. "You never believed in her, and you never believed in her dreams. You didn't even care what else happened in her life so long as she 'married well' and didn't embarrass the family, both of which eliminated me in your narrow minds."

"Now, Rhett—" Delaney begins.

Rhett doesn't let him finish. As far as I can tell, his eyes are nothing but fire right now. "When did you ever do something as a family that didn't involve a photo-op for the paper or the company newsletter? When—"

Delaney butts in with a thunderous burst that makes both Lourdes and me jump. "Listen to me, young man. You never deserved my daughter."

Rhett shakes his head. "No, you never deserved her. She was better than every person in this damn family. I loved her! I am the only one of us three who did."

His words are like stabs, yet I can't take my eyes off him. And I can tell he isn't done yet.

"You didn't give a shit about her. You should have told me. I would have taken care of her. I would have been by her side every single day at the hospital. I wouldn't have even needed a bed. A chair next to her would have been good enough. Hell, I'd have slept on the floor if necessary just to make sure she was okay. She shouldn't have been left alone."

I can't listen to any more without letting this flood of tears out. I've held them back as best I can, but that is no longer possible. Lourdes squeezes my hand in return as I choke on a sob. Rhett looks over at me. He moves forward a little in his chair but stops.

"She was never going to marry you, son," Delaney says to him. I can't tell if Rhett is listening.

I can't focus on him. I can't think about him. If I have to think more about Jill and me and—

Both my stomach and my throat are tight.

It's my turn to take on the Jonases again.

I open my mouth, but nothing comes out except another sob. Shit.

I can't do this by myself. Thank God for my bestie.

"Lourdes," I squeak out while squeezing her hand.

I don't need to say more. She knows what I mean. What I always intended on telling my parents, even if I couldn't use my own voice for it. I plan on paying back every single cent they gave me. I don't want their literal blood money in my life anymore. Helping me start a new life doesn't make up for taking away my old one. It may take me decades, but I don't care. I have to have a clean break from them.

But before Lourdes has a chance to talk, Rhett asks, "How—how is this possible?"

No one speaks.

Lourdes again starts to speak, but Rhett interrupts her. "Whose ashes are in the urn?"

"The dog's," Delaney replies coolly.

I swivel to face him in disgust, but he won't look at me. "You told everyone the dog's ashes were mine? Did you abandon him, too?"

Delaney avoids my gaze, and now won't look at Rhett, either.

Vara gasps again. I turn to see her mouth agape and hand on her chest.

Why the hell is she more upset about the damn dog than her own daughter?

"Of course not," she says with dramatic effect. "He died of cancer the same week as your accident."

"We added some fireplace ashes for good measure. Wanted there to be enough in the urn," Delaney says, unshaken by this comment.

"What the hell is wrong with y'all?" Rhett's voice is low and gravelly.

I don't want to look at his face and see his pain, but I force myself to, anyway.

His steely, narrowed eyes are on Vara and Delaney. "I'm only gonna ask one more time, and I better hear an answer. Why didn't y'all tell anyone Jaymie survived?"

They don't reply.

He scrunches his facial features with a grunt. "How could y'all lie to me? You knew how much she meant to me."

I watch him as he says this. I hear the catch in his voice. I see the dampness in his eyes.

I have to get out of here.

Chapter 45

Rhett

"How did you even find her?" Vara asks me, motioning to Gwenn, who still holds on to Lourdes. Lourdes is crouched down beside her, glaring at Vara.

I don't bother saying anything to Vara. I don't care about her concerns. The woman I do care about won't look at any of us.

Tell her to ground herself, damn it! I want to yell at Lourdes while she tries to soothe Gwenn through what looks like a panic attack. What does she see? What does she hear? What does she smell? What does she feel?

I can't form these words in my mouth.

What does she feel?

I feel like a knife is being twisted in my gut.

Gwenn—Jill—rises to her feet and charges out the door, Lourdes right behind her. The sound of their footsteps diminishes as they run away. I want to go after her. I have to. But first, I turn to Vara and Delaney. My eyes burn.

"I hope y'all rot in hell for what y'all put her through." My throat is tight, making my voice hoarse.

"Rhett, you know not to tell anyone about this, right, sweetie pie?" Vara gives me her sickeningly fake smile.

I don't answer.

I sprint down the hall, only to find the front doors are already closed. In a rush, I throw the doors open and race down the stairs. Gwenn is hunched over Vara's award-winning rosebushes, her body shuddering. Lourdes is knelt down beside her, slowly rubbing her back.

"Jill?"

She sobs and crumbles to the ground.

I can't go to her. I can't do anything to help her. "Jill?"

"Don't," she finally says with a hoarse voice. She reaches out, and Lourdes helps her stand. They turn to me. "Don't call me that. I'm not her anymore. Vara and Delaney were right about that one thing."

"What does that even mean? Either you're her or you're not. And now we know that you are."

"I came to confront them. I did that. Now, I'm done. I'm done with all of this, full stop."

Does she mean me, too?

She starts to walk away. Lourdes's arms are around her, but it should be my arms.

"Jill—"

She shudders again at the sound.

"Gwenn. Gwenn, you can't just leave."

The woman I've been drawn to since the moment we met looks at me again. Her skin is red and tear-streaked. "I can do anything I want now. I'm no longer chained to the haunting knowledge of my parents abandoning me. That's enough. It has to be. It doesn't matter that it's so much worse than I thought. I'm. Done."

Lourdes and Gwenn continue on to the car. I watch them buckle in and drive away.

Jill/Jaymie and Gwenn are gone from my life for good, it seems.

Chapter 46

Gwenn

"So, your Rhett was Jaymie's Rhett," Lourdes says slowly, deliberately, cautiously. "You were Jill."

I don't have much breath for a reply, but I have to say something. My voice is still hoarse as it comes out. "Seems to be."

"How do you feel about this?"

"Using your psych degree again?"

"Worrying about my friend. I'll ask again. How do you feel about this whole thing?"

"I can't wrap my head around how Rhett fits into this. It doesn't make sense to me right now. But one thing is still a constant. My parents abandoned me because I wasn't perfect anymore. And I can't stop thinking about Rhett, too. The woman he loved most turns out to be alive and also still gone forever."

"You want to talk to him?" she asks me as she drives our rental car back to the hotel. My body is trembling far too much to be in control of any type of vehicle.

"I don't know what to say to him."

"It doesn't have to be much. It doesn't have to be anything at all. It's your choice."

"He and I became so close. We were just naked together in my apartment two days ago. How did I lose all my memories in Arizona, then befriend my old Georgia boyfriend due to a blizzard in New York? How does that happen?"

"Some would say fate or destiny. Some would say coincidence."

"What would you call it?"

Lourdes takes a minute or so before answering. "An opportunity."

Chapter 47

Rhett

I HAVE TO FIND her. Even just to hear her say the word goodbye. I deserve at least that much after discovering my dead fiancée is actually alive. After calling ahead, I know Mama is home, but I don't tell her the story. She doesn't know about Jill yet. I rush to her house and run inside. I search Macon-area hotels on my phone and start calling. Mama calls from her phone as well.

Only no one will tell us if Gwenn is one of their guests. Privacy issues and all that. It's the same from every person I speak to.

I call another number and hope for the best.

"Sorry, sir. We cannot give out personal details about our guests and staff."

Wait a minute. I know this voice.

"Sarah Post?" I ask. "Matty Post's little sister?"

"Who's this?" Her tone is cautious.

"It's Rhett Mason."

Sarah squeals. "Ohmigosh! How are you? I haven't seen you in ages. Not since poor Jaymie—" She stops. I know what she's thinking. What she wants to say but won't. "Well, what can I do for you?"

I want to tell her—I want to tell everyone—Jill is actually alive, but can't. Gwenn wouldn't like it. "I need to know if someone by the name of Gwenn Rhys is staying there. Please."

Sarah is silent.

"I promise there is a good reason for this. Nothing dangerous or cruel or illegal."

I can't figure out if she is going to help me or not. Silence was never a good thing coming from Sarah.

Then I hear the clacking sounds of a keyboard. "If you tell anyone I did this, I will deny it," Sarah whispers. "Gwenn Rhys is here, room three fifty-three. And Rhett?"

"Yeah?"

"If this is for the reason I suspect it is, Jaymie would be happy you've finally moved on."

"You have no idea how happy. Thanks, Sarah."

Chapter 48

Rhett

"RHETT?" GWENN WIDENS HER eyes. "How did you find me? Did you follow us?" The door is only open a crack.

"Does it matter?"

I wait in fear for her to say the word "yes." For her to shut the door in my face. For me to have to take that long walk back to the parking lot and back to my life without her.

"No, it doesn't." Gwenn shakes her head. She opens the door and beckons me inside. Lourdes is in their living room area, clearly not going anywhere.

Can't say I blame her. I wouldn't leave Gwenn alone after all she's been through. I wish I didn't have to leave at all, but I know it's coming.

We all sit down. I have a chair, as does Lourdes. Gwenn perches on the end of a bed.

"What do you want?" Lourdes asks me.

I know she's just being protective, but I can't talk to her right now. Gwenn is the one I'm here for.

I move my eyes to Gwenn. "You're my miracle. So . . ."

She doesn't respond. She only looks away from me.

"What do we do now?"

"What do you mean?" she asks, making eye contact once again.

"You're—"

"Don't," she interrupts me with a hand slightly up in the air, as if it's another way to stop me. "Don't say it. I'm not Jill or Jaymie or any other name she might have had." She sucks in more air. "I have a different face. Different voice. Parts of my body are not the same, between surgeries and skin grafts. She was just the shell to build me."

Her words are like knife stabs.

"But you're still her! She's you. You're the same person."

"No, I'm not! I have zero memories."

"Okay. Great. So maybe it isn't true. Maybe Jill is alive out there, she's just not you. Can you at least give me that? Or maybe it is better for her to be dead. Huh? Then all this shit might not mean anything." I'm yelling by the end. I can't help it.

"It is true," she whispers by way of reply.

"How do you know if you don't remember?"

This is a logical question to me, but she scoffs. "I know what the hospital staff told me. I know what I remember after waking up, including a visitor I didn't recognize who knew me, and the info I've been able to gather. I know what little Vara and Delaney have told me. You want me to . . . what? Get blood samples from them for a DNA test?" She shoves her arm out into the air toward me. "Might as well take some blood right now. I'm already open and exposed. What's a little more bloodshed in search of the truth you want?"

"I want you to be who I know you to be."

"Who exactly is that?" Lourdes asks.

"No," Gwenn says at the same time. "You want the suddenly alive dead girlfriend."

I open my mouth to speak, but she shuts me down.

"Don't you dare. You are going to listen. I had a physical traumatic brain injury as well as a sort-of emotional one. I was told the shock of the accident, the injuries, and being alone probably forced my temporary memory loss into permanence. I'll never get any of it back. Ever."

I nearly choke on my saliva. "You can't say that. What about therapy?"

"Already in it, and you know that."

"Hypnosis?"

She hardens both her expression and her voice. "You're not seriously suggesting I allow myself to be hypnotized, are you? Or that it would even work?"

"All I know is you are my miracle."

"Stop calling me your miracle! How could you possibly want me to be her without being her? What, am I supposed to fake it all? Lie and say, yeah, it's all coming back now? What good would that do?" She almost yells this last question. Then she takes a moment to breathe, eyes closed, hand clenched.

"You always did like my eyes. Gray, just like Jill's. Now we know why." She cries harder. "The only thing left of her that's recognizable. I'd change my eye color right now if I could."

"Don't say that." My voice is raspy.

"Why not? You already thought of her when you looked in my eyes. Now, that's all you'll ever see. I'm never going to be Gwenn to you. Only your beloved Jill."

"Because that's who you are!" I snap.

She sniffles. "If only I had died back then. It would have been so much easier for you."

I nearly growl out the words, "How's that?"

"You and I never would have met. You'd have been blissfully wretched with Edin. She's as devoted to you as a manipulative bitch could be. The Jonases could have lived their rich, miserable lives not having gone practically bankrupt from hospital bills and hiding from me. It would have been a win-win."

"Gwenn, maybe . . ." Lourdes doesn't finish her thought out loud. Neither Gwenn nor I look at her.

"You want to talk about manipulative bitches? What the hell are you doing right now?" I've never spoken to a woman like this before, but I'm too pissed to apologize.

Gwenn doesn't flinch. "Just trying to save us all this moment right here."

"But you wouldn't be here," Lourdes tells her, her voice shaky.

"I know." Gwenn turns to her. Then she points a finger at me while still looking at Lourdes. "But he doesn't understand I'm me and not her."

"Maybe you should ask me how I feel before you go accusing me of things," I say.

Neither of them answers me. Then Gwenn opens her mouth. Her voice is much less shaky when she speaks again.

"Rhett, this isn't going to work." She stands from the bed and moves a few feet away.

I can't let her give up now. "We promised to always be together."

"She promised, not me. I told you I am done, and I mean it. Get out." She charges over to the door and swings it open.

I don't move.

"What are you waiting for?" she demands.

I stand now as well. "You must be out of your mind if you think I don't have a right to feel something about this. It affects me, too."

"Maybe you should go," Lourdes tells me.

Gwenn is still holding the door open.

I look at them both. "Fine."

Without another word, I storm out. Gwenn slams the door behind me. I stalk off, down the hall and to the elevator. Then I pass the elevator and run down the stairs. I have so much pent up inside me right now, but she won't give me a chance to say what I want.

I push the exit door open with much more force than is necessary. It clangs against the stopper and bounces quickly to closing again. The sunlight makes me squint as I rush over to Mama's car in the lot. When I get to it, I kick the front driver's side tire. Then I have to push the unlock button on the fob so the alarm doesn't go off. I wrench the door open and sit, but I don't close it.

Forget Gwenn, then. Forget everything about her or having ever met her.

Except that's it. I can't. I've already tried getting Gwenn out of my head. Nothing's worked.

I slam my hands on the steering wheel so hard, the people in the car next to me look over. I'm not going to let Gwenn shut me out. I lock up the car and run back to the hotel. Then I run up the stairs and bang on her door.

"You've got to be kidding me," Lourdes says when she opens the door.

I look behind her to Gwenn, who sits on a chair near the window, her face splotchy and damp and her hands full of tissues.

"It's probably a good idea for you to leave," Lourdes tells me.

Instead, I focus on Gwenn. "Your—Jaymie's cousin Ava-Leigh and I were the only two people who called her Jill. The only two people who understood her or even bothered to try. So try to help me understand."

"How?"

"Just tell me this: How did it happen?"

Chapter 49

Gwenn

RHETT STARES AT ME, waiting for an answer.

"There was a boating accident on Lake Havasu in Arizona. Delaney, Vara, and I were there visiting some friends."

"I know this. You always talked about the daughter, Shel Whitson, and how you hated your trips there. She was too stuck up for you to like. But what happened to you? How did you end up—" He chokes up. "Why were we told you died?"

I motion for him to come in and sit down. He obliges. I do my best to ignore the fact that he is still equating me with Jill and Jill's memories.

Once we're all seated and I've had a few seconds to control my breathing, I answer. "Vara and Delaney saw me in the hospital and left me there. I was no longer who they wanted me to be. My shoulder, arm, clavicle, and hip were broken. Five fractured ribs. I needed orthopedic surgery, neurosurgery, and reconstructive plastic surgery, including scar revision and tissue expansion. I needed nerve and skin grafts on my face, neck, and arms. I had been intubated because I needed a ventilator to breathe at first, but the tube caused vocal cord paralysis."

Rhett shudders at that word.

"Yes, it was as bad as it sounds. Then I needed surgery to fix the damaged vocal nerves, which is why I probably sound a little different than I used to." Hot, acrid tears stream down from my eyes to my jawline, but I keep going.

"Like I said, I had a TBI with no memories. Amnesia. Occupational therapists, speech-language pathologists, and physical therapists needed to teach me how to walk, talk, eat, think, hold objects in my hand, everything. I suffered vision problems and seizures. I endured fourteen months of constant rehabilitation."

He silently stares at me, wide-eyed and teary.

"It was excruciatingly painful. I couldn't do anything on my own without them for the longest time. Then, when I was well enough to leave the hospital but not so much that I could live on my own, I had to move into an assisted living facility for a while."

Rhett sniffles, but I try to ignore this.

"I still occasionally need neurological testing to make sure my brain isn't regressing back to the state it was in all those years ago. This entire experience has been grueling and expensive. For whatever reason, Vara and Delaney decided to pay all my recovery expenses and not have me legally declared dead. After their abandonment, leaving me with no one in the world, I almost wished I had died."

I take a few seconds to compose myself. This is so much harder than I thought it was going to be.

Rhett's eyes no longer hold in all his tears. A few drops escape down his cheeks. "That's when you moved to New York."

I nod. "I didn't know living up there was always my dream." I almost choke on those words as the reality of them hits me. "I took accelerated classes and all the required exams to become a real estate agent. That's a miracle in itself right there, me progressing from not even knowing what words are to being able to complete a real estate examination. That happened about six months after I arrived in Syracuse."

He winces at my calling that the miracle, but still, I keep going. "I changed my name through a DBA. Doing business as. My legal name is still Jaymie. I didn't think I could change it without Delaney and Vara being notified. I didn't know their names at the time. They must have paid a whole lot of money to keep me from finding anything beyond my first and last name. They furnished me with an outrageous amount of money, given anonymously through some high-priced lawyer."

"That's why their house hasn't been updated lately," Rhett whispers.

I shrug. "Might be. I don't care. Their money didn't mean shit to me. I wanted family. They didn't want me as the person the boating accident created. They sure as hell don't deserve me as I am now. New face, new voice, new accent, new life. New friends, who became my family, like Lourdes."

"Why didn't you tell me all this before? About the amnesia."

"How could I?"

"How could you not?"

"I did tell you it was too horrific to talk about, and it is. Anyway, I don't let people close enough for me to have any need to tell them. You should know that by now."

"And this is why you freaked out in the shed? Not the plane crash?"

I try to give the most straightforward answer I can without letting my emotions carry me away. Tears still roll down my face no matter what I say or do. "The facts of the first accident affected my coping skills during the second."

"I wish I had answers on why the boat wrecked. Why this all happened to you." Rhett's voice is thick. "I wish you had answers, too."

Tears drop onto my shirt and my legs. "It doesn't matter. Answers. No answers. It's all the same in the end, Rhett. Don't you get it?"

He scoots to the edge of his chair, closer to me. "Can I just—"

"No," I interrupt. My voice croaks. I clear it and wipe my eyes before speaking again. "I can't do anything for you. I'm legally changing my name as soon as possible. Jaymie is dead. Jill is dead. There is only Gwenn. I can't even see the top of Jill's pedestal, it's so freaking high. And I—I need you to leave now."

I stand. Lourdes and Rhett follow suit a few seconds later.

Though Rhett stands, he clearly doesn't understand.

"Please go now," I tell him. It's the second time I've kicked him out, but I don't have a choice.

He doesn't move. I look at his scrunched face and his hands on his hips. Those hands were on my hips less than three days ago. Had he wished they'd been Jill's, like he did with Edin? Had I been as big of a fool as Edin?

"Rhett. Please," I whisper.

Chapter 50

I EXIT THE ROOM into the hallway and immediately hear Gwenn crying through the closed door. She gasps for breath. I can't figure out what Lourdes is telling her.

My hand shoots up to touch the door, aching to hold Gwenn. To comfort her.

Instead, I do what she asked of me.

I leave.

Back at Mama's house, I find Granny out in the workshop, hammering together what looks like a wooden sign and post. She stops and looks up when I call her name. "Rhett, honey. What's the matter? Aren't you supposed to be with your friend Gwenn right now?"

I can't hold it in any longer. It all rushes out of me as hard as it did in the car at the hotel once I forced myself to walk away from her.

Granny sets the hammer down and comes over to me, wrapping her arms around me the way she did when I crumbled after Jill died. "What happened, sugar?"

I have no idea how much time passes before I have the strength to answer her. I gently move her back so she can see my face and know I'm telling the truth. "Jill's alive."

Granny sucks in air. She steadies herself with a hand on the steel countertop. Then she moves to hug me again. "Oh, sugar."

"And she wants nothing to do with me."

"Well, I'll be damned." Granny pulls back to look at me. "Oh, Rhett."

I haven't felt this low since Jill's first "death." Back then, Granny held me and let me feel my feelings, even when I ranted on about the Jonases. Granny holds me tighter than before and lets me feel my feelings again, even when I don't know what emotion is going to take control next.

Sometime later, while sitting on the steps of the veranda, with eyes and lungs that both burn, I tell Granny the whole story.

"Oh dear. Oh my," she repeats. Her eyes are wet and glossy, but she doesn't let any tears fall. She also doesn't have much else to say.

At first, anyway.

"How dare they? Those— I can't call them people. Those Jonases never were ones for love and devotion to anything but money. Oh, I'm fixin' to—" Then she glances at me in alarm.

"I should have done something," I say. "I should have gone to Arizona to see for myself that Jill really died like they said she did. I had no reason to take their word for it."

"What would you have done, honey? Asked to see her body in the morgue? You and I both know that would have broken you."

"No more than I already was. I never should have taken Delaney and Vara's word for it," I say again, these words nagging at me.

"Rhett, this is not your fault. None of it. You didn't know what they were capable of. None of us did." Granny pauses. "You'd be wise to remember this isn't Gwenn's fault, either. If it had been up to her, I doubt she would have chosen to be alone. Maybe after a while, once the shock wore off. It wouldn't have been easy for her no matter what."

I can't answer her.

"I'm so sorry, my sweet boy."

"How could they just leave her there, Granny? Someone else left her there, too, with no word on who they were or who she was. No doubt that stuck-up bitch Jill was forced to be friends with. She'd leave Jill there alone if Vara and Delaney told her to. She only cared about what the Jonases could do for her, same as her parents."

"Your mama will be back soon. I'm sure she'll agree with me that you and Gwenn are better off without Vara and Delaney and any of those other rich snobs. And . . ." Granny pauses and wipes at her damp eyes. "Well, darlin', maybe y'all are better off without each other, too."

"Granny, you can't—"

"Now, now. Just hear me out. You're always wondering what Jill would say about things. What would the Jill you knew say about this?"

I don't reply. I can't.

"I knew that sweet girl well enough to know I'm right about this. All those memories. All that heartache. Gwenn doesn't want anything to do with Jaymie. She doesn't want to be your Jill. You know you'll never be able to let Jill go. Maybe it's enough she's alive."

Chapter 51

Gwenn

GARBAGE.

Absolute garbage.

Ten year old Teen Vogue magazines, band posters, a ripped sports bra, stained running shoes, the driver's license they stole from the hospital. What am I supposed to do with all this? None of it serves a purpose anymore.

"Gwenn?"

"In here," I call out to Lourdes.

"For ladies' night in, I brought pad thai and plum wine. Lucy texted and said she's running late, but she'll be no longer than an hour." Lourdes enters my tiny bedroom and takes in the miserable mess I've made.

"You are a goddess," I say before smiling. It's harder to do than I'd expected, even if it is at my bestie. "And Lucy doesn't know what's going on here or what happened in Georgia, so it doesn't really matter that she's late. I've been avoiding that conversation with her."

Lourdes doesn't seem to hear my words. Instead, she looks at what lies on the floor in front of me, including two empty bottles of Pinot noir. "When did you start?"

"Drinking or sorting?"

"Both."

"Early this morning."

"Why didn't you call me? I would have helped."

"I took the day off," I say by way of an answer. My swollen eyes burn from all the crying I've done today.

"Oh. She's not coming after all," Lourdes says after she checks her new text. "Lucy says, and I quote, 'It's him! I've met the one. We shared the most perfect meet-cute in the grocery store just a while ago. I'll tell you both all about it tomorrow.' How many is that now, in the past six months? Seven?"

"Eight, at least, but who's counting? Tell her to enjoy the ride and not fixate on the shiny frosting."

"Will do." Then Lourdes turns her attention back to me. "How far have you gotten?"

"Toss. Donate. Undecided." I point to each pile.

"What's the last one?" She knows why there's no keep pile.

"Burn."

She nods in silent understanding. "I can't believe Vara sent all these boxes to you. To have kept everything Jaymie owned in totes in some storage facility all these years."

"I know. Me either." This brings to mind the short text Vara sent me the day before all the boxes arrived, only four days after I left Georgia.

Evil Mother

> I couldn't bear to part with a thing.

Well, I couldn't bear to go through it all right away. I needed some time. I definitely needed some alcohol. It was easier to begin without Lourdes only because I didn't like the idea of seeing her sad, empathetic expressions before we even started.

From the burn pile, Lourdes picks up a photo of Vara and Jaymie at her high school graduation. "Does your therapist know about the burn pile?"

"We've discussed it. I'm not burning it yet. I will give myself time, but I also won't keep it forever."

Lourdes then picks up one of the letters and begins reading it to herself. "What does 'DYTIBF' mean?"

"Do you think it'll be forever," I reply in a thick voice, having memorized those words. "Apparently, Jaymie had doubts." I can't bear to call her Rhett's name for her. "Even though they were lifelong friends and dated all through high school and beyond, Vara and Delaney threatened to take away her inheritance."

"Is this not the time to comment on the irony that they most likely lost it all now because they lied about Jaymie dying?"

I shake my head. "Maybe someday we'll come back to that. So, Rhett told Jaymie they'd be okay. They got engaged without her parents' blessing. They were just waiting to graduate college and find jobs before marrying. I guess he lined up a job down there. But it didn't sound like Jaymie was brave enough to go through with it. With all her talk to him of being strong and doing what they wanted, she caved to her parents more than she liked."

"Oh, sweetie." Lourdes sounds empathetic to both versions of me. "I'm so sorry you had to read all that."

"No. I did it to myself. I didn't fall down the rabbit hole. I jumped." I dig through the next tote and pull out a faded yellow stuffed bear. "This doesn't redeem them."

"Of course not. They're despicable, hurtful, just awful people. But does it redeem Rhett?"

I have no answer for this. I don't know if it does. It has been so difficult reading the sweet words he wrote in letters and notes and seeing those pictures of Rhett and the old me together on prom night and birthdays and random dates, knowing that will never, ever be me again. I will never be able to live up to my own legacy.

Chapter 52

Rhett

"It's done?"

"Yep. Finished the test drive fifteen minutes ago." I toss the keys onto Giovanni's mostly bare desk. No paperwork when there are no parts. "Call 'em up, and get it the hell out of here." I go to step away, but stop and turn back. "And next time, don't wait a month before ordering the right parts. At least half the guys are ready to walk."

The weasel laughs. "They won't, and you can't afford to."

I stalk away in search of Ricardo and find him under a car we've had at the shop multiple times. "What is it this time?"

"Bearings and an oil leak." He wheels out from under it and sits up. "Just finished."

"Me too."

He takes a moment to stare at me. "You aren't only talking about a car, are you?"

There doesn't seem to be any reason to reply. No more Edin, no more Gwenn, no more Jill. I don't want the first woman. I can't bring back the third. The second? I want her more than anyone or anything, but I have to be done with all of it.

Ricardo pushes himself up off the mechanic's creeper. He wipes his hands on a rag he pulled out from his left pocket. "Man, I can't tell you what to do. No one really can."

I move my head and shoulders a little, knowing this is only kind of true.

He motions for me to follow him. We start on our way to the break room. Tyler and two other younger guys are busy nearby lowering an engine into a ten-year-old SUV. By the sound of it, Ricardo and I might need to give them a hand in a few minutes, but we'll let them try to figure it out on their own first.

In the break room, Ricardo closes the door behind us. "What's up?"

I shake my head. "Not sure what to start with."

It's been weeks since Georgia, and nothing has improved. April is no better than March. Well, despite its ending, March also saw me happier than I'd been in years.

"Lady trouble. The weasel. Take your pick. Something's getting to you."

"Does your wife know you're this good at emotional conversations?"

He laughs. "It's why she fell in love with me. And why I'm sometimes the bane of her existence. So?"

I let out a breath. "Time to move on."

"To someone new?"

Damn. He really does know how to ask the cutting questions. I can see why this might piss his wife off sometimes. "Maybe. Maybe just somewhere new."

Ricardo nods. "At least out of this hellhole. You deserve better, man."

"Me? What about you? You don't deserve this crap, either. Maybe we should open our own shop together."

"One day, man. But for now? The weasel doesn't mess with me half as much as he messes with you. I can take it for a while longer." He's quiet. Then he asks, "Where you going to go? Back to Georgia?"

I take in a breath and then another before answering. "Some-where I can find peace."

Chapter 53

Rhett

I need to see you.

I STARE AT MY phone for several seconds. Of course I text Gwenn back as soon as I shake myself out of my stupor. How can I not? Gwenn and I haven't spoken since before I closed the door behind me in the hotel a month ago.

She asks if she can come over, and I'm not about to say no. I start pacing well before she's supposed to be here. So many questions in my head right now. I keep wondering what could possibly bring her here and if she's changed her mind. I've changed my own several times this last week.

I hear a knock and open my door, only to discover it's at the apartment across the hall. No sooner do I shut the door when I hear another knock.

It's Gwenn this time, holding a brown cardboard box that has its four top flaps in an interlocking fold, not taped. Though apparently newer, several of the box's corners look torn. Despite wanting to stare at the box longer, I can't avoid looking up in her eyes. They are bloodshot and swollen.

"Hi."

"Please come in," I say, but she remains at the doorway.

"This is for you." She holds the box out to me. Then I notice the shipping label with Vara's address on it.

"What is it?"

"Will you just take this thing, please? I don't want it anymore."

I oblige, gently removing it from her hands. Then I crouch down and set it on the floor. With slightly shaking hands, I begin untucking the flaps.

"I gotta go," Gwenn says as she starts to back away.

I let go of the box and stand. "Wait. Please stay."

Tears begin to fill her eyes. "Rhett, this is too hard."

"But is it worth it?"

She doesn't answer.

"I've been asking the same thing of me. What's worth it? And who is worth it?"

"Did you come up with any answers?" Her voice is strained.

"There's a reason you brought this over instead of shipping it. It would have been easy to send it here. You wanted to see me."

She sniffles, but doesn't bother wiping at a tear that falls. Not right away.

"You knew I wanted to see you, too." I step closer but don't touch her. Instead, I offer my hands to her, palms up.

Gwenn refuses to take them.

"What's in the box?"

"They didn't throw it all away. It was kept in storage." She takes half a second to glance down at it. "That box is everything relating to her I thought you'd want to have."

I tighten my jaw and ignore the painful burning in my chest. "Will you come in and talk with me?"

She opens her mouth, but the only thing that comes out is a stifled sob. Her eyes are still bright red and glossy.

I look at the box again. "It doesn't mean a thing to you, does it?"

"Once I finally worked up the nerve, I spent three entire days sorting through it all. I could have just tossed everything Vara sent me."

"Wh—" I start.

"I didn't," Gwenn interrupts. "In order to heal, yes, absolutely. But also for you. You spent years believing it was all gone." She sniffles again before continuing. "Please don't ask any more of me."

I want to reply to her. I want to tell her so many things, but first, I have to see what's in the box. There is no resisting this urge to find out what it holds. I need to know what exactly Gwenn saw, what exactly we're dealing with.

After kneeling down, I pop the flaps apart in the open doorway and pray Gwenn doesn't run off. On the top of the pile is a small, clear, zipped baggie, with Jaymie's name in black marker, containing a gold and sapphire engagement ring. The ring Jill never took off from the moment I proposed. It's split and bent open at the bottom of the band.

Gwenn sobs again. "It was cut off of me in the hospital. My hand was swelling too quickly, and they had to use a defibrillator on me. No one told me at the time that it was an engagement ring or what finger I wore it on. I didn't know until much, much later, when I was about to leave the hospital. But no fiancé ever showed, so I figured they'd moved on. I didn't have any name to search for like I did my family."

I carefully put the bag down and move to my feet to stand when, in all honesty, part of me thinks I probably deserve to stay on the floor.

Before I have a chance to speak, she says, "You're leaving?"

I follow her eyes to the large, open boxes on my living room floor. "I thought about it."

She lets out another few sobs that she clearly couldn't hold back though she tried.

"But no, I'm not." For a few moments, I give her a chance to breathe. Her breath is uneven and catches several times. "I'm finally getting rid of stuff I've held on to for too long and packing the rest away. Things Jill never would have cared if I kept or tossed. They aren't why I have my memories of her. There's no reason for me to look at all of it every day."

The woman I feared I'd never see again only blinks at me with watery eyes.

"You know what Jill would say?" I ask.

Gwenn scoffs through her tears and turns to leave.

"Please."

She stops.

"Please listen to me. Please stop running from me."

Slowly, she turns back to me. There's fire in her eyes.

"You know what she'd say? She'd say, 'Find the woman you want. You have to want each other. If you screw it up with the right woman, you're just gonna be a pawn for the wrong ones.' I have been a pawn since I started dating again. Now, I've finally found the right woman. I knew you were perfect for me before all of this came out. It's you I want, Gwenn. Jill is gone. I understand now. I accept it." I wait and see if Gwenn is going to move toward me.

She does. In fact, she puts her hands on my arms. She even gives them a gentle squeeze.

But the moment is fleeting. I already feel her wanting to move away.

"Please trust me like you trusted me before."

"Can you forgive me for not telling you the truth about my past, or at least what I knew of it?"

"You don't need to ask me that. I know why you did it. But if you want forgiveness, you've got it."

"Just like that?"

"Yes."

She pulls back and drops her hands. "I can't be who you want me to be."

"You don't have to. I loved you as Jill or Jaymie. Whichever name you want to pick. Of course I did. I spent my entire childhood and early adult years adoring her. But she is gone now. I will always love her, but she's gone. You don't have to go back to being a woman you no longer are. I don't want you to."

Watching her, I see she wants to shake this off, not wanting or perhaps unable to believe I'm being honest. I haven't given her much of a reason to think I have honestly let go of Jill, but I didn't spend all this time apart from her working on just that, only to not even explain my feelings the best way I can.

"Gwenn is alive. Gwenn is everything I want. I developed feelings for you long before we knew the truth."

She tries to back away but I grab at her hands. "Stop being so dang scared," I tell her.

"I'm not scared. I'm broken. Don't you get it? I've been broken for a long time. I'm slowly piecing myself back together, but you deserve better than that. You deserve to have a whole woman, not part of one."

"You are whole. Don't ever think you aren't."

She cries harder. "It's going to take me a lot of time to heal from this. A lot. I may never lose my anger over the accident. My therapist can only do so much. The rest is on me."

"I'm a patient man."

"You'll have to heal, too."

"So we'll both go to therapy. Hell, I know I should have gone back then. You and I can heal together. Or at the same time on our own. I just want you to give me another chance."

Gwenn blinks away a few more tears. It's an eternity before she replies. "I'm not sure I will talk about this with anyone apart from you, Lourdes, Lucy, and my therapist. This means it's likely no one from Jill's life will ever know. Can you handle that?"

"I can. I promise I can. It wouldn't be lying to them if they don't know the truth, since she really is gone. Granny and Mama will never say anything, since doing so would hurt you and me. We both know the Jonases won't tell a soul."

I take a much needed breath. "I like you as Gwenn Rhys. I like you as you are. I'm going to fall in love with you if you'll only give me the chance."

"Gwenn Mirielle Rhys, and I'm going to fall in love with you, too," she whispers.

"Do you mean it?"

She nods. "I won't give up on you, Rhett. I won't give up on us. We're partners, right?"

I pull her in for a kiss, most definitely not our last.

Epilogue

Gwenn

"I KNOW WHAT THEY are asking and what the assessment says, but that's only their opinions. What is this house actually worth?" My client's voice comes through my speakers as I listen to my voicemails. "It's already been on the market for three weeks. They can't expect to get that much for it, can they?"

I heave a loud sigh and resist the urge to drop my forehead to my steering wheel. Worsening my headache will not help the situation for me. Carefully, I press on the brake pedal at a stoplight and take a moment to roughly rub my eyes. I feel the need to scrub the day away, but I'm still at least ten minutes from home because of traffic.

The light turns green again, but it takes my brain a few seconds to realize I need to do something about that. The car behind me gives a honk as I move my right foot from the brake to the gas pedal. I glance down at my gauges and think maybe I won't be able to wait until tomorrow to refill my gas tank after all. My car's going to ding at me any moment.

There's a gas station about five blocks down, but it's out of the way. The chime I now hear tells me I don't have a choice. At the next stop sign, I flick on my right turn signal. Five long blocks later, I pull into the station next to a pump.

All while paying and refilling my tank, I wonder how to make my client understand that the assessor does actually know how to do their job accurately. Rhett would tell me to be firmer about it than I probably will be. He sometimes thinks I'm too soft with my clients. But he loves it when I'm soft with him.

Mm. I miss him.

I haven't spoken to him since this morning, when I regrettably had to inform him that I couldn't swing dinner after all when we were both off work because a family who originally turned down the idea of viewing houses suddenly showed up at my office and wanted to spend all day looking for a new home. The tenderness in his voice had me wishing I could have rushed out to Auburn right then, stolen him away from the garage and back to his apartment, and spent the whole day naked and happy instead of fully clothed and desperate to get that family to like anything—anything—they saw, even if it was just a little nugget to help me do more research to aid them in their journey.

Then, of course, I let my mind wander to all the other recent times Rhett and I have spent naked and happy together, even if it's rarely an all-day event like he always hopes for. Whew. This August heat isn't the only thing that has me fluttering my top's neckline just to feel a cool breeze.

With the help and guidance of our respective therapists, my relationship with Rhett has flourished, so much so that it was still April when we became an official couple. Since then, we've been able to look both back and forward with care and consideration for our pasts and the connection we have now. Our first utterances of "I love you" were whispered at a place we made special for just the two of us, no history on either side allowed.

Back on the road, my thoughts stay on Rhett. I worked a good three or four hours after he did thanks to my surprise visitors. I'm sure he's relaxing at his place with a beer right now, probably watching a game on TV. I think I might choose wine and an early bedtime.

Well, bed after drafting emails, writing down the words I need for my call to the confused client in the morning, and some scheduling of social media posts since I won't have time tomorrow or the day after. I really needed my newest assistant to stay and not quit me for a higher-paying job at an agency in Syracuse, but I can't do a thing about that now. And although it's Tuesday, the day of the week doesn't really matter for my job. I don't often give myself a day off, whether that's a Tuesday or a Sunday.

My phone rings. I involuntarily flinch, knowing my clients don't ever give me days off either.

"Hey, are you home yet?" Lourdes's voice comes through the speakers.

"Almost. Where are you?"

"At the shop. My delivery was late today, so I'm still organizing roses. Maybe we can do lunch on Saturday?"

"So far, yes. As long as my showing isn't moved up from late afternoon."

We work out a few details, then say bye.

Oh wait.

I forgot I have a showing that morning, too. Must remember to tell Lourdes tomorrow, I verbally remind myself.

At my apartment building, I find a spot to park in and gather my purse and work bags. I remain seated, though. I've been awake since two in the morning. It quite possibly might become a twenty-four-hour day for me.

Mustering up what energy I have left, I exit my car and lock it. Then I head to my door. With my key, the bolt tumbles open. I'm greeted not by the last remnants of dusk, but flickering light.

And rose petals on the floor.

I cannot see my living room carpet, as it's now red and pink. Flameless candles surround my coffee table. The table itself is bare. It's also been turned so that its longest side is not parallel to my sofa and TV, but rather the doorway. Rhett stands behind it in his nice slacks and white button-down shirt. Much fancier than the clothes he usually wears.

"Hey, babe," I say. I haven't even closed the door yet. "What is all this? I thought you went home after work."

Before any more sweltering air drifts inside, I shut the door and step closer to drop my bags on the sofa.

He stays behind the table and gives me a shrug with one of his sexy half-smiles. "Change of plans."

I take a step or two nearer to him, but with great effort. The cool, air-conditioned room isn't chilling the heat on my body. After forcing myself to breathe in, I say, "Oh?" I can't manage to squeak out anything else.

Rhett bends down to the massive gift bags I hadn't noticed are next to his feet. There are four bags in all, but from my perspective, I can't see what is in them. Slowly, he pulls something out of the first bag and places it on the near end of the table. It is a large, block-type letter "M" covered in flowers. Fresh ones, based on the scent in the air.

Then he silently and quickly pulls out another one. A flowered "A." He continues as it becomes harder and harder for me to breathe. It isn't long before he pulls the last one out and places it on the far end of the table.

M, A, R, R, Y, M, E, and a question mark.

I wipe my damp eyes. There is no holding back my smile. It's been growing since the first letter appeared.

In a flash, he steps around the table and comes to me since I can't seem to move my body in order to walk over to him. His arms quickly envelop me. I snuggle against him, so he speaks into my hair.

"From the moment I met you, I knew there was something about you. I could see a future for us as husband and wife. You know how hard it was at times to get to this point. So, what do you think?"

I still have my hands up by my face. At the end of his words, I move them up over his shoulders and link them around his neck. "I think I am so in love with you that I can't imagine feeling any better than this." Then I pull back to see his face. In doing so, I notice a rosiness in his cheeks.

He gives me another half-smile, but it only lasts a moment before breaking out into a full one. We lean into each other. Our lips have just barely met when he moves his head back and gently releases our bodies from each other.

"What are you doing?"

Rhett doesn't reply. Instead, he bends down to a kneeling position, one knee up and one on the floor. "Almost forgot." He reaches into his pants pocket and brings out a little black box.

The hinges give a tiny creak as he opens it to reveal a diamond ring nestled in the white cushion. I offer both my hands to the free hand he holds out to me.

"Will you marry me, Gwenn Rhys?"

More tears come. I nod and can't seem to stop. "Yes. Yes!"

He gives a short, happy laugh, then scrambles to his feet. Our lips connect for real this time, and the heat in my body spreads all the way down to my toes. I grip his shoulders and give a soft moan. He grasps hold of me and moans, too, as I slide my hands up his body to his hair. Then we pull back once more, just trying to catch our breaths.

"We're getting married?" he asks.

I give the same kind of short, happy laugh he did. "We're getting married!"

Bonus Epilogue

"YOU LIED TO ME."

"Sorry?" I say, not really sure what my husband is talking about. I don't remember lying to him about anything recently, and the few lies I did tell early in our relationship—for very good reasons!—I've already admitted to and apologized for, many times.

Rhett gives a slight shake of his head, but it's too difficult to understand what that means. Then he says, "Arizona."

"What about Arizona?" Then I take a few moments to think. As it dawns on me, I say, "I've never actually been to the Grand Canyon."

"That's right," he draws this out slowly, heightening his Southern accent.

"But we've talked about this. You said you understood why I let you believe I've been there before."

"I did. I do. However, I also think we need to rectify the situation."

I laugh, mostly because I really don't know what's going on right now. How do we rectify something that can't be changed? "It's a situation?" I finally ask.

"That's right. My darling wife deserves to see the entire damn state of Arizona on her terms, no one else's. I figure we start with the Grand Canyon," he adds with a cute shrug.

Is it strange that I want to burst into tears at his sweet words? If it is, I don't care. But I also don't cry. Instead, I'm smiling and grabbing him in for a hug. I'm still holding him when I ask, "When can we go? How? What about the shop?"

Rhett's owned his own auto repair shop for the past two years, and I still run my real estate company pretty much on my own as well, though now I have two assistants who excel at their jobs. I might even be able to hire on another broker within the next few months, I think. But still. We're both small business owners. It isn't easy to walk away from all that for even a week or a few days sometimes.

"Ricardo's got it. He's the best worker I'll ever have and a good friend, too. Your assistants can handle your clients for a few days, I'm sure. Right?"

I nod. "Of course." Then I laugh. "You already asked them, didn't you?"

"Might have mentioned it, but I told them you'd have to be okay with it first."

Embracing him even tighter now, I smile even wider. "Perfectly okay with it. I can't wait to go! We need tickets. And we need to pack. I'll have to see if there's any meetings I need to rearrange, but I don't think there's anything big coming up."

Reluctantly, I loosen my arms around my husband, but at least this affords me the ability to see his handsome face. "What's already planned?"

Because Rhett knows me. There's no way I can leave town without everything figured out ahead of time.

"All the stuff at the shop is good on my end. Ricardo knows what to do. Minka and Kallie can give tours and whatnot. You don't have any clients who are about to close in the next week, so that shouldn't be a problem. We already have tickets, boarding passes, hotel reservations, rented car, all that jazz. All we need are a few days' worth of clothes and toiletries, and we're good to go."

It really is as easy as he makes it sound. We leave town without any hiccups. The only worry I have is being on the airplane, but that's a fear that has gotten easier and easier over the last few years. Rhett holds my hand as I take deeps breaths with closed eyes, and everything melts away when we're in the plane. Once we arrive in Phoenix, the landing is a little bumpy, but other than that, our flight is uneventful, which in our case, is a much-welcomed thing.

Not only has Rhett planned a scenic drive and a few hikes we might like, we're also considering taking a helicopter ride over the canyon. It'll be the first time either of us have been in a small aircraft since that awful snowstorm four years ago.

"We can do this," he whispers in my ear as we take in the night view from our hotel near the canyon. He stands behind me, his arms enveloping me, my arms wrapped around his. "We can fly in that helicopter and know we'll be just fine. We're safe, no matter where we are. You and me."

"We're partners in this," I whisper in return, echoing words he said to me so long ago.

"That's right, darlin'. We've already gone through the worst. It's only good stuff from now."

I know he's right. We can make it through anything.

I pull him a little tighter around me. "Thank you. This is the best gift you ever could have given me."

Rhett kisses my ear, then down my neck, and I remember we get to have another first on this trip. At least a *first* in this state. This without a doubt will be the best vacation I've ever had in Arizona, and I couldn't be happier or more grateful for it, and for Rhett.

Bonus deleted scene: Meet cute

Gwenn

(THIS ISN'T ANY OLD deleted scene. This is the very first meeting of Rhett and Gwenn that didn't fit into the original story but is just way too good to not share with you.)

I grip my ticket in one hand and my small suitcase's handle in the other. Thankfully, I can have it with me as a carry-on. I hate checking my luggage. I'm always afraid I'll never find it again or it will be stolen or sent to far-off location or something.

All the rules about what to pack and what size, how much approved liquid in specific containers, is difficult enough. I freak out every trip that I got something wrong or that I'll be asked to answer a million questions and my mind will go blank or I'll have to remove every item from my bags and offer precise purchase dates and locations for every item.

Most of the once-full chairs are no longer occupied by the people waiting for the same flight as mine. Syracuse to Boston. Like me, everyone else seems to have taken up staring out the massive windows or wandering aimlessly around the small seating area.

From what I can decipher in the quiet grumbles around me, the other passengers are giving up hope of flying out of here in a reasonable amount of time or even at all. The snow is wreaking more havoc than I first feared, which makes sense considering the amount of snow I see out on the tarmac despite the crew's best efforts.

It's only an hour-long flight, though. I keep reminding myself of this. First weekend away from Syracuse in several years. Even though it's a working vacation, it shouldn't be too bad. That is, if the snow will ever let up. There hasn't been any official word since the original delay, which sends a tightening through my entire body, starting with my chest.

I don't want to stay in this airport much longer. I don't like not knowing how bad the snow will get. I hate being unprepared. I hate not being in control of harried situations.

And now my chest hurts even more. That familiar heat begins to spread. I suck breaths in and puff them out in short bursts, then long ones.

"We should have just driven," a Southern male voice from behind me says in my direction, startling me so much I forget to focus on my breathing. His tone is friendly and a little playful. Definitely not old. Pretty sexy actually.

I force myself to turn away from the massive window wall where I've been monitoring the snowstorm to glance over my left shoulder. A young man around my age stands a few feet behind me. "A blizzard is a blizzard, no matter the mode of transportation."

Though he isn't looking directly at me, I try to smile. I *want* to smile, but all the worries swirling in my brain make this impossible.

He shrugs in reply, like this makes no difference. He watches out the window as he speaks to me. "Big plans in Boston?"

Then he glances back over at me. We lock eyes, and he almost looks stunned. He blinks a few times in rapid succession and steps closer to me.

But then he stops short, having only moved one foot. He seems like he's maybe a little off-balance, too, physically. All it seems he can do at the moment is stare and blink. My instincts have me next to him in no time, my hand on his arm, having switched my ticket to the one that holds my suitcase handle.

Low blood sugar? I wonder. He's young, but it could be a stroke. What are the signs of a stroke? Aneurysm? Brain tumor suddenly bursting? Brain bleed?

"You okay?" I ask, maintaining eye contact with him. My chest heaves. I'm not sure I'm capable of helping him through this.

The man only stares. His mouth moves as if he wants to speak but doesn't. Then he shakes his head.

I feel my eyes get bigger.

Oh, gosh. He's not okay. What do I need to do? Call 911 or ask someone in the airport? Do I just yell out a call for help and see who comes running? Do I ask for a doctor to run over? I spin my head from side to side, looking around, trying to find someone who can help.

"No, no, no. I'm okay," he says suddenly, moving a step closer.

He places his hands on my arms now, too. We are almost holding each other at this point. I try to slow my breathing. I also try to make it not so obvious that it's as fast as it is, but I'm guessing he can see panic on my face.

"I'm all right," he says softly. "But thank you." Then he gives me a half-smile.

I feel my face spreading into a grin of my own.

"Good," I say. My breathing begins to slow. The anxious heat begins to cool. "If you're sure."

He gives another half-smile. "I'm sure. So, about your Boston trip?"

"Yes. Big plans." I smile after replying.

After the client meeting, I'm supposed to have dinner at one of the best restaurants in the city. Since I'm alone, I hope I have no trouble getting a seat at the bar if all the tables are booked. That is, if my meeting doesn't go over. If I can even get to my meeting.

The man half-grins again in return. We both seem to have just realized we're still holding each other and let go, but we don't step back. His body is only about six inches from mine. Heat radiates off of him. So much so that I think he might be the warmest thing in this airport. It's been a long time since I had any desire to snuggle up to such a man and take advantage of what his heat could do to me, and yet here I am, wanting a closeness with him.

"I'm Rhett," he offers.

"Gwenn," I reply.

There's an announcement on the PA system. "Due to inclement weather beyond our control . . ."

I know the rest. No need to listen. I also receive a new text on my phone giving me the same information.

"Just great." Rhett sighs and runs a hand over his bearded face.

I blow out a breath as well and rub my forehead. Rhett stares out the window.

"Maybe I can help," comes another man's voice. It isn't gruff, but it doesn't exactly sound young either.

Rhett and I swivel and are faced with a fortyish man in worn jeans, a blue, hooded sweatshirt, and an olive green cargo jacket addressing us.

"You got a plane?" Rhett asks.

"As a matter of fact, I do," he tells us.

"Is it safe? It'll fly in the snow? We won't be stuck here?"

The man answers in the affirmative to all three questions, but doesn't go into detail.

I look up at Rhett. He moves his eyes to me, too, then he looks back at the pilot. "You got other people going on this flight?"

The pilot nods. "A few. No sense waiting around here if you don't have to." Then he shrugs.

Rhett and I make eye contact again. I'm anxious at the thought of changing plans. It has me shaky. Then again, this pilot is offering us a chance to keep our original plans for Boston. And being trapped in the airport freaks me out.

Only one thing will change, I tell myself.

One difference for everything else to be the same.

As I debate the potential recklessness of this, I see the same thoughts expressed on Rhett's face. And yet, we both seem to come to the same conclusion. I know this at the moment we smile at each other.

Are we about to do what I think we are?

Want more *Lost Hearts Found?*

You can subscribe to my newsletter! You'll get all the news about my books and series first, as well as previews like cover reveals, first lines, and release dates. I might also have giveaways or books to share, other story excerpts, or what inspires my writing. One never knows! As a thank you, I'll also have special bonuses for you. Sign up at my website: https://lisakeiferauthor.com/newslettersignup

"I Won't Give Up" by Jason Mraz is mentioned by Rhett early on in the book. This song actually helped inspire me as I wrote. You can check out the playlist I made of variations and covers of "I Won't Give Up" on my Spotify playlist. The link to the playlist is also on my website: https://lisakeiferauthor.com/links

What happens when Lucy meets the man of her dreams, and decides to *not* date him? Find out in **June Days**, book 2 of Lost Hearts Found.

I would also like to ask that, if you enjoyed this story, please consider leaving a review (without spoilers please!). As an indie author, it can sometimes be difficult getting people to take a chance on my books. And thank you! I really appreciate it.

June Days preview

I AM, AS IT happens, not only a hopeless romantic but a helpless one. I love despite everything. Doctors could probably classify a whole new disorder based solely on me. It would certainly involve a new type of rehab or group, like Romantics Anonymous. I can just hear my introduction now: "Hi. My name is Lucy, and I'm addicted to romance."

I love to love, to fall in love, to be in love, to be showered with love. Once I fall, I'm all in. And I always fall.

Therein lies my downfall.

I definitely see the irony in how it happened in the exact same place we met the previous year. This location was one of my most favorite spots in the world. It's where I felt the most comfortable, the most secure, and the most at peace. We visited our home away from home every summer, from the time I was a toddler all the way up into my early teen years.

Then came the summer I was thirteen. We didn't pack up and go in June. We didn't pack up and go in July, either. It was our first summer vacation away from the only place I ever wanted to be. To be away from the cabin felt like being away from home, even as I lay in my bed in the place I grew up.

By the time I was eighteen, enough was enough. My sister Kenzie and I started a new tradition of traveling to the lake on our own every weekend in June. It didn't matter that, as a third grade teacher, I still had another month of school left.

I was on one of these trips with Kenzie at the start of the summer that pivoted my life in a direction I, the hopeless romantic, never saw coming.

Also By Lisa Keifer

Lost Hearts Found:

Accidental Pasts
June Days
Winter Blossoms
Throwaway Rules
Uncharted Avenues
Holiday Distractions

Acknowledgement

I want to first give a big thank you to my husband for always being so understanding. Creating a novel is a lot of hard work, and I wouldn't be able to do much of this without his support. Also, huge thanks to him for being my very own mechanic and allowing me to pick his brain on details I might not have known otherwise (though the shop Rhett works at is NOT based in real life!).

I also want to give many thanks to my family and friends for their support as well. They definitely know how to make me feel loved, and I love them all so much, too. Thank you especially to my bestie who is always there when I need advice or a second opinion or just an ear for listening and a shoulder to cry on.

A huge shout-out to my editor Joanne and her awesome insights, and also to my graphic designer Sarah, who created exactly what I saw in my head even if I couldn't put it into words.

Finally, thank you to you, reader, for taking a chance on this book. I hope it met or exceeded your expectations!